I0631690

THE CABIN AT BIG ROCK

JIM CARVER

THE EIGHTH BOOK OF THE SERIES
Life at the Lodge

Copyright © 2018 Jim Carver
www.authorjimcarver.com

All rights reserved. No part of this publication
may be reproduced, stored in a retrieval system, or transmitted,
in any form or by any means, electronic, mechanical,
photocopying, recording, or otherwise,
without the written prior permission of the publisher.

ISBN: 978-1-988284-07-1

Cover design by Iryna Spica
Typeset in *Dante* at SpicaBookDesign

Printed and bound with www.createspace.com.

Table of Contents

The Flaming Barge

I was in the yard behind the lodge chopping wood, when Trevor came through the rear door and grinned at me, saying, "Glad to see you're keeping busy. Sarah and I had some free time, so we thought we'd pay you a surprise visit. Since it's a Monday 'buffet night', we figured you and Pauline wouldn't be overrun with chores for guests, so I'd like to show you the truck I've bought and fixed up. Other than the fact she's been painted bright yellow with orange flames emanating from under the hood and running along her sides, she's a solid ride."

I chunked the axe into the chopping-block and said, "I'd love to see your truck, and don't worry about popping in, you're always welcome here."

By this time, he'd joined me in the yard, along with the three dogs. They were still frisking around him, although they'd probably already given him a frantic greeting in the parking lot. As I took a pace towards the door, Trevor put a restraining hand on my shoulder and said, "Let's finish here first," then he grabbed my spare axe from where it'd been leaning against a wood stack. He upended a thick log to use as a chopping-block and was swinging away before I could say another word. It only took ten minutes for us to split the logs I'd laid out, so I soon went into the lodge to say hello to Sarah.

After giving me a big hug and a kiss on the cheek, she said, "Don't go running off just now." Turning to Trevor in mid-sentence, she added sternly, "That means you, too." Then she giggled and looked excited, saying to him, "You'll have to tell them about our plans; see if he can take a day off."

"Sure," Trevor responded, "but first I want to show my truck to Henry, we'll only be gone for ten minutes."

"Oh yeah," said Sarah ironically and for the first time revealed her nickname for the vehicle:

'The Flaming Barge'. "He wouldn't want to miss a viewing."

Filling the kettle at the sink, Pauline said, "We'll all have a cup of tea together when you get back." Grinning at Sarah over her shoulder, but addressing us, she then remarked in an offhand way, "It'll be interesting to hear their plans, but you'd better hurry back, since Sarah looks about ready to explode."

Although they'd already seen the truck, the dogs accompanied Trevor and I as we hastened up the path to the parking lot. The Flaming Barge was sitting alongside my rather conservative vehicle and it really caught the eye. It was a Dodge crew-cab, supposedly a utilitarian truck, but its paint-job made it look ridiculous. With the orange flames spilling from under the hood then rolling along its sides, it appeared capable of rapid acceleration, plus performing the occasional wheelie.

As we walked around the vehicle, Trevor told me what he'd done to repair it. I tried to look knowledgeable, but other than some basic things, my understanding of mechanical workings leaves a lot to be desired. For instance: if a tire's not curved at each quadrant and forms a straight line at its southern border, I know what the problem is and I can fix it pronto. But talk of carboretor adjustments or of re-grinding a clutch component, leaves me thinking I'd probably understand brain surgery better. Anyhow, I nodded sagely as he opened the hood to show me the collection of gizmos and gadgets that powered his chariot. After inspecting it thoroughly inside and out, I proclaimed it to be a solid vehicle (as if I could know just by looking at it in the lot). Finally unleashing the big yellow elephant I'd diplomatically avoided mentioning, he asked, "What do you think of the ...er, colours? I was going to re-paint her, but then I had second thoughts."

Standing back to peruse the truck, I said, "I think I understand your reluctance to change her appearance: it's like calling a fat guy 'Slim'. It's entirely inappropriate, but it fits somehow."

Trevor laughed and said, "That's a good way of looking at it, but I might change my mind, or Sarah could insist on something less conspicuous. I don't think she likes to be seen in the truck when we're in town, especially at stop lights. She probably believes the other drivers expect blue smoke and screeching tires from us when the light turns green, but that's not the case, of course." He looked at the bright yellow vehicle with its flames again, then said, "We should go back to the lodge. Sarah and I have something we'd like to run by you and Pauline."

"Sure," I said, taking a final gander and grinning ruefully, "let's join the ladies."

Glad Moments at the Lodge

The dogs had disappeared into the bush, so we headed down the path to the lodge without their company. When we got inside, Moon was sitting at the main table with Sarah, while Pauline was pouring boiling water into the earthenware teapot at the kitchen counter. Pauline told me later that Moon had simply shown up shortly after the couple's arrival, explaining to Sarah, "I heard your voices, so I came down."

This statement was perplexing, since voices can't normally be noticed from the lodge to her place, unless someone's shouting, of course. I recalled no bellowing or loud cheering upon their appearance, so I inferred she'd been telling a fib for some reason. She'd flicked a somewhat guilty glance at no one in particular, then she carried on normally. I'd been out in the parking lot when all this had happened, so when we walked into the lodge, I watched them embrace and exchange cheerful greetings. But this raised what I thought were permanently dormant questions about the two of them.

Both Moon and Trevor are First Nations, but their similarities go beyond this. Even though they don't look alike, they move the same way, as though they're part of a different world. I don't think Moon and Trevor are blood relatives, while Pauline believes otherwise. This difference in opinion hasn't been the source of serious friction between us, but there's intense curiosity, nonetheless. Although I'd really like to know more about their relationship, I try not to press the issue. On the other hand, Pauline is always attempting to slip in a hopefully revealing query about Trevor, but Moon easily sidesteps her questions and goes wandering off on a conversational tangent. She'd be a natural for politics.

After the five of us got settled at the table with the compulsory pot of tea and plate of cookies,

I immediately saw Sarah was sitting unnaturally, with her right hand clamped into her left armpit and seemed too stiff for our relaxed little get-together. Since her face was flushed and she couldn't stop smiling, I asked, "So, what's up with you?"

She gently bumped shoulders with Trevor as they sat there, then she took her hand from under her arm. Spreading her fingers on the tabletop to reveal a ring, she asked me breathlessly, "What do you think?"

After peering closely as she twiddled her digits proudly, I asked, "Did you wash up before tea time? Your hand looks a mite grungy."

Too happy to give me a dirty look, Sarah then showed her outspread fingers to Pauline and Moon, saying, "Trevor proposed yesterday and isn't the ring beautiful?" The women all squealed with delight, while Pauline nearly pulled her across the table as she grabbed Sarah's outstretched hand to examine the piece of jewellery.

This revelry among the women left me nodding happily at Trevor and saying,

"Congratulations!" Then I rolled my eyes and said, "You're a brave man, taking on that one." I gestured at Sarah as she was still leaning across the table showing off her ring, then added, "She'll be a handful, she has her own ways."

Smiling ruefully and raising his voice slightly so I could hear over the women still cooing about the ring, he replied with feeling, "Don't I know it," then he said nothing more, although he was shaking his head almost imperceptibly. Apparently casting aside anything negative being said about his betrothed, he added cheerfully, "I bought the ring at your buddy's shop; Keith Johnson and I had an interesting chat about his booking-agent duties for you. Later, I'll tell you more about our conversation."

By this time, Sarah had extended her hand to just under my nose, while demanding I look at the ring instead of making rude comments about cleanliness. It was a simple gold band with a good-sized diamond held in a platform setting: very pretty.

As I nodded with approval, Sarah looked fondly at Trevor and said excitedly, "It's perfect!

It's from the mid-eighteen hundreds and even has a fitting inscription." She carefully removed it from her finger to show me the underside of the gold band. In flowing and old-fashioned script were written the words: 'For My Beloved Sarah'. Sarah put the ring back on and said dreamily, "I wonder who she was and where she lived." With a preoccupied expression on her face, she momentarily stared at it, then put her arm around Trevor, saying, "Oh well, we'll never know." She kissed him on the cheek and hugged him closer, then she said, "It doesn't really matter, I suppose, but it'd be nice to know."

Rather than have Sarah pull us all into speculation and make-believe, Moon said, "Yes, it's frustrating that we don't know." Not looking frustrated at all, she then asked, "When's the big day?"

Sarah shrugged, glanced at Trevor, then took a bite of cookie and spoke fervently through her munching, "If it was up to me, it'd be tomorrow." The commitment and romance inherent in this statement were commendable, but the sheen of this dedication had been slightly tarnished by the cookie crumbs on her lips. Unaware of this, she carried on, "Trevor doesn't want to get married until he's more settled financially." Shaking her head, but smiling at him lovingly, she told us he'd just paid off a number of old debts, but he'd incurred some new ones.

At this point, she looked at me with a half-pleading and half-belligerent look on her face, saying, "My father and Trevor don't get along, to put it mildly. Dad was against our relationship right from the start; I could make some nasty accusations about him, but I won't." Making a dismissive gesture and crinkling her nose, Sarah said, "Never mind him: we'd like to have the wedding here in the lodge." Smiling at Pauline and Moon, she added, "You two would be my bride's maids of honour, while Henry could be best man. It'd be fun! And I know my mother will want to attend, whenever that might be." She sighed dramatically and shrugged, then asked, "Would that be okay with the three of you?"

Pauline answered happily, "That sounds lovely, so maybe I'll even get to see Henry wearing a tie for once."

Making sure I could sport this kind of natty attire, I asked, "It goes around the top of my head with its tail hanging in my face, right?"

Ignoring my sartorial query, Pauline turned to me and said brightly, "We'll have to make a nice cake for the occasion, but it seems we'll have to wait."

Moon nodded and gave the couple a smiling perusal as she refilled her tea mug, saying, "I'm happy for the two of you; you belong together."

Planning to Visit

The four of us nattered on about the glad event, but Trevor remained silent and looked pensive. He kept glancing at me as though he'd like a private word; he was still cheery, but he was obviously concerned about something. Clearly having noticed this, Moon drained her mug and returned it decisively to the tabletop. Getting up from her chair, she smiled at Sarah and Trevor, then said, "I have work to do in the garden, but keep me updated on your plans." She briefly hugged each of them, nodded goodbye to Pauline and I, and made her departure.

After a moment Pauline stood up saying, "I should be joining her, since the veggies for the buffet have to be picked and prepared." She hurried to our bedroom, then reappeared a minute later dressed in her working clothes.

"I'll go up with you," said Sarah, "and maybe the dogs will keep us company." After making a big deal about parting with Trevor, she headed up to the garden with Pauline, leaving her loved one alone with me in the now peaceful lodge.

Trevor inhaled deeply and put his hands flat on the table. He seemed quite calm, considering the storm of emotion he'd provoked among the women with his proposal to Sarah. Not meeting my eye at the moment and beneath all the still waters, there was a slight edginess about him. I could hear his foot tapping under the table as we sat across from each other. After ruminating for a while, he raised his eyes to me and smiled sheepishly, saying, "Sorry about that, I was thinking about things."

"No problem," I replied, then grinned at him and said, "when I married Pauline, I knew it was the right thing to do, but I was nervous anyway. There'd been a lot on my mind, so I too would go for a mental walkabout occasionally."

Pleased that I understood, he nodded and topped up our tea mugs. He was only in his early twenties, while Sarah was two years younger, but neither seemed to have serious doubts about spending their lives together. Yes, he was a bit jittery, but overall I admired his stolid bearing in the face of his impending nuptials. When I was his age (I'm only ten years older), the ways of females were a mystery to me. Thoughts of marriage hadn't even occurred to me, anyway, since I'd been too busy drinking to regard any of my lady companions as life partners. There could never be a silver lining to the fact that a drunk driver killed my father, but at least it made me quit my love-hate relationship with booze. Snapping out of my grim musings after a moment, I asked Trevor about his immediate plans.

"That's what I wanted to talk about," he replied, adding a dab of honey to his tea. Then he locked his intense dark eyes on me and smiled, saying, "I have a business proposition for you; I think we can both make money."

"Tell me more," I said, nodding encouragingly, "as long as murder and mayhem aren't part of the scheme, I'm all ears."

"No, no, nothing like that," he answered and chuckled, but he quickly grew more serious. "I recently bought a property a bit smaller than Three Duck Lake, about twenty five miles on the other side of town," he told me. "I can't really afford it right now, but I think it'll end up looking like a steal." Giving me a pained face, he added, "I bought the truck, but the access road has to be cleaned up. The mining cabin there is well-built, but it's old and needs repairs, so that's an additional expense. I've taken Sarah up there a few times and she loves it." Seeming uncertain yet proud, he concluded by telling me they'd not have to buy a house, since they planned to live in the cabin once it'd been fixed up.

"It sounds nice," I responded, "but how are you going to pay the bills? You could become a moose rustler I suppose, but the money's not steady and you get injured a lot." I gazed sadly at him, then rolled my eyes at the unfairness of everything.

Laughing at my lame joke, he shook his head and said, "I've staked a claim on a rough piece of ground about two miles from my own property. A creek runs through the middle of my claim and I've panned gold there. I know there's a lot more to be found and I don't think the owner's aware of it. To him the land is probably just a real-estate investment he plans to sell in the future for a profit." Grinning at me, Trevor informed me that other than Sarah and I, no one else knew about the gold, probably because it's deposited in such steep ground. He took a swallow of tea, then added, "I had a word with Brian, my boss at the garage. Since I can recommend a good replacement for myself, he agreed to give me the summers off. Maybe eventually I'll build a number of cabins around the lake, like here, then spend my warm-weather time taking care of clients. Apparently, according to your buddy Keith, there's a ready-made demand in all the spill-overs from Three Duck Lake."

"How do you plan to get to work in the winter?" I asked. "Isn't there so much snow that it doesn't matter how good the road might be?"

Sighing deeply, he answered, "Yes, there's that too: I'll need a tracked snow vehicle to get up and down from the cabin." He shrugged, then added, "I'm sure I can rig up a system involving the truck, but anyway, that's all down the road a bit." He sighed again and said, "It's just another expense." His words lingered over the table in the quiet lodge, then seemed to blend into the faint shouts of a client outside on the path.

Wordlessly, I got up to retrieve the leather folder from a kitchen drawer, and wrote him a cheque. Handing it to him, I said, "Hope this helps and if you need more, don't ask."

He took it gratefully and read it, saying, "That's very generous, thank you." After regarding me happily for a moment, he said, "I should be able to start paying you back next week, but I'm afraid it'll cost you some work. We'll need Pooch and his saddlebags too. The three of us can drive out there, then climb down the ravine to the creek and spend most of the day panning. After that, we can get back to the truck and drive to the cabin: Sarah's made it comfortable enough."

"I'm looking forward to seeing everything," I said, "there should be no problem in taking next Monday off."

At this moment, Pauline rushed into the lodge and asked me where her spare work gloves were hiding. While we searched for them, I told her of Trevor's plan: "He's agreed to a 50-50 split with me on any gold we pan from the creek," I said, "and I'm sure Sarah's given you details about the road and cabin." After finding the gloves tucked away securely at the back of a drawer and handing them to her with a flourish, I said, "He's going to pick me up next Monday morning, then we'll do some panning on the way to his new place. We'll spend the night at the cabin, but he'll drive me back here on Tuesday morning. Think you can manage without me for a day?"

Not looking alarmed at all by thoughts of my absence, Pauline said, "Moon and I can stumble along, I suppose." After a moment of apparently untroubled cogitation, she turned to Trevor and said, "You can have breakfast here: will 7 a.m. be okay?"

Nodding cheerfully, he responded by telling us that living in his small apartment in town, he rarely made himself a proper breakfast, so he'd look forward to it. Pauline smiled at him, then left to return to the garden. Trevor and I finished our tea, with me reiterating my curiosity about the property, while he looked pleased. Soon after, we went up to the garden to watch the women work, with neither of us volunteering to help. We played with the dogs for a while, then Sarah and Trevor drove off in the Flaming Barge, tooting its somewhat feeble horn in farewell.

Fangs in the Drink

*F*ollowing supper that evening, Pauline and I were at the sink when she said, "Sarah told me she's fed up living with her folks: she wants a place of her own. She'd like to move into Trevor's apartment, but it's too small and shabby for her. So this cabin seems to be perfect for her, though I wonder how she'll get along by herself out there."

"She has lots of interests and can entertain herself, so I don't think being alone has ever been a problem for her," I replied.

"Yeah sure," said Pauline with a grin, "but she likes to show off too much to be solitary for long." She chuckled to herself and shook her head slowly, saying, "She'd never admit it, but I think she regrets quitting school. She misses the superiority she feels when she's among her peers, along with the fascinating exchanges she had with her teachers, of course." Then Pauline looked at me and giggled outright, saying, "There's always her book-club meetings, although I can't see her being a member for much longer."

Surprised at this bit of news, I asked, "She belongs to a book club?"

Smiling grimly now, Pauline nodded and told me the ten or so middle-aged ladies of the literary society wanted some younger blood in the mix, and along came Sarah. It only took a meeting or two for her to discover most of the women enjoyed discussing nursey or medieval romance novels, with rich and needy patients or heaving bosoms on every page.

Supposedly to challenge them a bit, Pauline informed me Sarah had brought two books to the following session: Ardrey's 'Territorial Imperative', plus Sallinger's 'Catcher in the Rye'. Pauline tried to grimace and said, "When she took them out of her pack and recommended them as topics for the next meeting, apparently the ladies had looked at the two books like hubby had just dragged something nasty onto the kitchen floor." Momentarily unable to continue speaking, she grabbed a tea towel, and dried a few dishes. Once she had her mirth under control, she told me there'd been a frosty silence while the ladies had distastefully regarded the two tomes now on the table with the more 'proper' books. Fiona Swartz, president of the learned ladies' group and who Sarah described as 'a stodgy old broad with a moustache', told her disdainfully that 'pornography and politics' weren't on their reading lists.

Pauline rolled her eyes and told me Sarah had said angrily, "Obviously, none of them had read either book; they'd probably heard they were controversial, so they shied away, the silly old biddies."

Shaking her head and saying ruefully that Sarah would be unlikely to attend further meetings, Pauline laughed again. "Never mind all that," she continued, "Sarah's just brimming with excitement at the thought of her new life; she'll be a busy girl for the next little while, so there'll be no time for fistfights at the book club."

We finished washing the dishes, and went out to the wharf to see the sun go down. As we relaxed with our glasses of lemonade, we idly watched as a rowboat carrying three people was being paddled towards cabin 'Larry'. Shortly after disappearing into the quickly darkening bend in the shoreline, we heard an expletive vehemently shouted over the calm waters. The word flew through the evening like a crippled duck, then there was a flurry of heated vocal exchanges and finally, silence.

This quiet didn't last long, however; a few minutes later we were approached by a peeved and thoroughly damp individual. He was wearing a soaked shirt and pants, from what I could see in the gloaming; his shoes were wet too. With his hair plastered unbecomingly to his skull, he indistinctly told us he'd just dropped the lower plate of his dentures into the lake. Apparently, he'd immediately gone in after it, but to no avail. Then he looked at me as if he expected me to do something about it, and right now.

Remembering his name and discreetly moving back on the bench so he wouldn't drip on me, I said, "Sorry Mr. Pierce, it's too dark now, I'll look for your teeth come sunrise, so it seems you'll be fasting until tomorrow."

In his wetness, he looked crossly at me for a moment, but obviously being a reasonable guy, he then told me exactly where he'd lost his choppers and added belligerently, "I don't get up until 9 when I'm on holiday, you know," then he humphed indignantly. He glared at me as if he figured I was about to sermonise on the evils of sloth, so I quickly changed my opinion of his character. 'Perhaps he's not so rational after all' I thought.

He carefully picked through his sodden wallet with his pinky extended and an anxious look on his face. "I'd better separate all this before it becomes a solid block," he was muttering to himself as he peeled a card off some others. I couldn't help noticing he talked with a sputtering, spongy sound to his voice, like he was trying to converse with a large cigar sideways in his mouth. But I knew his missing teeth must certainly be the cause of his non-crisp vocalisations, so I gazed up at his caved-in-looking lower face with sympathy. Just as I was about to make an inane comment about there being a full moon tonight, a final beam of sunlight flashed through the trees momentarily, spotlighting Mr. Pierce, unfortunately.

A few strands of his dashing comb-over hairstyle were hanging limply over his left ear, thus revealing the bald spot at the top of his head. Suddenly seeming aware of his shambolic appearance and trying to restore some semblance of dignity, he turned away from the blinding shaft of light, saying firmly, "I should be getting back to the cabin."

Pauline had been startled at first by his sudden and rather waterlogged appearance out of the evening gloom, but now she surveyed Mr. Pierce's damp form with concern in her eyes. "Get into some dry clothes," she said mock-scoldingly, "you'll catch your death of cold otherwise."

"Yes dear," he responded in a husbandly way. Then, realising what he'd just said, he quickly corrected himself by saying, "I mean...you're right, I'll change, and since I can't eat without my teeth, I guess I'll have to drink all night."

This casual bravado had obviously been directed solely at Pauline, who looked her usual

lovely self in a madras blouse and jeans. Not-
withstanding the strained circumstances, he'd
been trying to charm her as do most adult males,
but I'd long ago decided to not take offense at
these flirtations. During his devil-may-care grin
at her, Mr. Pierce swept his damp tresses from
his forehead and discovered the flap of hair hanging over his ear. Plainly upset by this disruption
to his manly good looks, he smiled hurriedly
at her, then turned to me and said in his garbled and spray-filled way, "Hope you find my
dentures, see you tomorrow," wasting no time
with fond farewells and slightly waterlogged, he
disappeared down the path to the cabins without
another gummy word. Pauline smiled at me and
sighed; she raised her eyebrows, and gazed at the
dark water of the lake. She said nothing, but she
was shaking her head slightly.

The following morning, she was busy in the
kitchen area when I came out of the bedroom
at seven. Since she knows the last thing I want
to do is to go for a bracing dip in the chilly lake
immediately after rising, she hugged me and
said encouragingly, "Have half a muffin now, go

out to your little job, then we can have a proper breakfast together."

Stifling the urge to whine, I reluctantly let go of her to get the swim-fins and goggles from the shed out back. At first the dogs looked at me questioningly, since they'd never before seen me getting prepared for a swim. But they obviously decided that whatever was happening was good news, so they started howling, with Banjo as lead vocalist.

His sister Grace had inherited the intelligence of most Border Collies from her mother, so training her had been relatively easy. With Pooch being proud daddy of the two siblings but much bigger, his sometimes harsh treatment of them keeps them in line, mostly. But Banjo has the smarts of a mud puddle, so if Pooch had hands, he'd probably throw them up in despair at his son's obtuseness. Doubtlessly the frequent victim of startled and angry reactions from clients upon his unannounced appearance in a cabin, Banjo would nonetheless wander into any open door, supposedly expecting glad welcomes and lots to eat. Instead, I'm sure he often got a boot in the butt to indicate that his tail-wagging presence wasn't appreciated, but he never learns from all these subtle hints.

Anyway, the four of us made the short trek down to the wharf with much yipping and howling involved, mostly coming from the dogs. So, by the time we reached the water's edge, my morning blues had evaporated.

The boat was half-onshore, so the dogs piled in without any invitations from me. Pooch showed his disciplinary side by nipping and head-butting the kiddies into their correct places in the stern, then the somewhat settled canine crew turned their eager and expectant eyes to me. I pushed us onto the lake, then rowed the short distance towards cabin 'Larry's' wharf. As we were on the way, I kept telling myself that the anticipation of an unpleasant event is often worse than reality, but I obviously hadn't convinced the sissy in me. The water still looked awfully cold and uninviting.

The dogs watched with keen interest as I stopped rowing, then searched under the bow for the anchor. It was only a rope tied around a rock, but I thought it best to use it. I didn't need a sudden gust blowing the boat across the lake as I was busily surveying the bottom. So I splashed it in and almost immediately felt it hit ground, since we were only in twelve feet of water, a short way off 'Larry's' wharf. Then I did an awkward strip-act, wherein I disrobed down to my swim-trunks and the dogs tilted their heads in puzzlement as they regarded me. When I reached for the flippers, Banjo started singing heartily and the others joined in, so there was no longer any tranquillity on the morning lake. Sticking my arms into and beyond the excited trio of canines in the stern, I flipped in the step-sling attached to the boat, so I could re-board from the water.

Without dwelling further on my chick-en-hearted reluctance, I donned the goggles and jumped into the lake. I'd been expecting the shock of cold water, but this hadn't helped, since it felt like ice had instantly formed on my extremities. Pooch and Grace joined me, but for some reason, Banjo stayed in the boat watch-ing with his paws on the sideboard and his tail wagging. After swimming around for a moment to get my blood unfrozen, I adjusted my goggles, took a deep breath, and went under.

The lake-bottom was mostly gravel with a few larger rocks scattered around, but there was no sign of Mr. Pierce's dentures. Just before resurfacing, I looked up and saw the undersides of Pooch and Grace as they paddled around the boat waiting for me. Banjo had his head underwater as he leaned from the boat to intently observe my every action. By the time my head popped up, he was coughing and sneezing violently in the stern, since he'd apparently forgotten not to breath normally when dunking the noggin under the wet stuff. When he saw me holding onto the side of the boat, he rushed over to say hello. But even though I was wearing goggles, I didn't want him hacking in my face, so I went under again. By this time I'd loosened up and was half-enjoying the morning excursion, but overall, I knew I'd prefer eating breakfast in the lodge.

On my second scan of the lake-bottom I didn't find the dentures, but something else grabbed my attention. A vertical length of rope tied to the boat was moving away at a leisurely pace; the anchor had obviously come loose. As I got to the surface, I could see the vessel had drifted some distance towards the lake's centre with Banjo still in the boat. With his paws on the sideboard, he was plainly excited but puzzled, as if he didn't quite understand why the clan was slowly coming apart. I was half-expecting a sad wave from him as he continued his slow and sideways journey, but he disappeared into the boat-bottom instead, so all I could see was the tip of his tail.

Since I was wearing flippers and the canine-captained craft was only a hundred feet away, I decided to swim after her. Normally, I'd let the boat drift to the Narrows, then tow her away using another vessel at some later time, but this was different. I'd got it into my head that it was my duty to reunite Mr. Pierce and his teeth pronto, so I didn't want to wait for 'some time later'.

Banjo was now watching as the three of us started on our quest. Pooch and Grace easily swam past me before we'd gone a third of the way to the boat, mainly because I swim like a turtle with a lead shell and hiccups. As I propel myself through the water with my patented combination of dog-paddle, breast stroke and free-style, there's lots of splashing involved. Along with all the noise and spray, I apparently stretch my neck up frequently.

On a recent occasion, Sarah watched my 'let's not drown' swim style and shook her head. When I finally floundered back to the boat after my short cool-off dip, she said, "The way you always bob up and down makes it look like you're trying to scrape your head on the sky." Grinning at me, she'd then added, "You're better off in the boat." Although I felt this pronouncement had been correct but rather uncharitable, I now say fervently, "Amen!"

Anyway, there were three pairs of encouraging eyes observing my splashy approach as I finally reached the boat. I climbed in and as I rowed back to the search area, I figured I'd find a more suitable rock on the bottom, and tie it to the anchor-rope. Using my razor-sharp deductive reasoning, I calculated that taking the rock up to the boat from its twelve-foot depth probably wouldn't work, so I'd have to do all the tying underwater. With this in mind, I stopped rowing and let the boat glide to our original spot. I untangled the rat's nest of loops and knots at the line's end, then dove in with it in my hand. We'd happened to stop directly over a likely-looking anchor stone, so I swam down to it.

Sitting beside the rock was Mr. Pierce's lower dental plate, looking vaguely sinister. The half-hoop of pink and white plastic looked utterly out of place on the gravel, so I paused a short moment to peruse it. Deciding the fake tusks appeared more obscene than scary in these surroundings; I scooped them up gladly and immediately abandoned my anchor-plans.

The three dogs were in the water when I resurfaced, so it was a while before we were all in the boat again. After finishing their 'let's shake half the lake onto Henry' ceremony, they settled into their places in the stern. Showing them the dentition, I said, "Look what I just found!" so they all sniffed at it curiously, but without much enthusiasm. Banjo seemed mildly interested and even licked them a few times, so I wondered how Mr. Pierce would react if he knew there'd been a dog tasting his teeth.

Once I'd rowed to our beach, my canine passengers scrambled out then loitered there, supposedly waiting to see if I was about to do something interesting. But no such luck: I just stood there wondering how best to return Mr. Pierce's escaped choppers to him. Since it was still much too early for him to have risen, I couldn't hand them over personally. And if I simply put them on the table outside his cabin, the chances were good they'd become either a macabre decoration or an integral part of a crow's nest. So I reached into the boat to take my pad and pencil from my shirt pocket, then wrote him a note reading, 'Found your teeth! Pick them up at the lodge whenever you want'...H. The dogs joined me as I jogged down the path to his still-shuttered cabin and slipped the message under the door. On the way back, I could smell Pauline's delectable coffee brewing, and since I could do without the intestinal orchestrations, I was glad

I'd eaten that half-muffin before heading out. Nonetheless, my gut managed to sound like a swooping French horn as I grandly entered the lodge and smiled at Pauline.

Since she was accustomed to my stomach making much ado about being fed, she ignored the soundtrack and asked, "Find the teeth?" I nodded and handed them over, so she washed them, then wrapped them neatly in brown butcher's paper. Putting the little package next to me as I sat at the table, she had to raise her voice slightly, so she could be heard over the gurgling brass band sounds issuing forth from my mid-section. "He'll be here for his teeth before we finish breakfast," she predicted, still disregarding the musical accompaniment.

She was right; I was just starting on my second helping of scrambled eggs, when Mr. Pierce appeared. No longer sporting his 'drenched and dishevelled' look, he thanked me for finding them, then grinned confidently at Pauline. As he took the little gift-wrapped bundle from me, I noticed his comb-over was now firmly cemented in place, and also that he seemed in a hurry to leave. Not bothering to re-weaponise his lower gums at the moment, he thanked me again and nodded in a debonair way to Pauline, then he left.

"You have a thing for him, don't you?" I asked her jealously.

She sighed longingly and tried to look guilty as she replied, "Yes, I believe I do. I think I've been swept away by his 'man of the world' manner, plus his hair-style, of course."

Unable to keep up the pretense, she giggled as I told her scoldingly, "You shouldn't speak sarcastically about our guests, they're our bread and butter, you know."

Not mentioning the huge hypocrisy of my statement, she looked at me with narrowed eyes and said, "You started it." She poured my morning coffee into what she sometimes calls 'the barrel', and I'm always surprised my large mug hasn't visited the lake-bottom yet. She watched as I slathered raspberry jam onto a thick slice of toast, adding, "Anyway, he's married and he's leaving on Friday, so any relationship is probably doomed." She gazed off into the distance for a moment and slowly shook her head in pretended disappointment. Seeming to recover quite abruptly from her sad speculations, she said cheerfully, "Oh well: ships passing in the night. I guess I'm stuck with you." She grinned at me, and had another piece of toast.

The Poplar Road

Days at the lodge blend into each other, and it seemed no time until the guys arrived for our regular Friday night poker game. I got miserable cards all evening; I'd rather not discuss the details, but it's enough to say I didn't win many hands. Keith didn't seem very sympathetic to me as he departed for the night with the other guys. "My heart bleeds for you," he said with deep feeling and a cheerful smile on his face.

"It's comforting to know someone really cares," I replied, looking into his insincere eyes and patting him unctuously on the side of his upper arm. "Thanks for being so supportive," I gushed gratefully, thinking that maybe later, I'd construct a small doll replica of him and stick pins into it.

As though reading my mind, he chuckled, then regarded me happily for a moment (he'd won a lot of hands that evening: big deal!) Finally, he asked, "Did you have a chat with Trevor about the property he bought?"

"Yeah," I replied, glad to change topics, "we're driving up there on Monday morning."

"It's a pretty little spot," said Keith, "but it's much wilder than here. Trevor would like to set things up like here at Three Duck Lake, but he's still unsure about the details. Anyway, first things first: a decent access road is needed." Halfway through the main door now, Keith added, "You'll love it, and the cabin there isn't bad either: keep me informed!" With that, he headed towards the parking lot carrying a substantial amount of my cash and whistling merrily.

Ecstatic to see a guest glad and relaxed, I shut the door so I could perform my role in the one-scene play I like to call 'it's YOUR fault'.

"So, how come you dealt me dirty laundry all night?" I asked Pauline peevishly. "You're the dealer," I whined, "so you're responsible for all the crippled and nearly-dead cards stopping by to smell up my little corner of the world this evening." Looking at her sharply, I added, "Try concentrating a bit more when you shuffle."

"Yes dear," she replied as she rolled the felt covering from the table, "you'll get better cards next time."

And that was it. The topic was never brought up again. Of course, I didn't seriously believe she had anything to do with the moribund nature of my cards. The poker gods must have been in a graveyard mood, plain and simple. Blaming her was my way of laughing off the loss, while I strongly suspect she always views occasions like this as prime opportunities to stop me from describing all my sad hands.

We were busy all weekend, with the grand finale being a crawfish curry for Sunday night's dinner. After eating and cleaning up, we waited for Moon to come down, then we played a couple of games of Scrabble.

I couldn't sleep that night, so I bounded joyfully (ha ha) out of bed at 2 to write in my journal. Pauline got up at 5 and had a quick cup of tea with me, saying she was headed up to the garden, but that she'd come down with Moon as soon as

Trevor arrived. She left with the dogs, so I added a few more profound words to my journal, and went out back to lackadaisically chop some wood. I heard the Barge pulling into the lot a while later, so I ceased my lethargic labours and went out to meet him on the path to the lodge.

"Good morning!" he exclaimed cheerily, "ready to go?" Not waiting for me to respond, he then asked, "What's for breakfast?"

"Pauline remembered you were quite fond of her sourdough pancakes, so that's what we're having," I reported. "I packed my personal gear last night, along with Pooch's saddlebags, so we're itching to go."

"Good!" he said, "but there's no big rush, let's have breakfast first. It'll sure be a nice change from my usual bowl of cereal."

Pauline and Moon came down from the garden and greeted him fondly as we all gathered momentarily on the path. After we'd gone inside, Trevor seated himself with an anticipatory look at Pauline as she served the fruit salad. She said, "While you tuck into that, I'll get the pancakes going; the batter's already been made."

A moment later, she put a cut-crystal carafe filled with a golden-brown liquid beside him on the table, saying, "That's real maple syrup." She thought flavoured corn syrup pretending it just came out of a tree was two-faced, so she'd have nothing to do with the stuff. The carafe looked as if it should contain an expensive liqueur as it sat on a silver tray in some posh club and definitely not in this rustic setting so soon after sunup. But it'd been a gift from a friend, so Pauline uses it whenever she can. Anyway, since maple syrup is almost as expensive as good booze and is presented so nicely in the pint-sized bottle, it turns out to be a rather fitting container.

The pancakes were big, so two of them were more than enough for me. I watched in awe as Trevor easily polished off four of them, and looked disappointed when Moon told him there was no more batter. "How on earth is Sarah going to keep you fed?" she asked rhetorically, "you've had enough!" This was exactly how a mother might treat her child, so Pauline raised her eyebrows surreptitiously at me, but said nothing. We finished our coffee a few minutes later, then

I reiterated my concerns at leaving the women to run things for a day. Moon replied in an appropriately anxious voice, "We'll try to get along," but she seemed to be suppressing a shrug.

After Trevor had thanked Pauline effusively, he had a private little chat with Moon, then helped me with my gear and Pooch's saddlebags.

With its intimidating appearance, the Flaming Barge seemed out of place in the lot, like a parrot at a sparrow convention. As we loaded our bags into the truck and Pooch sniffed excitedly at its tires, Trevor said, "I can't wait to show you the place, and I think you'll find the creek on my claim quite interesting too." Now giving me a deadpan look but winking conspiratorially, he opened the rear door for the dog and said to him, "The whole seat's yours boy, you'll be riding in comfort today." After Pooch had jumped in, Trevor slammed the door shut and jingled the keys, saying to me, "We seem to have everything, so let's hit the road."

As we drove off, I couldn't help noticing again that he behaved much more maturely than I did when I was in my early twenties. There was a relaxed assurance about him that was difficult to describe to myself, so I quit pondering and just enjoyed the drive.

Thick forests of pine and cedar lined the dirt road as we drove along, so I sat back to appreciate their serenity. Sitting on the seat behind and looking through the windshield, Pooch yawned loudly in my ear and thus startled me back to the present world.

"We have to stop in town," Trevor said as we turned onto the two-lane blacktop, "it'll only take a few minutes." Buildings started appearing roadside as we drove through the outskirts, plus there was some traffic: all pickups and no cars.

We pulled up alongside a vehicle at a stoplight, so I was sitting just to the left of the driver in the other truck. Since he was scanning our paint-job as if it bruised his sensibilities, I turned my baseball cap backwards, then gave him a V-sign with my fingers as our eyes met. I asked Trevor if he could really stomp on it when the light turned green, so he grinned and nodded, then looked around for any meddling cop cars. Feeling as if I was sixteen again, I nodded at the other driver, who was now regarding me like I was an escapee from the Home for the Mentally Decrepit. When the light turned green and Trevor floored the accelerator maniacally, I was pressed into the seat as the big V8 roared into action, then quickly thrust us forward. I was still plastered to the seat as Trevor speed-shifted into second gear, but I managed to take a peek into the passenger-side outer rear-view mirror. Our fellow-driver had his windshield washer spurting furiously, while his wipers were flaying the glass at top speed. Apparently, he'd picked up some gravel or dust somewhere, then he'd chosen to clean it off at a busy intersection. What an idiot!

Turning to Trevor and waggling an admonishing finger at him, I advised him he shouldn't drive so aggressively, he'd get a bad reputation, otherwise.

Not mentioning the fact I'd been the chief instigator of our little drama at the stoplight, he said sadly, "Yeah I know I shouldn't, but sometimes I just can't help myself. And it sure doesn't help my gas mileage when I goose her like that; this thing's a thirsty elephant."

He parked in front of the hardware store and said, "I have a few things to buy, so can you pick up one of the Daily National newspapers at the corner? I'll only be a few minutes, in the meantime."

I went to fetch the paper and also bought some liquorice in the general store. As I was dawdling along the street on my way back, I saw him come out with a filled shopping bag clutched to his chest. He opened the back door of the crew-cab, and once Pooch had thoroughly sniffed at its contents, Trevor put the bag on the floor. Nodding at a spool of quarter-inch rope that'd been squeezed into the top, I asked, "Plan to practise your knot-tying skills a lot?"

He laughed and shook his head, saying, "For some reason, Sarah doesn't like clothes lines made with baling wire."

I rolled my eyes and responded, "Sometimes women can be so picky: go figure. If an occasional rust stain appears on a blouse or on their undies, then so what?" I finished my Declaration for Slobs Worldwide with a mystified grimace and a puzzled tone to my voice.

Trevor chuckled at my apparent failure to understand, then closed the truck door and said, "Let's get rolling," so we both climbed into the vehicle.

It didn't take long to leave the outskirts of town behind, as we drove down the blacktop for a few miles. Then we turned left onto a dirt road that was obviously headed towards higher ground. It started to rain steadily but lightly, more like a heavy mist, really. As he studied the sky ahead, Trevor said, "It doesn't look like those clouds want to move, so I think we'll be socked-in for the day. I'm worried about the steep ravine getting slick; we can do this some other time, you know."

"It's hardly raining at all," I replied cavalierly as he switched on the windshield wipers, "I'd like to see the place, anyway."

So we drove on, through rocky ground with occasional clusters of pines coming close to the deteriorating road. "No one comes up here," Trevor said as we bumped along, "except maybe hunters and moonshiners." I offered him some liquorice, so we both chawed as the road got worse the higher it got in elevation.

Finally, he stopped before we got to a deeply-rutted muddy area and said, "Time for four-wheel drive! Get out, will you, and twist the lock on the hub of the front wheel. It'll be slow going from now on." Looking worriedly at the messy patch of ground, he added, "The next half mile of road was built on topsoil, so it gets sloppy. I'll have to get the cat driver to clean it up." He didn't complain about this large cash outlay; it wasn't necessary, since his head-shake and sour look were eloquent enough.

The road certainly wasn't as bad as some I've seen, so we didn't get bogged down at any point, but we weren't breaking any speed records either. After we'd skidded and heaved up the long-abandoned mining road, we came to a wider spot appearing to be a turnaround or a few parking spaces. Trevor stopped and turned to me, saying, "We literally go into the trees from here, so can you see where the road carries on?"

I looked around, focussing on a gap in the pushed-up roots and tree-trunks encircling the small area. "There?" I asked hesitantly as I pointed, "there's just enough room for a truck to get through, but the forest's beyond. So, who'd want to drive right into the trees?"

Trevor chuckled and said, "Take a closer look, the tire tracks should tell you something." Upon second perusal, it was now obvious to me that the road beyond the gap was a seven foot wide line of poplar saplings leading into the bush. Since the tracks continued and all the other trees were scraggly pines or tamaracks, I surmised this was somehow the road.

"You mean THAT?" I asked incredulously as I pointed again at the gap.

Trevor leaned forward to retrieve a topo-map from the glove box and said, "Here, I'll show you." Unfolding it, then propping it up on the steering wheel, he took a felt marker from his shirt pocket and drew an 'X' on the map, saying, "We're here. From this location the road's been built on bed-rock, so there'll be no more muddy patches." Using the marker as a pointer, he indicated our route, telling me we had two miles of tree-pushing to do. "We go along the side of this hill with the ravine and creek to our right, then we gradually go downhill to the lake and cabin," he said.

"What's with all the trees growing on the road?" I asked.

"Mother Nature's taking over," he responded, "the road's not been used for years and there's been all that empty space to fill. The area plainly suits the poplars, so now there's a seven foot wide and two mile long grove of them." He smiled, but then he quickly grew serious and said, "They're very pretty, but they're nothing but weeds, really, and they'll have to go."

He'd had a mildly resentful expression on his face as he'd spoken, and I couldn't help but remember seeing exactly the same thing on another friend's face. He lived in town and had been threatening harsh punishment to any crabgrass that dared plant roots in his lawn. I didn't mention this humorous little similarity to Trevor, of course.

Continuing with his report on the poplars, he was saying, "They can only grow to six or seven feet, because they're on rock and there's nowhere to sink their roots. There's a heavy-duty front bumper and grill-screen on the Barge, so there's no problem pushing our way through."

He returned the map to the glove box and said, "You'd better roll up Pooch's window; otherwise, he'll be slapped in the face with branches if he tries sticking his head out."

As I turned awkwardly in my seat and was cranking the rear window shut, Pooch took the opportunity to lick me on the nose, then woof gladly right into my face. After thanking him for the adoration and the face-wash, I straightened up, and offered Trevor some more liquorice. So we sat chewing the candy in the shelter of the truck, while the misty rain seemed suspended in the air outside. "We'll get lazy if we sit around here much more," said Trevor as he started the Barge and got settled behind the steering wheel, "let's go!"

We squeezed between the logs and pushed-up earth, then we didn't have much trouble driving through the saplings. They disappeared under the front of the truck, scraped their way to the rear, then popped up behind.

"Aren't you afraid that doing this might scratch your inspiring paint-job?" I asked, as poplar leaves and branches dragged along the closed passenger-side window.

Looking reluctantly accepting, Trevor replied, "I suppose that's the price I'll have to pay." Then he drove on for a bit, until we came to a length of pink flagging tape tied to one of the small trees in our way. "This is where we park," said Trevor as he stopped just short of the tape, "we head down the ravine to the creek from here." Turning in his seat and grinning at me, he asked, "Ready? It'll be steep and wet climbing down there, so maybe we should go straight to the cabin. We could go fishing; it'd probably be nice out on the lake today."

Although the suggestion had been tempting, I put on a stoic face, as if ease and enjoyment weren't part of my daily routine. "We're here now, so we might as well go down. I'd like to see the creek on your claim."

Since the saplings were tight against the truck, opening the doors was a hassle. Once he'd managed to exit the vehicle, Trevor said, "I wanted to clear an area here, but I soon saw I was just ruining my axe." Apparently, he'd tried chopping at the trees close to the ground, but he'd ended up slicing into the hard rock. This tends to dull a blade somewhat, plus along with little fragments of jagged metal flying off the axe-head, it's dangerous too.

Trying to cut the little trunks square and at road-level had been impossible with an axe, so he'd thought of using a chainsaw. But these noisy tools get pouty and belligerent if they're forced to chew stone for even an instant. They like to cough and belch out clouds of dirty blue smoke if this happens, just as a warning to the careless user. If it happens again, the work-saving instrument will whip its chain around an extremity and/or explode. Since Trevor could do without the drama and loud hissy-fits of a chainsaw, he'd thought of a much quieter tool: manual bolt-cutters.

By the time we got to the rear of the vehicle, Pooch had gone exploring the new turf with his tail held high in curiosity and excitement. Trevor retrieved the scissor-like tool from the truck's bed, then experimented with it by clipping down a few of the small poplars surrounding us. "It works fine," said Trevor, as he easily cut through a sapling trunk and tossed the tree aside. "I just happen to have two bolt-cutters in the truck, so can you give me a hand?" So we took fifteen minutes to clear away a thirty-foot stretch of road. Some of the saplings could actually be pulled from the shallow fissures in which they grew, but most had to be cut down. When we'd finished, the cleared area looked decidedly odd, with the nobbled road surface in the gently falling rain looking unnatural and conspicuous, but now we had a parking space free from the clutter of the small poplars. And because we'd cut them off square at road-level, there wasn't a carpet of up-thrust wooden spikes to damage the truck tires.

I called for Pooch and he appeared out of the bush thirty seconds later, looking pleased with his discoveries. Trevor insisted on putting the saddlebags onto the dog, so in ecstatic gratitude, Pooch slathered his tongue over the man's eyebrows as he bent down to perform the task. Wiping the dog spit from his forehead, then donning his own pack and seeing I was now wearing mine, Trevor said, "Let's go!"

Bears, Gold and Squirrels

We walked just ten paces before the ravine revealed itself in its scary steepness. As I peeked through the evergreens growing at its edge, it appeared to be a near-vertical four-hundred foot drop to the white-water creek below. The sides were bare glistening rock, while small trees and moss inhabited tiny ledges here and there.

"It looks worse than it really is," said Trevor, seeing my doubtful expression, "just follow me and you'll be okay." Then he strode confidently through a tangle of branches he'd obviously cleared on a previous trip and headed down.

The ravine's slope wasn't close to being vertical, but it was plenty steep enough anyway.

At first I worried about Pooch's inability to use handholds on his way, but heights plainly didn't faze him. He followed a zigzag course behind Trevor, then he decided to take a more direct route. He ran straight down with his saddlebags rattling alarmingly, but he was sure-footed and confident. As I stood clutching the trunk of a small pine and worrying about my foot-hold in the spongy moss, the dog hurdled impediments as though he was unconcerned that eventually he'd have to come to a stop. As I watched his casual fearlessness, I decided there must be a few mountain-goat genes in his makeup.

Trevor was well ahead of me now; he moved through the bush with the same unhurried nonchalance as Moon. He looked as if he was just poking along, but actually he was making good time. I found this very annoying, especially when he stood beside the creek with Pooch and looked up at me as I struggled down the ravine wall.

Even though we were only 50 feet apart, the roaring creek almost drowned out our words as he pointed out the best route for me to take to the bottom. An added thrill occurred when I inattentively grasped the stem of a devil's club plant, so as its spines went through my glove and into my hand, I let go of it double-quick and nearly fell to the rocks below.

As I finally made my way down and was standing beside Trevor, he grinned widely and said, "See? That was easy. Now all you have to worry about is climbing back up again!"

It was truly a wild place, so for a moment I felt as though we didn't belong. We were standing on a relatively flat area only 30 feet long, but it quickly rose in elevation as I looked upstream. With the creek roaring down a six foot waterfall just behind us and with the silvery mist mixing with the spray, it occurred to me that sometimes we voluntarily put ourselves into rather uncomfortable situations. I looked up at the ravine wall I'd just descended and immediately wished I hadn't, since joyful thoughts of re-climbing it popped into my mind.

Trevor put a hand on my shoulder and pointed downstream, saying, "The creek drains into my lake right beside the cabin. It's less than a mile and a half, but the going's so tough that it's a two hour hike each way to reach my claim. It's much quicker the way we did it, so now, let's find some gold!"

He explained that his claim included some of the lower portions of the creek, then added, "I've looked, but there's nothing there. This is the area that's grabbed my attention; there's gold here and I've already found some." Indicating our present location, he told me it was a potentially good spot, but that a little past the falls upstream seemed even better. Seeing me scan the rough terrain up there with doubt in my eye, he reassured me by saying, "Don't worry, there's a fairly easy way up there, but we have to cross the creek first." He grinned at me and said, "C'mon, I'll show you."

The creek was only six feet wide, so it was easy to find a stepping-stone to the other side. As we slowly climbed upstream, we were forced closer to the opposite ravine wall. I discovered a bounteous crop of trip-inducing juniper bushes had somehow found a home there, so I stopped to voice my admiration (or maybe something

not even vaguely complimentary) for their har-
diness and strength of purpose. Up ahead of
me, Pooch had got himself and his saddlebags
wedged between the unbending trunk of one of
the pretty bushes and the ravine wall. Although
being seen talking angrily to a plant might
raise questions about one's mental well-being,
nonetheless I found it necessary to leave the
junipers with no doubts about my true feelings.
Once I finished speechifying, I took three paces
towards the dog and tripped on a ground-hug-
ging branch. Not only do they hide your feet so
you don't know where you're placing them, but
the plant seems to push you back, if you bother
to get going again, that is. While standing or
lying there and weeping in frustration is always
an option, Pooch needed help, so I carried on.

After getting the dog unstuck, he made haste
to catch up with Trevor, who was well ahead
by now. I looked at the ravine wall on this side
of the creek and saw it was much steeper than
the one we'd descended. I shuddered as I imagined myself trying to get down; serious climbing
gear would doubtlessly be required, or maybe

even a parachute. Anyway, I don't think tricking around with gravity is particularly fulfilling: I prefer picnicking in a sunny meadow.

As I emerged from the bushes to get closer to the creek, I saw Trevor had taken off his pack and was untying its drawstring. He was obviously eager to start, and his excitement was contagious. "Take a couple of these bags," he said, holding them out to me, "they're just ten-pound potato sacks, but they're better than the plastic sample bags for holding paydirt, so any water drains out through the burlap."

Since Pooch was now snuffling at his pack as it sat on the rocks, Trevor said to him, "Glad you're here, boy. I need some things from your saddle-bags." Retrieving a gold pan and small folding spade, he said to me as he rebuckled the bag, "I'll leave your stuff here; take it out when you need it." Looking quietly elated, but trying to put on a serious face, he told me he wanted to show me something. Walking carefully to the creek, he said, "Watch out for these big rocks, some are loose."

We'd only gone a few paces before a second waterfall appeared around a bend. It was smaller than the first I'd seen, but much more impressive. Water gushed and roiled down a thirty-foot slab of raw rock, then spilled noisily over a gap in the stone to flow into an oblong pool about a dozen feet across. It was very loud here. Shouting into my ear, Trevor told me his claim line crossed the creek only a few yards above the falls, but said, "If anyone wants to explore that area, then good luck to him. He'll probably need wings, along with a strong belief in life after death." He chuckled as he looked up at the wild waterway as it raced down, then added, "There can't be much gold in the creek up there, anyway. It's all been washed down here!" He smiled confidently, then we watched the water cascade over the rock's edge and fall three feet into the pool. After a moment of quiet perusal, he said loudly, "Let's move away a bit, so I don't have to shout."

After we'd retreated from the creek, he pointed out a vague mark on the ravine wall and said, "You probably saw this high water mark; this creek was once a big river." I nodded, even though I hadn't noticed. "That area around the first falls we saw has gold," he said, "I think it was deposited when this was a river. Then for some reason, the water receded and I'm hoping most of the gold was washed into this pool," he gestured at the area, but we couldn't see the falls, now that we were standing a few paces beyond the bend. He finished by saying, "I think a lot of gold has tumbled down the creek over the ages, only to be trapped in the pool. It's settled on the bottom and can't be swept away, that is, until I arrived on the scene."

"How deep is the water there?" I asked.

"Right under the falls is about five feet, but I guess it averages around three." He plainly wanted to start panning, so he said, "I'll explain how I plan to get at it, tonight at the cabin." Shifting focus a bit, he then pointed out an area creek-side where basketball-sized rocks were almost on dry ground. "I'm going to turn them over and see if there's anything interesting there." He'd unfolded the spade and was tapping his gold pan impatiently with it. "By the way," he said, "don't waste your time with the six-inch layer of black mud; you need to dig down to the gravel." As he was about to head off, he stopped and asked, "Can you and the dog go down to the other waterfall? If you stay on this side of the creek and go just beyond our cross-over point, you'll see a grouping of rocks just like the one here. Check it out, will you? See if any little presents have been left for us."

"No problem," I replied, then after making sure Trevor had all his gear, Pooch and I headed down to the first falls. Finding the area he'd described to me, I took off my pack and pulled the small spade and gold pan from Pooch's saddlebags, then lay them on the rocky ground.

As though he knew the object of the game, Pooch watched, as I pushed one of the stones aside. The indentation of the rock soon filled with muddy water, so I couldn't see a thing. I started digging out the layer of mud, while Pooch observed my actions with his ears up. As though seeming to say to himself, 'Hey! I can do that!' he stuck his paws into the hole, then proceeded to energetically excavate. Big clods of mud flew between his hind legs as he dug, so I stood back a pace to watch. From previous experience, I knew it was very unwise to observe him from the rear as he shifted earth. If you did so, rocks the size of apples and speedy sprays of dirt would go zinging past your ears, until, inevitably, you got hit. So I hunkered down at his nose and stopped him after he'd dug to the gravel layer. As though understanding he should go no deeper, he began removing the stones and top soil from an area that hadn't even been under the rock I'd moved.

During his sizeable excavations, I noticed the wind had picked up a little and was blowing the misty rain so it billowed across the creek. Then I saw a big black bear just bopping along, supposedly looking for a frog or crayfish, or anything else that'd make a nice morning snack. Since we were in a cross-wind, he hadn't scented us, though I don't think this made much of a difference; he simply hadn't been paying attention. When I coughed loudly and banged my spade on a rock, he stopped abruptly and rose to his hind legs for a better view. He was twice the size of the bears at Three Duck Lake and he didn't seem in the least concerned by our presence. Fortunately, Pooch was still busily digging and was unaware of the beast; I really didn't need him mixing it up with a five hundred pound bear. For a moment, I thought the animal would come closer, but he probably got the dog's scent, and finally loped back the way he'd come.

Relieved the bear had visited and departed while Pooch had been distracted, I grabbed the spade and started digging into the gravel the dog had exposed. There was a gritty substance like sand with big grains mixed in with the gravel, so I shovelled it into my pan. When I was carrying it the two or three paces from the creek, Pooch volunteered his valued assistance by sticking his nose into the pan and nearly knocking it from my hand (he gets excited when he sees me carrying a full dish of ANYTHING).

When I finally made it back to the water and dipped in my pan, I started swirling the value-less stuff away. Slowly revealed were three small gold nuggets, each about the size of half a grain of rice. Yes, they were tiny, but my heart went pitter-patter anyway: my first pan! And I was used to seeing gold dust, not little lumps of the stuff. Trevor had told me he hadn't seen much of the fine powdery gold like at Three Duck Lake, but it was coarser here. I pinched the little nuggets from my pan, put them into a small aspirin bottle with a screw-top, then I refilled my pan. My second effort was totally unsuccessful, but I patiently tried again. After about an hour of panning, my little bottle had a number of the small nuggets rattling around in it, but I hadn't once used one of the burlap bags for paydirt. All the gold seemed to show up as coarse grains, so there was no point in packing dirt into Pooch's saddlebags and weighing him down.

The misty rain strengthened slowly, then it just pelted down. Pooch and I took shelter under an overhanging section of ravine wall, and it wasn't long before Trevor came from up the creek. He was drenched, but he didn't have a 'poor me' expression on his face. In fact, he looked pleased in a damp and bedraggled sort of way, as he nodded to me and asked, "Any luck?" I showed him the small nuggets in the bottle and he smiled, saying, "I found some too, I'll show you later." He carefully looked over my shelter and said, "There isn't room enough for two guys

and a big dog. Let's have a mug of tea and something to eat. But not here: I know a better place
just down the creek a bit."

So we picked our way cautiously over the
wet rocks to an area where the trees were much
bigger. Four pines seemed to be connected
underground, while on the surface bordered by
their trunks, the needles were dry and brown.
"Those are ground-squirrel nests: these animals
know where it's dry," Trevor said as he stepped
up onto a piled heap of evergreen needles. Looking expressionlessly at me, he asked, "Feel guilty
about messing up their homes?"

"That's the tree-rats' problem," I answered
rather uncharitably, just glad to get out of the
downpour. "Anyway, the bushy-tailed little
rodents will have everything straightened up
soon after we leave," I said as I joined him.

We stood watching as Pooch checked out the
half-dozen or so burrow holes and tried to shake
the water off his fur, but he quit halfway through
because of the restrictive saddlebags. Then he
flopped gratefully onto the dry pine straw and
lay his head down, but kept his eyes open.

"Comfy?" I asked him as he lay there. I knew he hated the rain passionately and he probably took my question as a personal affront. Taking off my pack, I told the dog I was happy to be getting out of the rain too. Then I searched through his saddlebags and gave him one of the doggy-biscuits. I also retrieved the large paper bag Pauline had packed for our lunch. I ran through the downpour to the creek to fill the kettle/teapot, while Trevor dug a fire-pit sheltered by the trees, just at the edge of the dry pine needles. As we lined the hole with flat rocks, he warned me, "Don't use the rounded ones from the creek, it's true they can explode, I've seen it happen."

As we waited for the water to boil, we ate our lunch of cheese and bread, watching the heavy rain from our shelter. Occasionally a drop would hit us, but overall we were protected, so the thought of going out into the weather again just didn't occur to us at the time.

"I have something to show you," said Trevor as we sat at the fire side by side. He took a pouch from his pocket and untied the drawstring, feeling around in the small bag with an index finger.

"Hold out your hand, palm up," he said, then he dropped in a thumbnail-sized object.

I'd been warming my hands at the fire, so the flake felt cool on my skin upon first contact. It was a nice nugget: close to a quarter of an ounce, by my estimate. It'd somehow been squeezed into a bird-shape and was almost polished-looking on one side, while the other was rough. "I'd like to give it to Pauline for all her kindnesses, plus the good meals, of course," he said with a grin. "It has nothing to do with our 50-50 deal: it's just a present." After speaking he pondered for a moment, then added, "In a way, it's half from you too."

"That's very thoughtful of you," I said, handing the little piece of gold back to him, "she'll really appreciate it."

Just then, a hairy little rodent-head with beady black eyes and tiny ears raised in high alert, popped up from one of the far burrows. Even though Trevor and I were only a few feet from the dog, the squirrel was only regarding Pooch: with indignation, it seemed. The dog was accustomed to having staring contests with the little beasts, so he only raised his head as they locked eyes. He knew the squirrel would disappear underground the moment he (Pooch) stood to investigate, so he remained lying on his comfortable mattress. Heaven knows what 'thoughts' were going through the rodent's molecule-sized brain as he chattered angrily at the unresponsive canine. Pooch twitched his ears and raised his furry eyebrows at the vocalisations, but this plainly wasn't the excited reaction the squirrel had been expecting. Furiously, he came right out of the burrow, then stood beside it and perused the dog for a moment in a disrespectful sort of way. After this annoyed stance, he got down on all fours, shot his busy tail straight up and feinted at Pooch, as if he was about to attack a 170 pound dog. Finding the rodent's behaviour intolerable, the canine rose to meet the challenge, but then the little beast instantly disappeared down his burrow. As Pooch investigated the escape hole, the little critter popped up from another burrow and to chatter tauntingly at him. So, even though he knew engaging in this game of hide-and-seek was a no-win proposition, the dog scampered over to the new location, while Mr. Squirrel quickly retired to his subterranean abode once again. Rather than futilely digging at this new hole, Pooch simply lay over the entrance, presumably thinking this would put an end to all the 'now you see me, now you don't' nonsense. Of course, the other holes might pose problems to his scheme, but the little tree-rat certainly couldn't use this hole in the near future!

Trevor and I chortled at their antics as the squirrel's pointy little head appeared out of another burrow, then Pooch repeated the part where he got up to lie over this new hole. "You know better than that, you big dope," I said to him in a scolding voice, but not even looking at me, he just wagged his tail briefly and woofed.

"I'd like to see how he intends to lay on all six burrows at once," said Trevor, "but suddenly, I have to go." Turning to me with a rather embarrassed expression on his face, he asked, "You don't happen to have any toilet paper, do you?" Wordlessly, I handed him a plastic bag containing a third of a roll squashed flat. I never forget to pack the stuff when I'm going into the bush for the day.

I always remember, since the lack of toilet paper brings to mind some supremely uncomfortable moments. The worst was when I was working on a geological survey crew during winter in the Northwest Territories. It's bad enough pulling your trousers down when it's a breezy -30, but using snow to clean yourself after, takes the whole experience one step closer to hell.

While Trevor was gone, I really started to notice how chilled I felt. The rain had drenched me, so the food and fire hadn't helped much. Deciding not to douse the flames until he got back, I sat close to the fire and tried to get warm. Pooch was still lying on the entrance of a burrow, but his little underground buddy was nowhere to be seen.

Portunus

I watched the wood-smoke go straight up, then form an ever-changing cloud under an overhead tree-branch in our shelter. As I imagined the smoke leaking slowly through into the rain, I felt a sudden surge of warmth course through my body. Still looking at the smoke, I leaned back on the tree trunk and saw them in the cloud: three stone steps leading up to a stout door with thick hinges. It was almost like viewing a movie, as I saw a young man wearing a cloak and a peculiar wide-brimmed hat, climb the stairs to enter a stone-walled room. Two others were sitting at a table in guttering candle-light and seemed to have been expecting him. The visitor didn't sit with the other two, but stood in front of the table and said, "I've been keeping an eye on the one who's moving here: he's a First Nations person, you know."

One of the seated men, obviously the oldest of the three, nodded and tapped his pipe into an ashtray. He was wearing a coat the exact colour of wood smoke, while his white beard seemed to swirl as he spoke: "Surely he'll be better than the drillers who were here some time ago. Their loud machines and greedy attitudes didn't fit, so it's a good thing they didn't find much." He chuckled dryly and added, "Of course, we were always able to subtly steer them into drilling in the wrong places. Eventually they left, but I must say I found their persistence quite admirable." Refilling his pipe, he added, "It's inevitable this area will attract attention; there's gold here. Let's just see what happens when this young man and his wife move in."

The standing figure faded into the wood-smoke, then seemed to become better-defined as he said, "He's on the right track to discover the mother-lode, he's only a few feet from becoming very rich."

"Yes, there's a thick vein of gold in the rock above the pool. The white quartz-fault indicating it in the wet stone is visible, but it's hidden under the torrent." As the older seated man finished speaking, he took a draw off his pipe and disappeared behind the cloud of smoke. "The nuggets in the pool will keep him busy in the meantime," he said, "but he'll eventually find the vein, I think." He paused, then his voice took on a fondly mocking tone as he gazed up at the standing man and addressed him, saying, "Don't look so anxious, Portunus; I know it's your duty to watch over the area, but be patient. We'll see the guy's true colours soon enough."

The scene was blown away by a gust and somehow, I wasn't completely disbelieving. I suppose I was half-asleep lying there by the fire with the rain pelting down beyond the protective trees, so this might excuse my easy acceptance of the figures in the smoke. Despite my wet clothes, I think I momentarily and totally fell asleep.

Seemingly without warning, Trevor was sitting beside me and returning the plastic-wrapped roll of toilet paper. "You don't sleep with your eyes open, do you?" he asked, looking weirded-out. When I shook my head in answer, he explained he'd shouted to me upon his return, but that I hadn't responded. Apparently, I'd appeared awake as I sat leaning against the tree trunk and watching the wood smoke rise, but I'd actually been somewhere else. I felt slightly embarrassed by my flightiness and was just opening my mouth to assure him that everything was okay, when an overwhelming chill enveloped me. I tried speaking, but I could only make teeth-chattering sounds, so I stopped attempting to vocalise.

Looking at my wet clothes, then out at the still-pouring rain, Trevor said, "I'm freezing my butt too. Let's put out the fire and get back to the truck; we could wait forever for the weather to cooperate." Making light of it, but appearing slightly grim nonetheless, he added regretfully, "Looks like we'll have to leave our shelter to go out into the rain again."

After regarding the unrelenting monsoon for a moment longer, I got vertical and immediately wished I hadn't, since the rapid increase in elevation had caused my grey matter to swoon, so I nearly stumbled into the fire. Plus, the wet bits of my clothing that hadn't been pressed against my body were now coldly holding my person in a clammy embrace.

Dismissing the discomfort with a force of will, I packed our gear and lunch things into Pooch's saddlebags, while Trevor put out the fire. Then we headed into the downpour, crossed the creek (our stepping-stone was now nearly submerged) and looked up through the rain at the ravine wall. Trevor said, "Climbing up that thing will warm us up for sure." After studying my unhappy and sodden appearance, he rather insultingly added, "And try not to grab onto a devil's club stem this time."

It wasn't a pleasant trek: even Pooch slipped a few times on our way up, but Trevor had no difficulty with the wet conditions. The two of them disappeared ahead of me before we were a third of the way, so I found myself climbing solo. My boots didn't have traction on the wet moss, so I stopped my ungainly upward progress to have a look-see at my miserable situation. After standing there under my dripping hat, I concluded I'd rather be in the lodge drinking a mug of cocoa. Then I heard a truck door slam and realised I was closer to the road than I'd thought. Trevor yelled down to check up on me, then told me to get right into the vehicle once I'd reached it, since he'd already removed and stashed away Pooch's saddlebags. 'Ain't he wonderful!' I said sarcastically to myself, 'maybe he's rotated the tires too!'

Since I'm not at my best when I'm drenched and have just survived a death-defying ordeal, I didn't make any pithy comments about my stroll through gold country. I have to admit though, the Barge never looked better: rain was splashing on the painted flames billowing from under the hood, but more importantly, she was a good shelter from the storm.

Although the climb had made me sweat, I wasted no time in getting into the truck, slamming the door shut and dripping on the front seat. Trevor was already behind the steering wheel, with the engine going and the heaters blowing full-blast. Pooch had been stretched out on the rear seat, but upon my arrival, he stood to shake himself, thus giving me another bracing shower. Then he tried licking me on the face, but I dodged him, so all he got was an ear.

With the windows shut tight, the heaters roaring and the three of us decidedly damp, it was quite ripe in the vehicle, but no one complained. After we'd languished in our funky mobile sauna for a few minutes, it stopped raining and the sun came out. Shrugging at Mother Nature's little games, we rolled down our windows, but a cool breeze had developed, so we soon cranked them closed again. Trevor mentioned we could go down again, since the day had improved. I said, "You've got to be kidding!"

Laughing at my reaction, he answered, "Yes, I am. Since I detect some reluctance in you to revisit the creek, we'll head for the cabin instead. I have clean sweatpants and tee-shirts there that'll fit you." As we got underway, he added, "Getting into dry clothes will be nice, anyway; today I just wanted to show you my claim. We can work it seriously some other time."

New Home

*A*fter the Flaming Barge had pushed through the poplar saplings for another mile, we came to a clearing overlooking a lake. There were three buildings: the cabin and outhouse, plus what looked like a core shack. The wild creek we'd recently left had become civilised as it flowed languidly into the lake, just to the right of the cabin. As we jumped out of the vehicle a cool breeze hit our wet clothes, so we made haste to get inside. After the blessed relief of donning our dry après-gold panning outfits, Trevor made a pot of tea on a Coleman stove, while I looked things over.

The cabin was solidly-built and meant to house four, I think. It had two rooms: the kitchen/living room with two bunk beds decorating a wall, while through a door were sleeping quarters containing a large double bed. "I put in new glass for the windows," Trevor informed me as we drank our tea at the table and gazed out at the lake. "The bed has to go," he continued, "according to Sarah, it's too soft and springy. She also suspects the previous occupants weren't very hygienic and probably had bugs, so she'll only sleep in one of the bunks."

I responded by rolling my eyes and asking peevishly, "Does she figure the insects have set up a community that's lasted generations with nothing to eat? There's been nobody here for years, as you well know." Shaking my head in exasperation, I finished dealing with this paranoid female quirk by asking rhetorically, "Anyway, what's the big deal with some lice or a flea or two?"

Trevor chuckled, but was clearly unwilling to delve into silly female preferences further, so he changed topics by saying, "Bring your tea mug along and I'll show you around."

The moment I stepped outside with him, I was somehow reminded of the cinema scene I'd watched in the wood smoke as I'd waited by the fire. Surprisingly, I hadn't thought of it since it'd happened a few hours ago, but then again, maybe it wasn't so shocking that I'd forgotten. I was used to these momentary lapses in my reality and I'd learned to relax: just to go with the flow. Though things might still be frightening in the way they present themselves, my reluctant acceptance is sometimes helpful, but I still get jittery. Also washing the smoky little incident from my mind was the cold rain, proving, I suppose, that misery usually outweighs everything else. So, not wanting to add to Trevor's list of concerns, I didn't mention my visions for the time being.

He was looking out over the lake proudly, saying, "She's tear-shaped, with the pointed part being where the creek flows in." Gesturing at a bare rock bluff jutting right into the lake across from the cabin, he said, "Impressive, don't you think? It rises 230 feet above lake level, then it goes 60 feet deep into the water." After a short pause, he added, "It's exactly a half mile from our shore to the base of the bluff." Smiling to himself and nodding, he clapped his hands once, as though breaking a spell. Then he turned to me and said, "C'mon, I'll show you the building on the other side of town."

Leading me to the shack standing a short distance behind the cabin, he said, "It'll be a useful place to store stuff, once I get rid of all the core samples, of course." They were four-foot lengths of rock about two inches in diameter, lying on their sides in flat plywood boxes. Some of the samples were unbroken, while others had obviously been split so the minerals inside could be examined. With four of these rock columns per partitioned box stacked to the ceiling in places, Trevor asked, "Can you help me with these?" We spent a few minutes rearranging things, so a pile of heavy boxes wouldn't topple over onto Sarah one sunny day, because this might cause her some distress: women! "I can probably use the plywood from the boxes, but I don't think the samples themselves will be handy: they're just tubular rocks," he said. "You're good at improvising and thinking outside the box: any thoughts?"

After peering at the samples, I nodded and said, "You could use them as heavy wind chimes

that click and thud in the breeze: very romantic. Since you have lots of them, you could hang
them all around the outside of the cabin: I'm
sure Sarah would be impressed."

Obviously not overly keen with my suggestion, he responded, "Oh well, I'll think of
something: it's not important for now." After
so cavalierly casting aside my brain-wave of an
idea, he pondered for a moment, then said, "I'll
be right back," and hurriedly left the shack. He
returned a moment later carrying the hardware
store bag and said, "Just some nails and bolts,"
as he put it on one of the stacks of sample boxes,
"but I couldn't forget this!" He took the spool of
rope along with a couple of pull-wheels from the
bag, saying, "Our clothes line!"

We went outside to remove the sagging and
knotted baling wire that'd been strung between
trees, then we replaced it. It wasn't easy getting
everything aligned; after playing a long-distance
game of 'cats in the cradle' with the rope and
while adjusting pulley-heights on tree trunks,
we finally got the thing operational. Trevor
looked at his watch and said, "I'd planned to take

you out in the boat to show you the lake and to catch supper, but there's no time. It gets dark real fast around here."

"Don't worry about it," I said, "Pauline packed us an evening meal. She cooked some rice and veggies for us, then insisted we take along one of her big jars of chicken stew. She told me we might not catch anything, so we'd have no main course for supper." I also related that she'd said, "Trevor would go nuts without a proper meal, you know how he enjoys his food."

"Smart girl!" he exclaimed, "always prepared! It's early for supper, but I'm starving, so let's eat."

The stew went well with the rice and the bag of chocolate chip cookies was soon emptied for our dessert. By the time we'd finished, the light was fading fast and Trevor said, "There's about a half hour of light remaining, so that'll give me time to show you one more thing." Taking a fly rod that'd been leaning on a wall, he smiled and said, "Let's go down to the creek."

The evening chill hit me the moment I left the ambient warmth of the cabin. The hulking bluff across the lake seemed ominous in the stillness and silence, so Trevor's voice was startling as he said, "I'm used to the quiet of the bush, but sometimes it gets eerie around here."

I followed him down to a level patch near the creek. The current was still robust, but the water wasn't rushing along suicidally, like a bit further up. It was about two feet deep where the creek met the lake; a perfect place to fish, one would think.

I watched as Trevor expertly cast the wet fly into the calmer flow near shore. "The creek has three bends which slow it down, then it reaches the lake," Trevor said as he looked upstream. He cast again, but since there were no takers, he changed flies. "I bet whoever lived here before, panned this area a lot and found exactly nothing. Going the first half-mile upriver isn't so bad, but then it gets hairy-scary." He chuckled, then added, "I think they just gave up. Why bust your butt going up a creek which you've already seen contains no gold?" He cast a few more times, still without success. Looking irritated, he turned to me and said, "This is a good spot: I've always caught something here before," then he changed flies again. It was practically dark after he'd cast some more, so he finally shrugged and reeled in his line, saying, "No joy here, let's go back to the cabin."

On our return, he stopped to gaze at the imposing bluff across the lake. The rocky monolith was now only a dark blotch hovering over the far shoreline, but seemed to assert its presence nonetheless. "I want to climb to the top of it," said Trevor, "maybe I can get there from behind or somewhere along its flanks. The view of the lake and the surrounding countryside must be stunning, but that's not the reason I want to get up there." Almost talking to himself as he regarded the bluff, he murmured, "It's the challenge and my curiosity of course, but I feel compelled to be there soon."

"Just be careful," I said, after we'd looked across the water at it for a few moments, "remember, you're responsible for two now."

After I made this fatherly and completely unsolicited pronouncement, he probably looked annoyed, but it was nearly dark, so I couldn't see. Just then, Pooch returned from his explorations around the lake. As he approached, all I saw was a big pink tongue flopping up and down in the gloaming, but I recognised the appendage, so I feared not.

He'd just given us his usual effusive greeting, when I said to him, "Your din-din is in a bucket in the cooler on the back of the truck. I'll go get it for you."

Not trusting me to accomplish this important task all on my own, Pooch accompanied me so he could keep a close eye on my progress. I retrieved the five-gallon sealed container and read the label: 'Pig liver and kidney in broth'. Although it sounded tempting, I'd already eaten, so I gave it all to the dog.

While Pooch was avidly enjoying his evening repast in a corner of the cabin, Trevor lit a candle, then got the wood stove going. When we were finally sitting at the table, he said, "Let's weigh the gold we found today; I can start repaying your loan."

Using an old-fashioned balance-scale, we discovered we had exactly an ounce and a half: not bad for less than two hours of panning. And that wasn't even counting the larger nugget he was giving to Pauline. I felt somewhat piratical as we sat there in candlelight evenly divvying up the small gold pellets. Trevor gave me half, then looked up prices in the newspaper I'd bought earlier.

Making notations on a pad, he muttered to himself: "That's what you loaned me and that's what I've paid back." Then he looked at me and smiled, saying, "Let's keep this on a strictly business basis; I'm taking 20 percent off my contributions because of the impurities in the nuggets. As you know, they aren't pure gold."

"Why 20 percent?" I asked.

"I have a friend in town who has his own little foundry and who's tested the gold I've brought to him so far," Trevor answered. "He says that's the average slag-content of the nuggets." Grinning at me, he added, "I'm being very careful about who I tell; he, plus Sarah and you, are the only ones knowing of my discovery. Pauline will also know of course, but let's keep it at that. I can do without claim-jumpers hiding in the trees, then stealing my gold."

"I guess this means I can't blabber joyfully about it to Joyce at the post office," I said glumly. "But you're right: 'loose lips sink ships' and all that. Mum's the word!" Then I looked at him and asked, "How do you plan to get at the paydirt in the pool? It's four or five feet deep in places and the water's cold: I mean it's frigid."

He chuckled and said, "Yeah, it's meltwater from the higher elevations, so it's quite cool. You don't swim where the creek enters the lake; I don't think I've ever heard a louder shriek than when Sarah dove in for the first time." Taking a colander and burlap sack from a dufflebag on the floor, he said, "I'll loosen the gravel and sand with a spade, then scoop it all up with my kitchen utensil. I can dump it into the bag until it's full, then pan it. I think I can stand getting into the cold water, but what about you?"

"No problem, matey," I answered, rubbing my hands together and trying to leer greedily, "I'll do anything for gold."

Bluff

Trevor had dragged a thick wool throw-carpet from under the bed for Pooch. The rug was now lying near the stove with a large dark dog on it, just like at the lodge. Pooch pricked up his ears, lifted his head and looked alert, plainly listening to something. Although Trevor and I could hear nothing, the canine insisted on being let out to investigate: brave dog! But he whined outside the door less than two minutes later, so I had to let him back in. Instead of making friends with whatever had been bumping along out there, he obviously wanted to lay on his bit of carpet near the stove, the big chicken. As I wondered what'd driven the dog back to the cabin so quickly, Pooch laid down and without any fuss, went into snooze-mode.

Trevor chuckled at the dog's unwillingness to go exploring in the nighttime, then stared into the candle with a faraway look in his eyes. He still had his usual confident bearing, but he seemed puzzled about something.

"What's on your mind?" I asked.

He gave me a startled look, as though the sound of my voice had just brought him back to the here and now. Apparently not recognising me for a moment, he regarded me blankly, then got himself in order again and said, "Normally, I do things without thinking much and they seem to work out. But this marriage thing has me bent all out of shape." He seemed oblivious to the fact that his shoulder-length black hair was dangerously close to the flame as he sat hunched at the table, so I moved the candle away. The crackling sound of the fire in the stove dominated the following quiet, but the silence was somehow different from the lodge's. It wasn't ominous or frightening, but just different.

"Pauline tells me lots of guys were interested in Sarah," I finally said. "Maybe you're not ready to commit and you feel rushed."

He nodded and said, "I had to put my cards face-up on the table, because there was one persistent guy in particular who she seemed to like, so …." His voice faded and he shrugged, doubtlessly thinking of the dastardly oaf who dared to have designs on Sarah. He got up from the table to put another log into the stove, then returned and said, "I proposed to her right at this table." Grinning sheepishly, he added, "The Lake had no official name, so I filled out a few government forms and paid a small fee. So, from now on, it'll be called 'Sarah's Lake'."

"You were laying it on a bit thick, don't you think?" I asked, "How could she possibly say 'no' after that?"

He chuckled half-heartedly, then levelled a serious look at me, but didn't say anything. He obviously needed the marital know-how of an older guy like me, so I said encouragingly, "Sarah's headstrong and stubborn: good luck to you! She's also sweet and loyal, plus she can make you laugh. Tell me, how'd you like to see her with someone else?"

"There's no way," he answered, "I'd go nuts."

"It was the same for me when I first met Pauline," I said, "I couldn't imagine things without her and that feeling only grows as time goes by." Looking at him appraisingly then nodding, I told him he had his act together and that he wasn't making a mistake by marrying her.

Seeming consoled by my positive words, he lifted my little bottle of gold from the table and studied it quietly. After a moment, he said, "I've been distracted by other things long enough, so tomorrow I'm going into the pool to see if it's as rich as I think." He rattled the little nuggets in the glass bottle, then set it down on the table again.

Feeling silly bringing it up, I told him of the three-man scene I'd witnessed in the wood-smoke. "According to them," I said, beginning to regret mentioning it, "there's a thick vein of gold in the rock above the pool. But apparently, there are enough nuggets under the water to 'keep you busy' for a while, so I guess you're right about that part of the creek." Trying to be dismissive, but not even convincing myself, I added, "That is, if you believe there's any merit to my little daydream."

Disregarding my skepticism, he asked, "Were any names mentioned?"

"Yes," I answered, secretly relieved he hadn't questioned my sanity, "One of them was called 'Portunus'. Familiar with the name?"

"Never heard of him," Trevor responded, "I'll have to ask Moon."

"It hadn't occurred to me you'd have to deal with the spirit-world out here," I said. "I suppose I took it for granted that this place is too isolated to be of much interest to anyone: silly me." I looked at him in speculation for a moment, then asked, "Have YOU seen anything here that's out of the normal?"

"Not really," he replied vaguely, but I didn't believe him; I think he was just trying to steer me away from actuality. Although he knew I'd had 'other world' experiences at the lodge, I got the distinct impression he believed I couldn't handle this new situation.

Ignoring his doubts, I asked, "Mind if I stay another night? I'd like to see what's in the pool."

"Won't Pauline be worried if you don't show up at the lodge tomorrow?" he asked.

"We can drive there first thing in the morning, pick up something for supper, then spend most of the day panning. Tomorrow's a Tuesday: another 'buffet' night, so I think Pauline and Moon can squeak by without me."

Trevor chortled and said, "Sounds good: I can use the help and the company."

We talked about the impending marriage, but we were plainly more excited about investigating the pool's contents. At about 10:30 I got up from the table and said, "It'll be a busy day tomorrow, time for some shut-eye."

Trevor nodded, then told me to take the bed in the other room. "It's relatively clean I think: hardly any bugs at all." He was grinning as he pumped up a gas lamp, then he said, "I'll read the paper for a while, so I'll close the bedroom door. I'll open it again after I douse the lights. The bunk beds out here are quite comfortable, so I'll be fine."

I unrolled my sleeping bag and lay within it on the bed. Sarah had been right in describing the mattress as being too soft and springy; it was also bouncy, with its material apparently also used in the construction of catapults. Amazingly I quickly fell asleep, then I had a vivid dream about all my teeth turning gold. I was trying to see my reflection in the pool to study them, but ripples kept destroying the image. As I leaned over the water for a better look, I fell in, with the cold instantly numbing me. When I awoke, I was lying on the floor with my head under the bed and my sleeping bag fully ten feet away. Whether I'd fallen from the mattress, or had simply been taking one of my nocturnal walkabouts didn't matter; I felt chilled to the bone.

Wondering how on earth I'd managed to escape from it in the first place, I got into the sleeping bag again as I sat on the edge of the bed. After checking my teeth carefully with fingers and tongue to make sure they were my natural choppers, I lay down. When I closed my eyes, the fire in the stove seemed to crackle louder, while Trevor's snoring reminded me of Sarah; she just wouldn't put up with strangled vacuum-cleaner sounds coming from the other side of the bed.

I chuckled, then scrunched the sleeping bag around my head and tried to sleep. But it was no good, my eyes snapped open against my will, so I watched the flickering the fire was projecting through the stove's vent hole. The small orange spotlight squirmed on the other room's floor, sometimes seeming to pulse in rhythm with Trevor's breathing and not helping at all in my attempts to revisit dozy-land.

I lay there knowing that trying to get unconscious again would be a lost cause, so I finally got out of my sleeping bag. I tiptoed through the open doorway to check on the wet clothes I'd hung over the stove earlier: they were still clammy-feeling. I think it was their delicate fragrance instantly taking me back to lying in a four-man tent in a bush camp somewhere very close to the middle of nowhere.

Easily beating out fingernails scratching on a blackboard, or a baby crying furiously just behind you all the way on a long bus trip, is the super disagreeable sound of rain pattering steadily on your canvas rooftop. You're toasty and dry in your sleeping bag now, but you know shortly, you'll be cold and wet then stay that way for the rest of the day. I remember being irked further by the sight of the disreputable cluster of still damp work clothes hanging above the stove. The prospect of donning undried pants and shirt that desperately needed a wash had brought an extremely limited amount of joy to my heart, so now that I had a choice, I left my attire alone as it hung there damply. I decided to keep wearing Trevor's things, then change after we'd returned to the lodge. As I quietly put a couple of logs into the stove, he snorted and shifted in the bunk, but he didn't wake up. Accustomed to seeing me vertical in the wee hours, Pooch raised his head from the carpet and gave me a tail wag, then went back to sleep as I made my way to the main door.

The difference between the dimness in the cabin and standing under the stars was startling. The full moon seemed centred over Sarah's Lake, with its reflection in the water too bright to look at for long. It wasn't just cool: it was cold. Trevor had mentioned lake-level here is 2,500 feet above the lodge and that there's much higher ground in the vicinity, of course.

I hurried into the cabin to grab my sleeping bag to use as a cloak, but I'd been blinded by the moonlight. I had to wait for my eyes to adjust once I'd closed the door behind me, then Pooch came over to say hello. I asked him with an encouraging inflection in my whisper, "Care to come outside with me, boy?" He answered by trotting over to his rug, flopping down with a weary sigh, then closing his eyes. What a loyal companion!

Trevor's snoring now sounded like the grunting of a wild boar eating something tasty he's found on the forest floor, but I could at least see again. So I grabbed my sleeping bag off the bed and went out once more. Draping the bag stylishly over my shoulders and down my back, I sat in one of the lawn chairs set up in front of the cabin, then studied the surroundings.

Occasionally I could hear the creek burbling, but this only accentuated the chilled silence of everything else. Away from the lake, the trees melded together to form dark fur on the bodies of the steep hills, while the shining water somehow didn't seem to belong in the picture. An itinerant cold breeze from higher ground ruffled the mirror smooth surface of the lake, so I wrapped the bag tighter around my body.

For some reason, I'd been trying to ignore the slab like rocky bluff directly across from me, but I finally focussed on it. The granite wall's grey colour seemed to glow in the moonlight like an unmoving ship's sails, while its massive shoulders loomed towards the stars. I could understand Trevor's wish to get to its top to enjoy the view, but the thing was downright scary at the moment. My trepidation was irrational; after all, it was only a big chunk of stone on the far shore, but it definitely had a brooding presence.

I caught a whiff of wood smoke from the cabin, so I momentarily thought of returning to bed. But I was comfy sitting there, plus I didn't have the energy for the arduous twenty foot hike back there, so I stayed put. The next thing I knew, the sun had risen and Trevor was standing in front of me as I reclined in my chair.

"Did my snoring chase you out last night?" he asked. "Sorry about that."

"Hah?" I responded, using my conversational skills to hide the fact I was still half-asleep. As the meaning of his question finally registered in my dormant brainpan, I said, "No, no, no:

it wasn't that. It was only my insomnia acting up again."

Just then, Pooch came belting out of the bush and gave me his morning greetings. He did this by happily wagging his tail, then woofing directly into my face. Since I was seated and still slow with sleep, I couldn't completely dodge his affectionate slurps. He managed to get me on the forehead before I could duck away; he loves to catch me sitting!

Trevor was frisking with the dog when the rising sun's rays hit the flat surface of the big bluff at exactly the correct angle. The glare was incredible; it was like having a powerful searchlight shone straight into your eyes. As we both turned our heads away, Trevor said, "It'll only be like this for a couple of minutes, until the sun moves enough." Grinning at me through the suddenly harsh light, he said, "I've seen this from the creek; you can look at the rock from there without melting your eyeballs. It's the same from the other side. It seems a spotlight is on the cabin for a period each day. Think that means anything?" He was being lighthearted and had laughter in his eyes, but I had the feeling that deep down, he had concerns.

After nodding to myself and looking thoughtful for a moment, I tried to ease his burden by saying, "It probably means you're doomed, but don't worry about it, you'll be fine on cloudy days."

Sensing my casual attitude towards his destiny had been unenlightening for him, I quickly changed subjects by saying, "Let's just go now, we can have breakfast at the lodge, then drive back to our parking spot in the poplars." Like a switch had been hit, the intense glare ceased and the bluff reappeared. Also like hitting a switch, was Trevor's reaction to the mention of food. Obviously, all thoughts of bluff, cabin or lake had instantly evaporated. Rubbing it in a bit, I said, "Pauline bought three large smoked hams the other day." Then, as if it really didn't matter, and I was just making conversation, I added, "We could have some with eggs for breakfast, I suppose." I'd been busily folding my sleeping bag into a neat bundle (for no good reason) as I'd spoken, but I'd kept him under observation from the corner of my eye. He hastily took the truck keys from his pocket like a quick-draw champ, then smiled at me.

Once the three of us had boarded the Flaming Barge, there wasn't much conversation as we slowly pushed our way through the saplings; it was much too early for scintillating speechifying anyway. When we reached our cleared-out parking area, for a laugh Trevor shifted into second gear, then immediately went back to first as we got to the small trees on the other side. When we got out of the truck to turn the hubs back to two-wheel drive, Trevor said, "I'm sure looking forward to one of Pauline's breakfasts."

"She might be busy in the garden," I said as we got back into the vehicle, "so maybe I'll have to do all the cooking." He didn't seem enthralled by this prospect, but he was polite enough not to comment.

As we got to the outskirts of town, I started to hear what I thought was a Salvation Army band in dire need of a lot more practice and perhaps some new instruments. With coronets blaring and tubas hooting, they'd apparently bumped into a mariachi band, so each group was now battling to see who had the loudest trumpet player. Too bad they were each playing in different keys. After further listening to the discordant sounds, I realised we were the source of the cacophony. Trevor was the Sally Ann group, while I was Mr. Mariachi. It was obvious I now had stiff competition for the title of 'King of the Midriff Musicians', so the intestinal 'Battle of the Bands' continued all the way to the lodge, without either of us saying much.

As we pulled into the Three Duck Lake parking lot, he was making sounds similar to the fog-horn like bellow from one of those elongated Swiss mountain horns. "Careful with the sound effects," I warned him as we made our way down the path, "you'll excite the dogs."

Right on cue, Banjo and Grace appeared out of nowhere and welcomed us back. Even though he'd been with us all along, Pooch joined in with the greetings, so we soon had a trio of jumping and barking canines. We all headed up to Moon's garden without bothering to go into the lodge.

Back to the Lodge

I snuck up behind Pauline as she was weeding a patch of fallow ground near the hedge, put my hands over her eyes and asked, "Guess who?"

After pondering for a moment, she queried excitedly, "Are you the cute new clerk who's just started at the post office?"

"No," I answered, "he died, so try again."

Giggling, she turned to face me and said, "We heard the orchestral sounds you and Trevor were making on your way up here. So, by any chance would you like something to eat?" Not needing a reply, she told me to have a cup of coffee with Trevor, then she'd be right down to join us.

Moon was at the other side of the garden talking to Trevor. She waved to me and said, "See you down there in a few minutes," then she returned to her conversation.

After we'd all got settled at the table in the lodge, Pauline looked at Trevor and said, "Now, first things first. What would you like for breakfast?"

An occasional rumble was still coming from each of us, but Pauline ignored it. "Well," Trevor said with a happy sigh, "Henry mentioned ham and eggs, so that'd be excellent!"

"How'd you like the eggs done?" she asked.

"Sunny side up, please," Trevor replied, then he started chortling.

"What's so funny?" she asked with a puzzled look on her face.

"Sorry about that," he said, "I was just remembering a French Canadian guy I heard ordering breakfast in a restaurant. He'd been trying out his English, but he made a few hard-to-detect errors that might lead you to believe he wasn't exactly fluent." Trevor laughed again, then continued, "I don't know how the waitress managed to keep a straight face when he asked for 'tree fried heggs facing the sun,' but she wrote down his order without a peep."

Trevor's French Canadian accent had been perfect, so all of us were laughing now. I hasten to add that I'm fully aware of how feeble I must sound when I try to speak French, so no disrespect is intended.

After a fruit salad of grapes, chunks of mango and orange with a sprinkling of walnut pieces, Pauline brought us the main course and the ham was delicious. The thick steak didn't stand a chance against Trevor's avid onslaught with his knife and fork. Once he'd cleared his plate, she gave him more ham, so the vast cargo-hold continued to be loaded. After polishing off his second helping, Moon gave him a stern look, so he showed some discipline and didn't ask for a third.

As we drank our coffee, he described his plans for the new place and also mentioned his gold claim. "That reminds me," he said, as he fished the small pouch from a pocket and smiled at Pauline. "I have a little gift for you," he said. Trevor took out the flake, asked her to hold out her hand, then dropped it into her palm. With shining eyes, she examined the polished-looking side first and told us it looked like a bird. "It's just a small token of my appreciation," he said,

"I found it on Henry's first visit to my claim, so think of it as a souvenir."

"It's very pretty and quite substantial," she said as she handed it over to Moon. Gazing into Trevor's eyes and grasping his forearm as she leaned across the table, Pauline said, "It's very sweet of you. Thanks so much." Most men would wilt under a blast of her sincerity, but he only coloured slightly as he somewhat bashfully nodded at her.

Giving the flake back to Pauline, Moon was bright-eyed too, as she said, "Very nice: it looks like your claim will pay off."

Addressing Trevor with an 'I told you so' tone to my voice, I said, "See? Now she knows too. This is exactly how word spreads." We both stared at Moon, who didn't look at all like a coffee-klatch gossip or a chatterbox of any kind. I gestured rudely at her with a sideways movement of my head, then asked him in a loud, suspicion tinged 'whisper', "Think she's trustworthy?"

"I guess we don't have any choice now," said Trevor with a laugh, "we'll have to take our chances."

I grinned at her, but she remained stoic and unemotional. I think she was annoyed by our japes. Hastily changing subjects, I said to Pauline and Moon, "You'll both be bitterly disappointed to hear you have to spend another day and night without me." There wasn't any boo-hooing from them after my announcement, so I carried on, "Trevor and I want to get back to the claim, then maybe leave enough time to go out onto the lake. We'll spend the night up at the cabin, then drive back here tomorrow morning, so I can then resume my duties."

Bless her heart, Pauline didn't ask 'What duties?' but said instead, "You'll need something for lunch and supper, so I'll pack a basket for you." After thanking her with a peck on her cheek, I turned to Moon and told her of the three guys I'd seen in the wood- smoke.

She gave me an appraising look, then said, "You shouldn't be seeing these things: you're a white guy." Seeming to belatedly recognise the racism of her statement, she shook her head and said adamantly, "No no, that came out all wrong: I didn't mean to be insulting, but ….."

"Don't worry about it," I replied, "I know what you meant."

She smiled at me, then nodded and said, "You mentioned the name 'Portunus'; I know him, but only by reputation." She topped up her coffee mug and carefully added a half-spoon of honey, saying, "From what I've heard, he's a handful, who takes himself very seriously and won't compromise if he thinks he's right. He was given a section of high ground to oversee, and it seems he considers it his own. I hope you don't have to deal with him."

A number of clients showed up for breakfast, so Pauline and Moon got busy, while Trevor and I made ourselves scarce. We went down to the wharf with the dogs, where he caber-tossed a large log into the water and Banjo gamely tried retrieving it. Pauline came rushing down about fifteen minutes later carrying one of the large picnic baskets. Telling us she had to return to the lodge pronto, she wished us good luck at the claim, kissed me on the cheek, but hurried back, saying, "See you tomorrow!"

We headed to the parking lot; Banjo and Grace tried getting in with Pooch as I opened the rear door of the truck for him. I promised to see them tomorrow, but they clearly wanted to go for a ride NOW and didn't understand why they'd not been invited. They ran behind as we drove through the trees to the road, then they quit following as we turned right and picked up speed. I must say I felt a twinge of guilt watching them in the outer rearview mirror, as they gave up and disappeared into the bush.

Cold Gold

As we motored along not saying much, it struck me that in this little enclosed world of the vehicle, everything was right and proper. Therefore, anything wrong or misbegotten is plainly someone else's fault: unless you suffer the misfortune of having a pea-brain at the steering wheel, that is. If that's the case, praying sometimes works. But Trevor's a good driver, so I just sat back and watched the world go by.

When we reached town and were stopped at a light, a middle-aged lady driving a dark blue sedan pulled up alongside, just to my right. She immediately started scanning the Flaming Barge's lovely paint job with sour-faced disapproval, so this somewhat irked me. So I waited until our eyes met, then I jabbed a finger towards the rear of her vehicle and looked worried. I turned to Trevor and said, "Pretend I've just told you there's something terribly wrong with the rear of her car. Look at the woman for a moment, then at her vehicle's hind end and shake your head." Half-standing behind the steering wheel and craning his head to the right, he even piqued Pooch's interest; so now all three of us were gawking at the car's rear. But a couple of angry toots from behind indicated the light had turned green, so we had to leave without further ado.

It didn't take long to reach the parking spot on the mining road we'd cleared of saplings the day before. After donning our packs and making sure our tea and lunch things were in Pooch's saddlebags, we headed down to the creek. It wasn't raining and this made a big difference; footing was better, so the insecure feeling of always being on the verge of a bad fall was mostly absent. Although I made much better time than on my first foray, Trevor and Pooch still had to wait for me at the bottom. "Ready to go swimming?" he asked with a grin as we stood beside the roaring creek, "The water's nice."

I knew the plan, but exactly the last thing I wanted to do was to strip off and go for a dip. I chose not to voice my reluctance as I gazed at the torrent of meltwater, but I think he knew my feelings anyway.

"Let's go straight to the pool," he said, so we crossed the creek on our stepping-stone, then headed upstream.

When I'd first seen the pool, it must've been near its low-water level, since now it looked much bigger. The recent heavy rain had caused the falls to grow too, both in volume of water tumbling down the rock, plus the sheer noise of it as it spilled into the standing water. I dipped my fingers in and it was very cold.

Trevor had stripped down to swim trunks, then he'd fished out his spade from Pooch's saddlebags. After getting out the colander, he handed me a couple of empty twenty-pound potato sacks, saying, "We'll fill these, then pan the paydirt."

I nodded and unenthusiastically sat down to remove my boots. I took off my jeans and revealed my seldom-used but snazzy maroon swim trunks, then put on a pair of old sneakers. The moment I took off my tee-shirt, I could feel the cold spray of the falls on my chest, which was decidedly unpleasant.

Before I could indulge in an inner dialogue with the topic being 'cold or gold', Trevor said, "Might as well do it now," then he dove into the pool with the spade and colander in his hands. Surfacing quickly, he gasped and shouted something about brass monkeys, then he hastily returned to stand beside me again. With a grim countenance and through suddenly-blue lips, he said, "It's a little chilly, but it's doable." Turning his sodden head towards me, he asked, "Ready?" and I nodded with no hint of eager anticipation. "I'm going to dig right under the falls, so I'll need you and the bag close-by." Handing me one of the burlap sacks, he added, "Don't look so glum, think of the gold!" then he dove in again.

I waded into the ever-deepening frigid water and headed towards the falls. Trevor glanced at me, then went under with his spade and colander, leaving me standing there holding the bag. I know going in slowly is probably the worst way to enter cold water, but I couldn't just dive straight in. By the time I pussy-footed to the fall, my shoulders were nearly submerged in the ice water, I felt totally numb and nearly stepped on Trevor as he worked on the bottom.

If you've ever felt inclined to jump naked into a large snow drift after being toasty in bed, other than confirming your status as a certified loony, you might understand the shock. I was already shivering by the time he resurfaced with the colander filled with dirt and gravel. He dumped it into the bag as I held it open for him, then he went under again. After doing this twice more, he said, "I can't stay in any longer, so let's see what we've found so far."

Although it was a huge relief to scramble from the raw water and feel the sun's rays on my skin, I was still shivering uncontrollably. I set the bag of paydirt down and said, "I'm going to get a fire going," then I headed into the bush looking for starter material.

"I don't think that's such a good idea," said Trevor, leaning forward to wring out his hair, "we'll get all warmed up, then it'll be tougher to go back in. Why don't you just prepare things, but not light it? Meanwhile, I can pan what we have in the bag."

I nodded, and started making a fire-pit a few feet from the creek. Rolling rocks aside and digging a shallow hole warmed me up again, so I began to feel almost human again. As I was dragging a large log from the undergrowth (I figured we'd need a big fire), Trevor was panning the contents of the burlap bag.

Then I heard him say wonderingly as he studied the gravel in his pan, "Jesus H. Christ!"

I'd never heard him blaspheme before, so I knew he must've been overawed by the showings. Nonetheless, I asked, "What's the 'H' stand for?"

"Humphrey," said Trevor without shifting his gaze from his pan, "come look at this!"

I quickly joined him and couldn't believe what I saw in the pan. He'd sluiced out the dirt and gravel, so now all that remained was black sand, with lots of gold nuggets of varying sizes.

"Yumping Yiminey!" I exclaimed in a supposed Scandinavian accent. Abandoning it, I finished by saying, "There must be two ounces in that single pan!"

The gold was mostly in the half-grain of rice size we'd seen before, but there were also a few much larger nuggets. Trevor kept tipping the pan side to side, so black sand and water rolled over the gold, with the movement somehow making the sight more striking. Grinning widely as he regarded my astounded face, Trevor said, "It's your turn to go under and do the digging; think you can manage?"

Looking again at the gold and feeling the excitement stirring my frosty outlook, I nodded enthusiastically, saying, "No problem!"

I was still too chicken-hearted to dive straight in and face the horrible shock all at once. So, doing an 'old lady with a pebble in her shoe' impression, I waded cautiously into the pool. A few teetering paces later, the icy water was at knee-level and I couldn't feel my feet. Trevor was right behind, watching my stilted progress silently, so I didn't want to let the team down by appearing to be a total wuss. A sudden dip in the pool bottom immediately lowered me to waist level, so visions of dropping plums into liquid nitrogen came to mind. Pooch normally loves being in the water with me, but as I tried uncrossing my eyes, I could see him at the far side of the pool. Apparently deciding the water was too cold, he was on dry ground watching me intently, supposedly to view my next move. When I called his name, he got up on all fours and wagged his tail, but he didn't join me. Since I plainly didn't need him, he wasn't about to step into the pool: smart dog!

Trevor was right behind me with an empty burlap bag, so I accepted the inevitable: I dove underwater with the colander and spade in my hands. After suffering the initial glacial shock, it wasn't so bad, unless you aren't curious at all about how ice cream feels. It was surprisingly loud down there, as the falls were creating a never-ending roar, while my spade clattered noisily on rocks as I cleared them to scoop with the colander. After getting it filled with dirt and gravel, I resurfaced dramatically to empty it into the bag Trevor was holding open for me. Since there seemed nothing to say, I didn't linger for a chat, but dove to the bottom again.

Coming up in thirty seconds, I spilled another colander-load into the bag and said, "That's enough! I'm not going under any more. You'll have to find a better method: it's too cold this way!" I wanted to stride purposefully from the pool, but since I couldn't feel my feet, I tripped and fell face first into the icy water. Even though I found this quite irritating, I didn't indulge in a frenzy of water-splashing and profanities, since I was too numb for theatrics. Awkwardly getting up, I went directly to the fire pit, took matches from the jeans I'd hung on a nearby branch, then got the flames crackling. I removed my wet swim trunks and put on my pants, while Trevor panned the paydirt I'd recovered from the pool's bottom.

It was a warm summer day, but my teeth were chattering as I donned my shirt and hunkered down by the fire. Trevor clearly wasn't as incapacitated by chill as I was, drat him. I like spending time with the guy, since he's never made me feel as though we're in some sort of competition to see who's better at this or that, but .... .

He came over and sat beside me with his pan in his hand. Smiling broadly, he said, "Have a gander at this!"

If anything, there was more gold than in the first pan I'd seen. Again, it was mostly in the form of the small grains, with larger nuggets scattered throughout. One of them was much larger than the piece he'd given to Pauline, plus there were a few flakes of colour in the black sand. "I haven't seen such rich pans before," he said, handing it to me, "I'm going to get out of these wet trunks and into my dry clothes. I'll be right back!"

While he changed, I sat by the fire admiring the gold we'd found. It was a very pretty sight, but it wasn't inspirational enough to get me into the creek again. Sitting by the fire had warmed me, so I felt almost comfortable once more, but not inclined to splash around in the meltwater anymore.

Pooch was sticking his nose curiously into the pan, since, after all, I was sitting, plus I had a dish in my hands. In order to prevent him from snorting up some gold pellets, or having them decorating his chops, I pushed him away as Trevor rejoined me.

"You're right," he said, "we can't work this way." Then he nodded to himself and said, "We were in the water for maybe ten minutes, but that was enough for each of us." He held his palms out towards the fire as he sat there beside me, then he added happily, "Oh well, live and learn. I think I know of a way to make things better."

Since he stopped talking and just stared into the fire with a pleased expression on his face, I had to voice the obvious question to break him out of his reverie. "How so?" I asked. He blinked, then switched his focus to me, as though he was surprised I was here in this wild place. I could tell he had no idea of what I'd just said, so I asked again, "How do you propose getting the gold from under the ice-water without freezing and becoming an over-aged soprano in a boys' choir?"

"Maybe a scuba wet-suit would work, know anything about them?" he asked me with his eyebrows raised.

"They come in many different colours and are probably really expensive; that's all I know about them," I answered informatively, "have you thought of using survival suits?"

"That's an interesting idea," Trevor responded, "but aren't they designed to keep you afloat?"

"Could be," I answered, "I don't know a thing about them."

"Thanks for all the useful info," he said, "Now I won't have to do much research."

"Glad to be of help," I said, ignoring his sarcasm, "let's make a pot of tea and have something to eat!"

Sarah's Lake

I'd taken the saddlebags off Pooch and had left them by the creek. The moment I jingled a buckle while opening them, the dog magically appeared out of the bush to see who was messing with them. I fed him a doggy-biscuit and admonished him for not joining me during my adventures in the pool, but he was too busy eating to pay me much attention. After our break, Trevor and I panned the borders of the pool, but there was no talk of actually going in again. We found some more of the gold pellets, but our pans weren't nearly as good as the ones we'd got from under the falls.

We worked around the pool for about an hour, with me rolling rocks aside and Pooch doing his excavating, until Trevor said, "Let's go back to the cabin. I want to show you the lake." He was pouring the contents of his pan into one of the bags, when he asked, "Notice anything about the pool bottom when you were down there?"

"I was too cold to be paying much attention," I answered.

"There's a layer of overburden under the rocks and I bet it's full of gold. We've barely scratched the surface, so imagine spending hours in the pool and not just minutes," Trevor said excitedly as he put the saddlebags onto Pooch. I don't think Trevor had a case of raging gold fever, but his enthusiasm was certainly contagious. As he packed the paydirt away, he said, "We can clean and weigh it back at the cabin tonight, then I'll learn what I can about scuba suits or whatever, tomorrow." He couldn't stop smiling as he gazed at the pool, then he added, "I know for sure now that a lot of gold's here. And according to those guys you saw in the smoke, there's more hidden in the rock above the falls." He was looking up at the angry water tumbling down the granite, while nodding and saying to himself, "I'll find a way."

Since I'd almost forgotten about Portunus and his two buddies, it was rather jolting to be reminded of their unearthly presence. So, as I was extinguishing the fire, I carefully avoided looking into the smoke, since mention of them had really discomfited me.

The route up the ravine wall was familiar to me now, but it was still tricky, so I took my time. As usual, Trevor and Pooch were waiting in the truck when I made it to the road. After I'd climbed in and caught my breath, Trevor said, "This changes everything, so maybe I won't have to build cabins for summer tourists after all. I can just work my claim, and since you'd have to be nuts to try getting anywhere near the pool or falls in winter, I can holiday at the cabin when the snow flies or keep busy at the garage; whatever's best."

He still hadn't started the engine and was leaning forward with his forearms resting on the steering wheel. He'd been dreamily looking out the windshield as he'd been speaking, so I knew he'd lost me again amid all his happy speculations. Easing him back to the present, I asked, "You still carve, don't you?"

He nodded, then turned to me and answered, "Of course, but I haven't had much time for it lately."

"You could carve whatever you want, then Sarah could varnish or paint it. She loves doing that kind of thing and she's good too!" I could see he found the idea appealing, so I carried on: "It could be your own little cottage industry. People pay big bucks for good Native art; you could sell a few pieces at the lodge, on commission of course." Looking rueful and shaking my head, I added sadly, "The proprietor there can be difficult at times, since he only accepts gold."

Trevor grinned at me and started the motor, saying, "That's a good idea! It'd sure fill in those long winter days. I'll mention it to Sarah."

Using the Flaming Barge to push through the saplings growing on the road, we got to the cabin. I guess it was the contrast between the leafy claustrophobia of our slow trip and the open space of the lake, but the big bluff seemed closer as it loomed across the way. It appeared to be leaning aggressively over the water and towards us, so I tried ignoring it. But it dominated the scene and couldn't be dismissed, so I found myself mentioning it to Trevor.

Apparently blasé about the big rock, he glanced at it and said, "The fishing's good at its base, let's go out in the boat."

He gave me a spinning rod that'd been leaning on a wall of the core shack, then a box of lures. "I'll be using hook and worm," he said, holding up a small earth-filled carton, "from Moon's composters, of course."

The boat was simply a four-man aluminum vessel with a pointy end and battered oars. Strictly functional and obviously with no regatta coming up in the near future, I noticed it lacked life-vests. "Sarah won't have any cushions if you're not safety-conscious," I said as Pooch jumped in without being invited, "otherwise, whatever can she use to soften her seat?" Trevor rolled his eyes in reply, but he didn't say anything.

Rowing to the left, we skirted the shore and scanned the bush, which was wild-looking and obviously undisturbed by human hands. There wasn't any level ground; it was all hummocky and mossy, with thick vegetation seeming to make it impassable. There was also a steep, ten-foot climb from the lake to the unwelcoming tangle further in, so I hoped for Trevor's sake that there were more accessible stretches of shoreline.

Breaking into my thoughts, he nodded towards the same area I'd been studying and said, "That's where I planned to build a cabin. Fifty feet in, there's a fairly level patch with only tight-packed small pines and bushes growing there. And the shoreline's not as bad as it looks, once I clear the bushes out, that steep stretch is only about fifteen degrees." He smiled with satisfaction and started rowing again, saying, "I was going to prepare the site for the building, but now, maybe all that work won't be necessary."

As we made our way around, I cast a lure into the water and trolled without success. Pooch was now lying in the stern with his big head on the bench-seat next to my leg. His chops were spread out and his dark eyes were closely observing my technique as I reeled in, then flipped the lure back into the lake. Surprisingly, he didn't seem inclined to watch the scenery go by, but was solely focussed on me.

"I've caught fish here before," said Trevor as he rowed slowly along, "but it's not a good spot. The water's deep here on the north half of the lake, it's about 130 feet." Shrugging as he pulled at the oars, he said, "I guess you have to be a big fish to swim through this part, there's nowhere to hide." Glancing over his shoulder as we rounded the lake close to shore and headed towards the bluff, he gestured with his head, saying, "The water's about 60 feet deep at the base of the big rock, then it quickly goes to 15 or less. There's a shallow inlet between the bluff and the creek inflow: that's where most of the fish like to hang out."

As he'd been speaking, I'd seen movement among some windfalls onshore. I'm familiar with how a deer or a bear looks in the shadows of the bush, it's home and they belong here. He might show fear or curiosity, but he wouldn't engage in guilty starts, then hide himself. It'd only been an impression, but the momentary movement had somehow seemed human, so

I glanced at Trevor to see if he'd noticed any-thing. But he'd obviously been lost in thought, and hadn't seen a thing.

"Much wildlife around here?" I asked, still looking into the bush.

"Yes," answered Trevor, "there's the usual gang of critters, plus one I've never seen before: marmots. There's a colony of them up there in the hill." Looking at Pooch, he added with a smile, "I bet you'd find them interesting, too." The dog lifted his head and wagged his tail, then seemed to take heed of his new surroundings for the first time. Although I hadn't convinced myself that what I'd seen had only been an animal innocently going about his day, I didn't want to spoil the easy conviviality in the boat, and didn't voice my suspicions.

We were now near the middle of the bluff; Trevor stopped rowing and shipped the oars. We looked up at the huge granite wall and only saw a narrow ledge halfway to the top, with nothing visible beyond. Trevor said, "It's about 50 feet to the bluff from here, but if you're right at its base, the rock overhangs the water so much that it even shelters you from the rain. The top half isn't vertical either," he added with a nervous chuckle, "it's an easy 50 degrees down to the ledge, but it must be scary looking down from the top. I'll have to get up there for a look-see."

Pooch gazed at the wall blocking out his view of the countryside, then jumped into the lake and swam towards the rather ominous grey granite. I dipped my hand into the water and discovered it was cold, but it didn't have the numbing frigidity of the creek. The dog sniffed various areas of the wall, then he swam back to us. This gave me concern; if you've ever tried getting a mature Newfoundlander dog into a boat from the water, you'll know why.

Immediately seeing the problem, Trevor said, "Don't worry, there's a landing area in the inlet; he can follow us until we get there."

As I called Pooch, my voice echoed eerily off the wall with an angry inflection I was sure I hadn't verbalised. I think Trevor heard the difference too, but he didn't comment. After a moment of uncomfortable silence, he said, "I don't want to hang around here any longer." He unshipped the oars and started rowing, saying, "We can get the dog back into the boat, then catch our supper in the inlet."

'A positive attitude usually wins the day!' I said cheerily to myself. Then I hoped Pauline had packed one of her magic jars of stew as an emergency supper for us.

We turned left into the pretty inlet and the place was a relief after the oppressive blankness of the stone wall. The water on the lake had been riffled by the breeze, but it was mirror-smooth here. Only about 60 feet across, it sported a patch of half-submerged reeds, with pine windfalls leaning from dry ground and lying among them. We climbed out of the boat onto the shore to wait for Pooch, who was obviously enjoying his afternoon dip. With hands on his hips and a proud look on his face, Trevor gazed at the lake as we stood there. Since I had a good idea of how he felt, I didn't want to spoil the moment with words, so I said nothing.

I was watching Pooch from the corner of my eye as he swam in and wetly stepped ashore. Trevor was still dreamily surveying his domain, and Pooch was plainly aware his pal wasn't paying attention. As for me, he was probably unsure of my seemingly casual manner: Pooch doubtless knows by now that my occasional stumble-bumness is just a distraction I use to hide my true brilliance.

Anyway, Trevor and I were standing side by side looking out over the lake, while the dog approached from the left. Trying to make himself unobtrusive, like an elephant attempting to be mouse-like, he casually stood in front of us and gazed across the way as if his mind was elsewhere. Then he lowered his head and half-closed his eyes. From previous experience I knew these were the first moves of his shake-cycle, so quick as a bunny, I stepped behind Trevor. He finally focussed on what was happening nearby, but he was much too late. Pooch unleashed a torrent of spray, like a garden hose's nozzle turned to 'monsoon setting' and, thanks to my cowardly manoeuvre, Trevor got caught in most of the spray.

Not commenting on his sudden drenching, I took a pace from behind him and pointed at an area of the inlet just outside the reed-patch, saying doubtfully, "That should be a good spot, but I've yet to see a fish caught in this lake. I didn't even get a hit on my lure as I trolled here." I turned to him indignantly, as though it was all his fault, but I don't think he picked up on my pretended annoyance. He was dabbing at his face with his hanky and gave Pooch a dirty look as the dog shook himself once again, then sauntered off into the bush.

Trevor walked over to the boat to retrieve his rod and the carton of worms, before setting up his rig. With red beads and silver spinner a few inches above the baited hook, he turned to me and said, "Want to see some fish? Watch this!"

Since there wasn't much weight at the end of his line, he only managed a 25 foot cast towards the middle of the inlet. He cranked his reel-handle just twice, before the still water erupted with a trout doing a somersault and noisily splashing along the surface. Then he dove and headed straight for the cover of the reeds. The submerged trunks and branches of the windfalls were obviously not a place for a fish on a line, so Trevor's rod bent double as he persuaded the trout to go somewhere else. This game lasted another five minutes, until he finally pulled the beast ashore. It was about ten inches and identical to the fish in my lake.

"Very nice," I said, "one his size is enough for my supper."

"Your turn now," replied Trevor, "try a lure."

I'd switched to an articulated plug that mimicked a small frog foolishly swimming through open water. I cast it just off the reeds and reeled in maybe ten feet of line, when the lure was savagely attacked. This trout didn't jump, but dragged the line deep and fought against the flex of my rod. He swam in a few tight circles, then took a zigzag course away from me, but it was a losing strategy. He tired himself out, but just as I was cranking the handle to land him, a rat's nest of twisted monofilament developed on the spool of the cheap reel. The line somehow got tangled and stuck down in the main housing, thus rendering the whole outfit fairly useless.

It was Trevor's piece of equipment, so he should be ashamed to own such shabby gear. I turned to express my vexation, like a symphony violinist miffed at the dime-store instrument he was expected to play, but Trevor had seen the problem and was grabbing the landing-net from the boat. While I was peevishly fussing with the recalcitrant reel, he grabbed my line and managed to scoop up the fish, saying, "He's smaller than the first, so one more and we'll have supper." Rather than play a frustrating game of 'let's unravel the line', Trevor cut out the raggedy knot, then pitched the rod into the boat. "Sorry about that," he said, as he gave the rig a disrespectful glance, "it was left behind by the previous tenants and now we know why." Shaking his head grimly but grinning, he added, "I'll catch one more, then we can have an early supper. I'd like to clean the paydirt we got at the creek and weigh the gold. We can go fishing any time." He re-baited his hook, then cast his line into the inlet. After only two more tries, he had another trout raising a ruckus on the once-quiet waters, while Pooch reappeared from the bush and watched all the action with keen interest. Trevor finally got the fish ashore without having to use the net and Pooch stood back with his tail wagging, but didn't interfere. He knew better than to get too close to a fish flopping on the ground with a hook in its mouth. I ordered the dog into the boat, while Trevor killed and cleaned the trout. Pooch likes to eat fish guts and they're probably harmless enough, but I won't let him. It's my delicate nature, I suppose.

Once we'd bundled into the boat and Trevor was rowing towards the cabin, we heard a piercing cry that had us all snapping our heads around to gaze up at the rock bluff. Trevor stopped rowing and said, "That's a marmot's warning call. For a rabbit-sized critter, he can sure shout loud. There must be a bear or a hawk around."

It wasn't necessarily the decibel-level of the cry, but its substantial resonance seemed to hang in the air like something solid. The high-pitched hoot had the penetrating quality of a foghorn combined with the screech of an eagle and somehow, I found the sound slightly unsettling.

Trevor was looking at the bluff and saying, "There might be a colony of them right at the top, so I'll have to check it out." He started rowing again with a contemplative look on his face, but I don't believe he was thinking of furry grey beasties running among the rocks.

We rounded the lakeshore about fifty feet from land, until we came to the creek inflow. I was tempted to try my luck with a worm and his fishing rod, but the wharf was just beyond, so I didn't.

As we tied up and Pooch scrambled out, I noticed it was a solidly-built floating dock with a wide strip of outdoor carpeting nailed to its platform. Trevor saw me perusing the vividly-coloured fabric and explained, "Sarah told me she gets splinters every time she's on the wharf, so ..." He chuckled as he looked at it, then added, "It was a partial roll. I think the guy at the hardware store just wanted to get rid of it, so I got it for a steal!"

'No wonder!' I thought. It was bright orange with black splotches and I was baffled as to the original purpose of its creation. Carpeting for the visually impaired, I finally concluded.

Tearing my eyes from the wharf-covering, I regarded Trevor balefully as he said, "Look at this!" and gestured at a pile of logs on the shoreline. The bush in front of the cabin had been severely cut back, with the felled trees now bucked and piled neatly. "Emergency wood for the stove," said Trevor, "it's good knowing it's here."

After we'd gone up to the cabin, he took the bag of paydirt from the saddlebags, then suggested we go down to the creek with our pans. By the time we'd cleaned the dirt and he'd put the pellets and nuggets into his pouch, it was nearly nightfall. While we'd been hunkered down by the creek, I'd had the uncanny feeling we were being watched from the bluff across the lake, so I felt relieved returning to the cabin.

Pauline had packed the picnic basket with enough items to ensure we'd not starve to death. I grabbed a few potatoes, a small bottle of olive oil and a container of coleslaw from the hamper, while Trevor peeked in and asked about a dish wrapped in wax paper. "That's a peach pie," I informed him and he nodded as though he was only mildly interested, but I knew different.

After our supper of delicious fried trout, I cut a large wedge of pie for myself, then gave the rest to Trevor. He was still eating it as he brought out the scales to weigh our gold: 7.5 ounces. Obviously super-pleased with the results, he said happily to me, "We didn't get much done today, but wait until I'm properly prepared; that pool's full of gold!"

"It's not right for me to get half, if you've done all the work," I replied, "that 50-50 arrangement only applies when I'm actually here: fair enough?" I hadn't been sure what he meant at first, so maybe my magnanimous generosity was inappropriate.

He looked surprised and nodded, then he asked, "Care for a root beer? I put a few bottles in the creek."

As we drank the pop, he lit a candle and doused the gas lamp, then poured the gold pellets from the pouch onto a newspaper, saying, "Let's divvy this up." While I watched him carefully weighing it on the scales, he said rather apologetically, "Sometimes I question my good luck. Do I really deserve to find all this gold just lying on the ground? Am I so self-absorbed that I'm taking all these riches for granted?" I'd never before heard him doubting his own conduct, so it was a mild shock for me as he continued, "I'm a Native guy, so I'm supposed to be close to the land and all that, but I feel I'm somehow taking advantage." He shook his head and looked guilty, then he grinned and said, "Don't get me wrong; I love the fact the claim has gold, but I feel I've just accidentally stumbled onto it and it belongs to someone else, like those guys you saw in the smoke." He sighed and added, "I'm probably being silly, but ..."

"I understand," I said, although I didn't really. "Don't question any good fortune coming your way, but simply benefit from it." Then I added philosophically, "The world is full of bad news, so when fate smiles upon you, taking advantage isn't a sin, but an opportunity to improve your circumstances."

As though responding to my encouraging tone, Pooch got up from the rug near the stove and checked to see if his dish had magically been re-filled. When he discovered it was still empty, he sighed in a world-weary way and returned to his place. He flopped down on his carpet as if all the strength had left his legs, then grunted irritably after doing so. He gave me an accusing look, as though all the disappointments in the world were my fault, sniffed indifferently at the wood-stack, then dropped his head to the rug with an audible thump. He stared at me for a moment, then shut his eyes and seemed to fall asleep instantly, despite all the inequities of life.

Carefully avoiding mention of the three specters I'd seen in the wood-smoke, I said, "This is a nice place and you belong here." He smiled gratefully in response, but there was a hint of worry in his eye. I think he'd seen something and didn't want to discuss it, but my suspicions didn't mean much. It was his land, so it really wasn't any of my business.

Just then, a single marmot call came from across the lake. The cry had the piercing quality I'd heard before, but now it seemed plaintive and odd in the nighttime. "Wonder what he's yelling about at this time of day," I asked casually, but Trevor just shrugged.

Sleeping Outside

I liked the cabin and the lake, but the big bluff seemed to intrude more than simply being part of the scenery. Since it's only a personal impression, I'd never tell him I find the place slightly unsettling. It's so wild-feeling compared to Three Duck Lake, mostly because of that huge fist of rock hanging over the water. Even at night, it somehow made its brooding presence apparent, so as I sat at the table and looked through my reflection in the window, I couldn't disregard it as it hulked darkly in the moonlight.

As we both sat staring out the window, Trevor said, "I want to tell you something that's no secret, but I know it's been bugging Pauline." He grinned at me, saying, "I think you're curious, but you can shrug it off. Not her: she really wants to know. It's no big deal that Moon's my stepmother, but she's very private and prefers not to talk about it." Smiling at my startled reaction, he continued, "If it wasn't for Moon, I don't know where I'd be today; certainly not here talking with you." Shaking his head sadly, he said, "I don't want to talk about my real parents; I don't know much about them, anyway." He placidly stared into the candle flame, but I noticed his hand, formerly calm and flat on the tabletop, had slowly turned into a fist. "By the time I was ten, I was pretty much on my own," Trevor continued, "and Moon took me under her wing. She made sure I got an education and she'd basically been my big sister/mother for years. She even used to take me to some of her summer bush-camp jobs, where she cooked. I'd make a few bucks helping repair some of the men's personal vehicles, that is, after the guys realised a little Native kid like me could be useful." Chuckling as he thought about it, then quickly becoming serious, he added, "She saved me and it's as simple as that, so I'd never mean her any harm. But I know you can be trusted to just tell Pauline and no one else, so keep it under your hats, okay?"

I nodded and replied, "I don't think Moon wants to blow her own horn. Don't worry, we won't tell her we know."

"Good!" he said, "now maybe Pauline can lower her eyebrows the next time she sees Moon and I together." He chuckled again and said, "I've told Sarah of course, and it's been tricky trying to get her to keep her trap shut about it. She'll be relieved to know I've told you now." He laughed, which turned into a yawn, then I followed suit.

He hefted his little pouch of gold and idly dropped it to the tabletop, where it landed with a small, pleasing thud. He stared into the candle for a moment, then told me he had a friend in town who was knowledgeable about scuba suits and such things. There was a long pause in the conversation, so we gazed out the window again. "We'd like to get a dog," he finally said, unsuccessfully trying to stifle another yawn, "but Pooch's too big, so we plan to get a Lab or a setter." He sighed and closed his eyes for so long that I thought he'd fallen asleep. But he snapped back to the here and now, saying,

"There's so much to do and so many plans to make, sometimes I think things are getting out of control."

"It's just marital jitters," I responded soothingly, "you have nothing to worry about. Except maybe the rest of your life."

"Thanks for the pep talk," he answered rather insincerely, "you always seem to know the comforting way to put things."

"No problem," I said humbly, "that's what friends are for."

We watched the guttering candle for a while, before Trevor muttered to himself, "There's a draft coming from under the door, so I'll have to fix it." Glancing through the window, he said, "It's getting breezy out there; the cold air from the high ground is coming down here." Smiling sheepishly after looking at his watch and seeing it was only 9:30, he turned to me, saying, "I know I'm not being much of a host, but I have to go to bed: I'm falling asleep here."

"Would you like me to tuck you in, then sing a lullaby? I asked.

"No," he answered quickly, "Sarah says you sound like someone trying to play the bagpipes and sing at the same time."

Acting hurt by this insult to my musical abilities, I sulked for a moment, then said huffily, "This time I brought along my ski jacket, plus toque and gloves. I'm going outside for a while," then I went into the other room to get the items from my pack.

Knowing my prima donna bit had only been an act, he yelled from behind the wall of the neighbouring room, "Try not to bother the marmots."

By the time I'd donned my warm evening outfit and Trevor was in his bunk getting his snoring activities started for the night. Pooch was lying by the stove and showed no interest in joining me. He thumped the floor with his tail a couple of times and gave me the glad eye, but he didn't even raise his head. He just closed his eyes and didn't seem bothered by the strangled outboard-motor sounds Trevor was beginning to produce. So I left them in their noisy tranquillity to go outside.

The cold wind hit me the moment I closed the door behind me, so I congratulated myself for dressing like a tea-cozy. Even though I had my pocket flashlight with me, I resisted any urge to go exploring by shifting one of the lawn chairs further from the cabin (to get away from the snoring), then sitting.

While I sat facing the lake and waiting for my eyes to adjust to the outside night, Trevor's still audible experiments with sound effects abruptly stopped. During the ensuing quiet, I gazed at the lake's wind-ruffled surface as it shimmered in the moonlight. I was just beginning to think he'd suddenly died, when the snoring resumed with a distinctly gurgling motif, like a malfunctioning sump pump. I chuckled as I wondered how Sarah would handle this festival of sound in the wee hours, when the full moon over the bluff grabbed my attention.

The way it was rising over the rock made it look as though the bluff had a silver and slightly orange dome, with the clouds in the night sky moving along briskly. I was certain there were flames and smoke within the shining disc, but the moon was so bright I had to turn my eyes away. Trevor's not-so-distant snoring, with the silent stars as indifferent witnesses, combined to somehow make the scene surreal. Adding to my vague discomfort, an owl or a big bat darted by closely, but I'd felt the beast's momentary presence more than I'd seen him. I breathed deeply to relax, but it wasn't working. The moon had risen free of the bluff and was now bathing the monolith with light that seemed too strong in the night. The cold wind strengthened while clouds eventually hid the sky, but the outcrop across the lake seemed to have its own ghostly lighting. Since the night was hardly comforting, I returned to the cabin, where Trevor was now giving the world one of his quiet periods. I said goodnight to Pooch, then I went into the other room and closed the door. Surprisingly, I fell into a deep sleep the moment I lay on the mattress, so thankfully I didn't know if Trevor had then resumed his after-hours concert.

Interlude at the Lodge

We drove down to the lodge for breakfast the following morning. We arrived during Pauline's and Moon's tea break and they needed no force to convince us to have something to eat. We had sourdough pancakes with bacon, and Moon had to give Trevor the old fish-eye to get him to stop inhaling bounteous quantities of nutrition.

While we were drinking our coffee, Trevor told the ladies about the richness of the claim and reiterated the need for secrecy. He could've gushed on about our findings, but he'd obviously decided to keep things low-keyed, so I followed suit.

Changing topics a bit, Trevor told us Sarah was still living at her folks' place and wouldn't move into the cabin until certain things had been accomplished: like marriage. Also, the road in had to be cleared, and since she refused to be totally isolated, some way to communicate with the outside world would be needed.

"It'd cost a fortune to have a private phone line installed," I said, shaking my head grimly, then a sudden notion occurred to me. "Have you considered using smoke signals?" I asked.

Acting as if my query had been serious, he answered, "It's too windy: it wouldn't work." Then he added, "I know a ham radio operator in town who says all I have to do is to buy a good CB, then call him. Apparently it'd be easy for him to patch me into the phone service after that. I give him the number and he dials it for me. Duck soup."

It was a plausible scheme, but the thought of having a CB radio as an integral part of the phone line, gave me pause. Trevor'd probably soon be listening to the captain's greetings to his passengers after a successful takeoff from Warsaw. It's frustrating trying to make yourself heard over somebody loudly reporting wind conditions or whatever in Eastern Europe, but when the words are all in a foreign language, the whole thing quickly loses any entertainment value. But I didn't mention these fun occasions the phone company would likely offer up, since he'd soon find out for himself.

"There's also the core shack that has to be emptied of samples, plus the bed I have to buy …," he started patting his pockets and saying, "I have a list somewhere," but he gave up looking for it to take another sip from his mug.

Moon had been quietly sitting there observing us as we'd been chatting, but then she turned to Trevor and said, "I've learned more about this Portunus, the guy Henry saw in the smoke. His father was Moroccan, and his mother had obviously been cheating on her British Army husband while they'd been stationed in Gibraltar." Moon shrugged as she continued, "Not much more is known about him. How he managed to show up here is anyone's guess, but one thing's for sure: no one likes him. He's done nothing to warrant the discomfort others feel in his presence, so I concluded he simply has a chip on his shoulder." She took a small bite of the chocolate/walnut cookie she'd had by her mug, then frowned and said, "I know his type; I was given a good description of what it's like being in his company. It's like trying to knit a sweater and he wants to know about each stitch." She laughed, then added with an exaggerated grimace, "He somehow got in good with the Overseer and was eventually given a parcel of high ground to watch over. He's done this, but Portunus isn't a benign presence any more. Apparently, just allowing the road and cabin to be built by the drillers, along with the human habitation, had caused a lot of fuss. The Overseer and Portunus had a falling out about it, so since then they've done their best to avoid one another." Topping up Trevor's coffee, while ignoring my pleadingly extended mug, she gave him a worried look and said, "Then you showed up, not knowing you're walking into a messy situation." She went on to tell us the Overseer was currently absent and would be away for a while. "So Portunus is on his own now. Heaven knows what he might do next, or if he'll even show himself again. Just be cautious!"

In answer, Trevor smiled confidently at her and said, "I'll mind my manners, but there's no way I'm leaving. I'll take you and Pauline to the cabin as soon as the road's been cleared. And as for Portunus, he can go hang. He won't be chasing me away from Sarah's Lake any time soon, and that goes for my claim too!"

While I admired his resolve, I couldn't help feeling leery about the situation. After glancing at Moon, I could see the concern on her face, but neither of us wanted to rain on his parade. I wondered about Trevor again; was he just an ordinary guy who'd accidentally stumbled into this ethereal spirit-world and didn't know what the consequences could be? Or was his seeming ignorance only a ruse? I didn't know. He was certainly being offhand about the matter, but I couldn't shake the feeling he knew more than he was letting on.

He winked at Moon, then thanked Pauline for the breakfast. "I have to drive into town to find out about scuba suits," said Trevor as he got up from the table, "and I'm taking Sarah out for supper tonight." Rolling his eyes in a long-suffering way, he added, "I'm sure she'll have more assignments for me, along with a number of 'suggestions'. She keeps me busy, that one." Taking the truck keys from his pocket and jingling them, he smiled at everyone, and made his exit.

Moon finished her tea and gazed at the door for a moment. With a contemplative look on her face, she said, "I should be going too; there's a lot to do in the garden." After deciding she'd soon join her, Pauline and I were now the only ones sitting at the table.

She was wearing her dark blue work shirt with its sleeves rolled up to her elbows, revealing a vivid scratch on her right forearm. This wound doubtlessly came compliments of the damnable, but absolutely essential blackberry hedge surrounding the garden. Without its thick and thorny presence, any moose or deer could just stop by to sample the tomato plants, greens and all, or maybe try the potatoes, moose love spuds.

So the scratch was simply an occupational hazard and not worth mentioning as we sat there. Although I'd only been away from my bed for two days, it was nice being back at the lodge with Pauline. I noticed she had a slight sunburn on her nose as she donned her maroon 'Crickets' baseball cap at a jaunty angle and stood, saying, "I should be going back to the garden, we can get together later."

Acting like a greasy sleazoid with questionable motives, I asked her, "Hey babe, want to go out in the boat tonight? We could 'watch the sunset', then just enjoy the peace of the lake."

Not seeming to notice the oily and untrustworthy manner I'd been adopting, she answered, "That sounds nice, but you'll have to promise not to sing, since you'll scare the loons."

"I don't believe you're really concerned about birds," I said, now acting hurt by the aspersions being cast my way. I added sulkily, "If it's so important to you, then I won't croon at the moon, but it's your loss."

She grinned at me, then bent to give me a lingering smacker on the lips, saying, "See you soon," and started to head up to Moon's.

"Oh, I nearly forgot," I told her, "Trevor informed me Moon is actually his stepmother.

So I guess we were both half-right about him, she's not a relative, but she has been his mother. And since she's such a private person, I've promised we won't tell Moon that we know."

The news gave her pause, but she tried to be nonchalant about it. She said, "That explains a lot," then left as though the matter meant nothing, but I knew she'd be dwelling on it.

Just after Pauline had left via the main door, the three dogs came happily through the rear, displaying their usual high energy. Banjo and Grace were ecstatic to see that I, the leader of the pack, had returned, so I went over to their spot by the stove to say hello. I don't think Pooch could resist joining in on the frantic and boisterous greeting ceremony, even though he'd been with me all along. Since he was much bigger than the other two, he could easily shoulder each aside, so it was mainly Pooch in front of me. However, I noticed Banjo had a large smear of earth caked on his chest, whereas the rest of him was in its normal almost-presentable state. As Pooch knocked him away from me once more, I couldn't figure out how Banjo had managed to get himself in such a state. I finally caught him and upon closer inspection, I could see the dirt seemed to have been worked deep into his fur. It was as if he'd gone for a mud facial and the beautician's aim had been off by a bit. Since this was unlikely, I asked him, but all I got in reply was a glad look and a lick on the face.

We all went down to the lake, where I played fetch with them and cleaned Banjo. While we were there, a family group of husband, wife and daughter of about twelve or thirteen approached. They'd just completed the pleasing walk around the lake; I could tell by the bored witless expression on the girl's face. I was certain she'd have preferred waving goodbye as she watched them hike into the lake, but maybe the notion was uncharitable on my part. The parents were cordial towards me, but didn't say much as their daughter played with the canines. Anyway, the dogs seemed to momentarily brighten her outlook, yet I noticed as they left, the girl was a few paces behind her parents and was walking as though she had a heavy weight on her back.

Percy's Magic

The guys came over on Friday evening for our weekly poker game and I did quite well, thank you very much. Keith, jeweller and booking agent, knew of Trevor's claim and asked about it. I tried to answer casually, but I think he knew I wasn't telling him everything. He just nodded vaguely, then he winked conspiratorially at me and said nothing. He'd had a good night at the poker table too.

After another busy Saturday, during which Sarah came to visit, the four of us were playing Scrabble in the lodge later in the evening. Moon had won the first game by a wide margin and I found this to be miff-inducing. She'd been victorious over the last six games of our ongoing tournament, so the other three of us were determined to put the kibosh on number seven.

While Pauline is a lovely and caring person, she can be quite vicious playing Scrabble. We all take the game seriously: especially Sarah. Since she'd been sitting to my right, she'd wanted me to set her up on the board, so she could defeat Moon. But I wanted to win too. I'd been blocking the double and triple word scores as much as possible, so this had irritated her to a degree. I'd just finished ruining her chances of scoring big and she was about to comment on the rinky-dink three-letter word I'd just put on the board, when a client came in.

It was Percy Prentice, the guy I'd met earlier down by the wharf, but now he was without the female representatives of his clan. He was wearing shorts and t-shirt, with a too formal looking jacket sporting bulging pockets. In other words, he appeared decidedly odd as he cheerfully approached us at the table. He was maybe 5'7" and had dark, slicked-back hair. He'd obviously been out in the sun for too long, since his face was a bright red and his lips were shiny with balm. He looked down at the board and asked, "I'm not interrupting, am I?"

"I was just about to take my turn," Sarah replied peevishly.

"Good!" he answered, "I haven't caught you in the middle of something. Do you like magic?"

"No," said Sarah after four milliseconds of contemplation.

"Super!" responded Percy, then he took a deck of cards from a pocket and fanned them out under her nose, saying, "Choose a card, any card and don't show me."

As though she was doing something distasteful, like pulling a porcupine quill from a dog's tongue, she took a card from the offered deck and was clearly so excited that she yawned.

"Now show it to your friends," said Percy, obviously not put off at all by her disdainful lack of enthusiasm. She held it up for Pauline and Moon to see, then she showed me the eight of hearts.

The Great Persini told her to put the card back into the deck, before he shuffled it. He bent down to the table to perform the task, but his manual dexterity left a lot to be desired. After cutting the deck and laying the two halves end to end on the table, he tried to mix them. But he somehow managed to catapult a number of cards onto the Scrabble board, where three of them landed face-up. Since they were all the eight of hearts, our magician for the evening said, "Oops, I guess that kinda spoils the trick," but clearly undaunted, he added, "here's another one that'll baffle you," as if this first demonstration of his mysterious skills had been a success. He took three silver coloured cups from a pocket and set them upside down on the table in front of Sarah. Then he gave her a ping pong sized gold ball and asked, "What do you think of this precious sphere, young lady?"

Looking terminally bored, she idly cupped it in her hand to judge its weight and said, "It's a big ball-bearing with a spray-painted gold surface." She shrugged as she handed the heavy little orb back to him, then she studied her letter tiles with a cheesed-off expression on her face. But Percy had put one of his silver cups on the table and it was hindering her view. As she moved it aside, a gold-coloured ping pong ball fell out and rolled across the table. It went over the edge and bounced once on the floor, before Moon snagged it and returned it to Percy without comment.

He sighed and gave Sarah a disappointed look, saying, "Please don't mess with my props, you'll spoil the illusion otherwise."

I thought she was about to give him her pithy review of his abilities and his act, but before she could utter a word, he said, "Oh well, never mind." He put the balls and cups into a pocket of his jacket, telling us he had something special to demonstrate now. From his jacket he retrieved what looked like a three-foot length of piano wire with a triangular wooden handle at each end. It was the type of thing an aggressive guy might carry on his person, so he could garrotte anyone with whom he had a disagreement. Percy lay the handles on his shoulders with the wire behind his neck, and informed us that soon he'd be holding the device in front of him and we'd not know how he'd done it. "Watch this!" he said. He'd hooked his thumbs through the handles and was tautening the wire just behind his lower skull. Having seen his previous performances, I was afraid we were going to witness a self-decapitation, so I was about to put an end to the show, when the main door slammed open.

Mrs. Prentice angrily burst into the room and any magic immediately ceased. She was wearing a short-sleeved blouse revealing pallid strips of white flesh above the sunburned redness of her forearms. She had on shorts and was barefoot; her legs and feet were shocking-red too. Levelling a stern look at her husband, in a parade ground voice she said to him, "Percival! Are you bothering these unfortunate people with your stupid tricks? Can't you see you're imposing?"

Raising his nose just a bit, he informed her the audience had been enjoying things until she'd stormed in.

Doubtlessly wishing to further discuss the part about 'enjoyment', Sarah opened her mouth to offer her point of view, but Pauline interrupted the flow of hostilities by saying, "That's a bad burn!" She got up from the table, walked over to our guest and put a consoling hand on her shoulder, saying, "It's Deloris, isn't it? I'm Pauline. We fair-skinned girls have to watch out for one another." She glanced at Deloris's fried limbs again and said, "I have just the thing," then ushered her into our bedroom, closing the door softly behind them.

I knew Pauline was going to take a leaf off the aloe vera plant she had growing in a pot on the windowsill. Then she'd cut it in half and apply the resultant fluid to Deloris's burn. This was both cooling and soothing, plus it sped up the skin's healing time, but Pauline's nursing abilities weren't the most impressive part of the scenario. It was the way she'd smoothed the waters of what could've been an unpleasant little confrontation, by being her normal empathetic self. I'd seen her do this on many similar occasions, so I once asked her if she'd made a conscious decision to play diplomat. She'd looked at me expressionlessly for a long while, then she'd said, "You can be quite cynical at times, can't you?"

"Yes, but not when you're involved, my lovely," I'd replied unctuously.

Regarding me suspiciously, she'd said, "I don't like emotional scenes, so I do my best to avoid them and that's all there is to it."

"Yes dear," I'd said and that'd been the end of the discussion.

While Pauline was in the bedroom administering aid to Deloris, Percy fascinated us all (especially Sarah) with his detailed description of all the fixtures he and his plumbing buddies had been installing in the houses of a subdivision being built. As he was telling us about all the calibrations on the most expensive showerhead, he could barely hold in his excitement. "It has 'mist to fire hose' and everything in between," he enthused, looking at me as though I could do with a good cleaning, maybe on the 'prolonged thunderstorm' notch.

"Does it have a 'suicide by drowning' setting?" Sarah asked idly as she rearranged her letter tiles on their little wooden platform. She gazed at the Scrabble board and I could see her eyes focussed on the three letter word 'tin' I'd used to block her access to a triple word score. Since she was still with us, I could tell she probably had a good second option and was eager to take her turn, but she gave me a dirty look anyway.

Percy was preparing to speak, apparently to respond to Sarah's rather insulting query, when the bedroom door opened and the two ladies rejoined us. Deloris had an aloe vera sheen about her and was clearly more relaxed than when she'd first come in. She glanced gratefully at Pauline and said, "Thanks so much, this is a big help."

"Try not to clean it off tonight," Pauline replied, "then come to the lodge tomorrow morning for another treatment, I'm up at 5."

After smiling warmly at Pauline, Deloris looked at her husband, who was now sitting comfortably at the table munching on a peanut butter cookie he'd found on a plate. Not nearly as shrill as before, but unable to totally hide the admonishment in her voice, she said, "Let's go Perce, I'm sure these good people want to finish their game."

Sarah, who'd been unsocially studying her letter-tiles, heaved a sigh and surreptitiously mouthed the word 'amen'.

We finally resumed the game, but Moon beat Sarah by a single point to win her seventh in a row. Sarah blamed her loss on Percy and told us she didn't want to play anymore, then huffily retired to her room.

After Sarah's abrupt departure, Moon simply said, "Number seven, eh? Oh well, it's no big deal." Grinning into our unsmiling faces, she added, "I should be going too, you'll probably have another chance to embarrass yourselves tomorrow night." She looked pityingly at each of us in turn, as if we were nice but ignorant folk, then she bade us goodnight and left.

Pauline started preparing our evening cocoa. She seemed puzzled by her own feelings as she asked, "What do you think of Trevor's new place?" Not waiting for an answer, she continued, "I know there's a lot of gold on his claim and also that the cabin's nice, so why should I have these lingering doubts? I haven't even been up there yet."

As she was pouring me a mug, I said, "I've had the same feelings about the country around there. It's much wilder than Three Duck Lake, but it doesn't seem indifferent to our presence. In fact, I sometimes think all our activities up there are being observed, which isn't very comforting. And that big bluff I told you about somehow scares me; it dominates the lake and appears to have a personality of its own," I said. "It's clearly a silly notion, but …"

"What about this 'Portunus'?" asked Pauline, "Moon told us he could… complicate things. Maybe your feelings aren't so silly."

She sat back in her chair and yawned without apologising, then she said, "Anyhow, Sarah and Trevor love it there, so what we think won't dissuade them much. They're a young couple about to spend their whole adult lives together, so they might listen politely to two cautious old fuddy-duddies like us, but I doubt if they'll change plans. And there's all that gold!" Pauline regarded me appraisingly for a moment, then asked, "How come we don't have a pool full of gold like them?"

"With my scintillating charm and likeability," I replied humbly, "who needs precious metals?"

She gave me another steady and serious look as I sat there drinking my cocoa, then said, "Yeah sure," without sounding at all enraptured by my presence. We talked about Moon being Trevor's stepmother and neither of us understood why she was so secretive about it. Pauline said, "Taking care of someone else's child is a noble deed, after all." She thought about it further, then shook her head and said, "I just don't get it. Moon's being silly about the whole thing."

"I agree," I replied, "but let's not blab to her about it, anyway. She must have her reasons, other than humility, for all the hush- hush about her relationship with Trevor. Let's comply with her wishes even though we think she's acting like a dolt."

Pauline sighed and nodded as she finished her cocoa, saying, "I'm going to bed." She got up from the table, while I went over to the wood-stove to say goodnight to the dogs. Then Pauline and I retired to our room.

Portunus Pays a Visit

The next few days at the lodge were routine but busy, so I didn't think of Trevor very often. Occasionally, the image of him in a wetsuit submerging himself into the icy pool water came to mind, and I wondered how he was doing. But clients and lodge duties came first, and my attention was usually elsewhere.

One morning the phone rang as Pauline was pouring me my daily ration of coffee. Because of my insomnia, I limit my intake to one helping per day, but the mug I use is quite large. She's taken to calling it 'the thing', as in, "Now that you've finished with the main part of your breakfast and I can clear away a few plates, there might be room for 'the thing' on the table." Nonetheless, I put up with all the disparagement because her coffee's excellent.

Anyway, it was Trevor phoning and I'd never before heard him sound so jittery. "Sorry Henry," he said hurriedly, "there's no time for small talk. I need you at my lake today, it's an emergency. I'm calling from town, so I can drive out to the lodge to pick you up. Can you take another day off?"

"Sure," I responded, "what's up?"

He paused, then answered, "I don't trust the phone, so I'll tell you when I get there."

When I asked if he'd like breakfast once he got here, he refused, so I knew something must really be wrong. "I need to talk with Moon," he said in a preoccupied way, "I'm sure she can help."

"She's visiting a friend," I informed him, "she'll be gone for a couple of days."

"Good timing Moon!" he muttered irritably, then he paused and asked, "is Pauline there?"

"She went up to the garden just before you phoned," I told him.

"It's good she doesn't know. Tell her I need your assistance with the wharf and the core shack. I don't want to alarm her, so I haven't even told Sarah about it. We can tell them the truth after today."

"What truth?" I asked.

"See you soon," he said and hung up.

I went up to the garden to tell Pauline that Trevor needed help with a few things. Since it was only a 'buffet night' at the lodge, I told her I might overnight at the cabin. "I'll pack a basket for you," she said, laying down the shears. She'd been clipping around the entrance to one of the cats' 'hedge-caves', and apparently 'PC', the Siamese, had been tolerating her proximity. But my sudden appearance had obviously freaked out the feline, so now she was huddled at the back of her 'cave' with her darting eyes searching for a way to escape. Silly beast.

By the time Pauline had returned to the lodge and prepared a basket for us, I heard the Flaming Barge pulling into the parking lot. I kissed Pauline and apologised for leaving her in the lurch. Rolling my eyes, I said, "Young love! Everything has to be done just right and by yesterday! Hope to see you soon," then I headed out the main door.

Yours truly hastening down the path with a large wicker container of food in my hand, certainly wasn't something the dogs could dismiss, so they accompanied me. Trevor was rearranging gear in the box of his vehicle, as the trio of canines easily jumped onboard to greet him. As I stashed the basket on the back seat floor and closed the door, he said, "I almost forgot; we'll need your binoculars, so can you go get them?"

I wanted to ask why, but I tamped down my curiosity and returned to the lodge to fetch them. When I got back to the parking lot, the dogs had disappeared and Trevor was sitting behind the steering wheel, tapping it nervously. After I'd climbed in and shut the door, he explained in a matter-of-fact way that he'd told the dogs to vamoose. Clearly they'd obeyed him, so I wanted to discuss this rapport he obviously had with the canine crew, but he seemed too nervous for a chat.

We drove through the trees and onto the dirt road leading to the blacktop. Then he started telling me about the two used wet-suits he'd bought. "Wearing one makes a huge difference," he said, "I can stay in the water for more than an hour. Since we're about the same size, you'll have to try one out. And the gold in the pool is impressive. I'll show you what I've found when we get to the cabin."

He was trying too hard to be positive, plus, he was driving too slowly. Normally he's a very good driver, but he was plainly distracted now, nearly rolling us into the ditch as he turned to speak to me.

"You don't seem to be with it at the moment," I said easily, "there's some traffic on the road, you know. So why don't you pull over and we can switch places? Then you can tell me what this is all about, without me fearing instant extinction by way of Mack truck." While most guys (including me) would be offended by such a suggestion, Trevor simply nodded and soon I found myself in the driver's seat.

He wasn't saying anything as we tooled along, so my patience was being stretched thin. When I glanced askance at him, a shock of fear went through me. He was peering sightlessly through the windshield and worriedly biting a finger nail. I was so used to his calm presence that his obvious emotional turmoil at the moment scared me. Trying to sound casual, as if I was only inquiring about the weather, I asked, "So, what's this all about?" My question seemed to wrench him back to the here and now, but it took him a few moments to respond. He sat up straighter, cranked the window down and stuck his head out. This wind-buffeting seemed to help him get his act together, but he still had an apprehensive look on his face as he started to speak.

"The weather's been nice recently," he told me, "so I decided to get to the top of the bluff with my groundsheet and sleeping bag, then spend the night there. I also wanted to scope out the best route up, so I did a lot of climbing back and forth before I could start cutting a trail. The view from the top was something else and the sunset was spectacular. I found it nearly impossible to believe the lake and surrounding countryside, plus the cabin were all mine." He chuckled ruefully and shook his head, saying, "At least I thought it was my land, but apparently that's not a given." He continued somewhat angrily, "This 'Portunus' has devised a test to determine whether or not I deserve the place," then he added, "from what I learned about him during his visit, he's unpleasant and self-important. In other words, he's not an inspiring guy."

"Visit?" I asked, "you mean you spent some time with him? Tell me about it."

We were driving through town now and somehow the pedestrians on the sidewalk seemed distant as they went about their day. Maybe I felt this oddness because they were doing their everyday chores, while I was heading into the unknown. Trevor seemed to know everyone in town, so he faked smiles and waved often as we drove through. Doubtlessly these folks must have wondered why he was sitting in the passenger seat, but we didn't stop to explain. As we got to the outskirts on the other side of town, he started talking again.

"I'd brought some food in my pack, so I ate well back from the edge of the bluff. I'm not particularly afraid of heights, but it's such a long drop to the lake that it's scary."

He told me he'd belly-crawled the last few feet to the edge, so he could look straight down. The bare rock dropped about 150 feet at a 50 degree angle to a ribbon of ledge that seemed suspended in mid-air. Nothing could be seen beyond this small level area, then the bluff-face angled down to the lake far below. Staying on his gut, he'd retreated from the drop-off after giving the tiny-looking cabin across the way another fond perusal. Getting to his feet and heading into the scattered cedars and pines growing just short of the edge, he found a patch of moss perfect for his groundsheet. He established his campsite, then carefully dug a fire-pit nearby. By the time he'd collected wood and had a blaze going, the sun had set and a cold breeze had started to whip the flames around. The tranquillity of the night and the cold stars seemed to sit beside him, so he'd relaxed in his own infinity. He spent a long time gazing into the fire and looking up at the stars, but it got so cold that he draped his sleeping bag over his shoulders.

While he'd been telling me about his night of camping at Sarah's Lake, I'd taken the left turn onto the single-lane roller coaster leading to the mining road. Though the way was so bad that it was imperative to keep the truck moving slow and steady in second gear, I wondered what would happen if I sped up and shifted into third. We were both wearing our seatbelts; for sure, we weren't going to end up plastered to the truck's ceiling after hitting a big bump. Since we'd probably be aloft for a while, I pondered upon the Flaming Barge's air-worthiness and decided not to stomp on the accelerator. I'm sure this loony notion passed through my mind simply as a distraction to the bad news Trevor was probably about to report, so I tried dismissing the nonsense to focus on his words.

We were now approaching the parking area from which the 'sapling road' had headed into the bush. "I've had it cleared," Trevor said, "it's easy going from here."

The cat-operator had done such a good job that I barely recognised the road now. The little trees had been scraped away and were mixed into the three foot esker of dirt and rocks lining the ravine side. I was happy to see that now a moment's inattention wouldn't send driver and vehicle on an impromptu visit to the creek far below. I glanced at Trevor to see if he wanted to switch places, but he was chewing on a fingernail and looked worried, so I didn't ask. We passed the pink flag marking the beginning of our route down the steep ravine; our bolt-cutter parking spot was only a stretch of rocky road now.

Trevor had been staring blankly into the bush and not saying anything as we drove into the cabin's clearing. After we got out of the truck, he spent a long time gazing belligerently, but also fearfully, at the huge slab of granite across the lake. Finally, he turned to me and said, "Sorry for being so mysterious, you must be dying of curiosity by now. Let's go down to the wharf and I'll tell you what happened last night." He wandered down to the creek and returned shortly with two bottles of root beer. He aplogised for not having a selection as he handed me one, then we each grabbed a lawn-chair and went down to the lake.

Carpeted in its ridiculous orange and black colours, the wharf bobbed in the occasional breeze like a Halloween place-setting that'd been frisbeed into the water. We set up our chairs on it, and sat side by side as we drank our pop. I was determined to act blasé about his apparent hesitancy to speak, but inside I was a tad irritated, especially when he got up and said, "Your binoculars: you left them on the front seat, right?" After I nodded, he hurried to retrieve them from the truck, leaving me glowering at the bluff, which seemed to be returning the favour.

The rock's reflection on the water's surface doubled its bulk, while the riffles caused by the breeze gave the image movement that appeared contrary to simple wave-action. Midmorning on a sunny day and I was feeling spooked as if I'd just seen a shadow shift on the shore of a dark lake. I shuddered, then suddenly decided I wouldn't like to live here, since the place didn't seem at peace with itself.

He came back with the binoculars, sat beside me, and focussed them on the bluff. He spent a long while studying the rock, during which I had to repress the urge to tear them from his eyes, clonk him on the head and demand an explanation. I couldn't help prompting him by asking, "You were going to tell me something?"

He apologised again as he handed the glasses to me, then asked, "What have I told you so far?" He seemed so shaken and at such a loss that I momentarily felt guilty about interrupting his thoughts. "You were sitting by your campfire at the bluff's top and you were star-gazing," I said, "and that's where you left me. So, what happened next?"

"Oh yes," he said almost to himself, "the stars and my fire." He regarded the slab of rock with an indecipherable look on his face, then he addressed me, saying, "It was nice up there at night. The stars were very close and my thoughts were clear. I was proud to be at the highest point of my own land, but I felt humble at the same time. Know what I'm talking about?"

"Yes," I answered, "I felt much the same when I first moved to Three Duck Lake. The feeling hasn't faded."

He nodded, but then he furrowed his brow and said, "I thought about all the gold I was finding, plus getting married to Sarah and I must admit to feeling self-satisfied." Smiling faintly and taking a swig of root beer, he told me he'd been staring up at the starry sky for a number of minutes, enthralled by the immensity of things. He'd got up from his seated position to feed more wood into the fire, glancing at the void sixty feet away. Whereas the sky had been filled with a rich scattering of twinkling silver-like coins in a wishing well, there was ominous blankness directly ahead. The ground simply ceased to be at the drop-off, so he was glad to be well back from the edge. Since the wind had weakened, he could see the wood smoke from his fire rising towards the full moon, but now it was colder. He watched as the last stick was consumed in the flames, then he made sure the fire was out. The wind had picked up again, but his groundsheet and patch of moss were in a slight depression, so he'd been mostly protected from the blowing cold. He looked at his watch and saw it was only a little past 9:00, but he decided to get into his sleeping bag anyway. With plans of spending the following day in his wetsuit down at the creek, he curled up in his warm bag and quickly fell asleep.

As he'd been telling me all this, I'd been wondering about the marmots up there and how they'd reacted to the 'paint-stripper on the fritz 'sounds of his snoring, but I didn't want to interrupt.

"The crackling of a fire and the smell of wood smoke woke me up some time later," he said. "I didn't see anything burning in my pit and anyway, once I put a fire out, it doesn't start again." He stared at the bluff, then narrowed his eyes and nodded to himself, saying, "So I got out of my bag and looked into the bush behind me. About forty feet away was a fire with a guy casually sitting beside it. I was surprised, to say the least." He smiled ruefully and shook his head after making this understatement. Anyway, Trevor told me when he'd cautiously gone to investigate, his visitor barely looked up at him as he invited him to sit. "My name's Portunus," he said as Trevor gingerly sat across the fire from him, "and I know who you are." Saying nothing more, but with a stern and officious air about him, he studied Trevor's face.

"I didn't know what to say or do," Trevor told me, "so we just looked at each other as we sat there."

According to him, Portunus had been wearing a strange, wide-brimmed hat. It was the sort of thing a man might sport on the golf course, or at the pheasant-shoot. But apparently it'd been stored wrong for a long period, since now the right side of the brim had a deep crease that made it rise above the other in an upward swoop. The tan leather headpiece would've been comical-looking, except for Portunus's piercing eyes beneath.

He had a flat nose and thick lips, but the rest of him was slender, a combination making it seem as if he was wearing a mask. Obviously of mixed heritage, he was part black, part white, with something else thrown in. "His skin blended with the night," Trevor explained, "so I really couldn't see much of his face under that stupid hat." He went on to tell me Portunus had been wearing a wool-collared jacket with an insignia of some kind on the breast pocket, but that he couldn't decipher it in the flickering firelight.

After his silence and the intrusive way he'd been studying Trevor, Portunus asked him, "Think you belong here?"

Making a big mistake by letting his sudden anger and indignation rule over discretion, he responded by asking, "Who are you, King of the world?"

Apparently, this query had somewhat irked his nighttime visitor. He impatiently tossed a stick into the fire, then levelled a hostile look at Trevor. Talking in a voice dripping with scorn, he said, "Just because you signed some papers and money changed hands, doesn't mean much." Mockingly, he added, "You, of all people, should know this."

Not wishing to get mired in a discussion of politics, Trevor said, "I was just spending a night out on my land, so why are you blessing me with your presence?"

Portunus smiled for the first time, revealing large and very white teeth, then answered slyly, "You don't have to ask, you know why."

Trevor shrugged and replied, "I don't really. Moon mentioned knowing of you and Henry saw you in the wood smoke, but that hasn't told me much." Since his initial outrage had cooled down a bit, he diplomatically left out the part about Portunus having the reputation of being a rather scummy fellow.

"Ah yes, Moon," he said with a total lack of fondness, "she lives a few valleys away with that married couple." Trevor had the feeling Portunus wanted to say more about her, but instead he commented, "That Henry is quite sharp for a white man, he's not as stupid as he looks."

Trevor turned and grinned at me as we sat side by side on the wharf. "I'm only quoting what he said. Personally, I think you're a wonderful guy."

Ignoring the large dollop of insincerity adorning this pronouncement, I said humbly, "It's always nice to be praised, even though it might be a wee bit backhanded." After a beatific pause, I asked what happened next with his new friend.

Quickly turning serious, he tried giving the bluff a casual look, but his eyes lingered on it for too long. He finished his root beer and put the empty bottle between his feet, but he didn't stop gazing at the bluff. "Portunus told me it's been called 'The Grandfather' or simply 'The Big Rock' for ages, and that I'd been disrespecting it by making myself at home," Trevor said.

"So, to prove I'm worthy and have pure intentions, he wants me to climb down to the ledge, then jump the remaining 150 feet into the lake."

I was stunned. The mere suggestion of doing such a thing gave me the heebie-jeebies. "What right does he have to put your life on the line?" I asked angrily. "You told him to go to hell, didn't you?"

Chuckling nervously and nodding once, he replied, "Yes, but not in those words. I told him it was a suicidal task and you'd have to be nuts to try it." He looked towards the steep slab of granite across the lake and shuddered as he continued. "Portunus told me the feat had been accomplished a number of times in the past. Apparently, the whole thing was the initiation for a boy growing into manhood. It was a rite of passage for male members of the tribe which used to live here. According to Portunus, it's my turn now." He studied a minnow that'd come from under the wharf and was now nibbling curiously at a thread from the rope tying the boat to the dock. The strand poked enticingly into the water, then receded as the soft breeze shifted the vessel a few inches. Trevor sighed, then told me when he'd refused to do such an outrageous thing and that he'd report these oppressive demands to the Overseer, Portunus had shrugged, saying, "He'll be gone for a month or a year, but who knows? A better question would be, who cares?" Gazing at the Big Dipper for a moment, he'd laughed drily, saying, "I don't blame you for being reluctant, it's a frightening prospect. Some have been killed or seriously hurt. I understand slipping at the top, banging your head on your way down, then falling the wrong way into the water are the causes of most fatalities." Obviously giving him lots of merriment, he said, "There's the story of the guy who nearly made it to the ledge, but he took a tumble and bashed his head on it on his way down. He was dead before he hit the lake." Portunus had finished relating this inspiring little anecdote with a satisfied smirk on his face, while Trevor had been trying to keep his cool. "You can refuse to show me any merit or courage you might have in your gut, but you can't just slink off to your cabin and dismiss me. I can make living here extremely unpleasant for you, and that includes the gold claim." He'd paused, then added, "If I don't see you out here at 3:00 tomorrow afternoon, then I'll know you decided against staying." With that, plus another smirk, Portunus had doused the fire, then he'd unhurriedly walked into the night and disappeared.

After Trevor had finished telling me this, the determined look on his face alarmed me, so I asked incredulously, "You're not actually thinking of trying it, are you?"

"Of course!" he replied irritably, "why do you think I rushed you out here this morning? Do you believe cops or a bailiff could help?"

"Sorry about that," I said as I saw how truly upset he was, "I was just reacting emotionally."

He was studying the bluff again with worried eyes, as if he was momentarily unaware of my presence. "It seems I don't have much of a choice," Trevor was saying resignedly to himself, "I'm sure Portunus wouldn't hesitate to make things miserable for me and Sarah if I don't oblige him. But it's weird I trust him to leave us alone once I've done the climb. I somehow know he'd never renege on his word."

I wanted to make a glib remark about Trevor's good fortune in dealing with such a prince of a guy, but the sight of the hulking monolith across the lake stopped me. The thought of climbing halfway down the thing, then jumping into the lake a long distance below, chilled me and rendered me speechless.

But Trevor had been right; what could he do? He'd called me, which was flattering, but I really couldn't do much to help. I thought of my own relationship with Three Duck Lake and how I'd defend my beloved piece of land come what may, but ….

I looked over at his wristwatch and saw it was 10:00. In only five hours time he was going to climb down the bluff, then plummet the remaining 150 feet into the lake. I saw he'd already decided to attempt it, so I didn't try dissuading him as he asked for the glasses again. After using them to study the rock-face closely, he said, "It shouldn't be as difficult as it seems, the toughest part is having your act together and not dwelling on failure." Handing the binoculars back, he said, "Take a look at the right side of the face. See the plants growing here and there? I think they're junipers." He pointed at the area, so I focussed the glasses on it as he continued. "Anyway," he said, "they're probably well-anchored to the rock, so they'll make climbing down the first section easy. Duck soup."

It didn't look ducky or the least bit peachy to me. I imagined trusting my life to an evergreen which might have strong roots deep in the rock. After a brief ponder, I decided I'd likely give that particular thrill a miss. The plants led down to a foot-wide crack angling diagonally down across the face, with another fault about 50 feet below and heading back to the other side.

"That top crack will give me solid footing all the way across," said Trevor, "same with the second one."

"But you can't hang onto anything," I pointed out as calmly as I could, "there aren't any hand-holds."

Trevor shrugged and said, "I guess I'll just have to lean forward onto the rock and hope it's not windy up there."

Since the two fault lines were about eight feet

apart on the left side, I asked, "How do you propose getting down to the second one?"

Trevor shrugged again and said, "I'll find a way."

Still being negative, I told him the lower fault travelled to ten feet above the ledge. "That's where the star of Portunus's happy little story came to grief and it's easy to see why. I bet there are lots of ways to die going for that last ten feet," I said. He nodded, but he wasn't looking at me, while his eyes had a glazed, preoccupied look. So I slapped him on the shoulder to get his full attention and said, "I know this place means lots to you, but it won't do you much good if you're dead. Can't you hold off? There must be an alternative to this madness."

One look at his face told me I was wasting my breath, as he'd clearly made up his mind.

"I appreciate your concern," he told me, "but it's something I have to do, so let's get on with it."

We got into the boat and rowed over for a closer look at the outcropping. After further studying his planned route down the rock- face, Trevor said, "No problem," as if he'd only been scoping out a tricky golf shot. I tried to be a positive presence, but a little voice in my head was giggling ironically at his apparent lack of worries. I also noticed a distinct tone of hysteria in his voice, but I remained stoic on the outside.

He looked at his watch and said, "We should be heading back to the cabin. I want to show you the gold I got, the last time I used the wet-suit." He was obviously trying to get his mind on other things, but it wasn't working. I could see this in the apprehensive way he regarded the looming granite wall as he unshipped the oars and started rowing. "I've stashed the suits down by the creek," he said, "no point in carrying them back and forth. You'll want to join me after you see what I've panned." He smiled as if he didn't have a care in the world, then he informed me he could repay a large chunk of the money he owed me. I nodded happily, but inwardly I felt jittery.

After we'd tied up the boat and entered the cabin, he said, "Now, first things first," then he handed me a lidded glass vial. "That's exactly seven ounces, and I picked up a paper on my way through town this morning. So let's calculate where your loan stands. I'll have it paid off in no time!"

Although it felt entirely inappropriate to be writing numbers and re-weighing gold pellets, we took care of the business side of things. After we'd finished, Trevor nodded towards the vial on the table and said, "The gold's an added plus, but that's not why I refuse to leave. I think you know the reason, so why waste time discussing it?"

I'd been about to try talking him out of his intentions, but his last statement had just confirmed his resolve. So my speech about his upcoming marital responsibilities went unspoken, and an edgy silence followed.

Trevor broke the jagged quiet by suddenly asking me, "Know anything about cliff-diving?" as if he'd just read an article about it and was mildly interested.

"As a matter of fact," I replied, "I know three things and number one is by far the most important. If you choose to leap from heights that'll get you plummeting at more than 100 mph when you hit the water, your future is limited. So it's best not to even think of engaging in such folly; take up stamp collecting or glass-blowing instead." I didn't chuckle after saying this, since I wanted to indicate my seriousness, but he didn't react in any way, so I continued: "Number two," I said in my countdown of things I know about cliff diving, "unless you'd enjoy communicating with everyone in a falsetto voice, your ankles should be locked together when you hit the water. Plus, pinch your nostrils while keeping your elbow tight to your chest."

"That makes sense," he said and nodded, "what's number three?"

"Jump," I replied, "you're just inviting trouble if you dive. I'd imagine accidentally performing a belly-flop from 150 feet would be quite uncomfortable."

He laughed nervously and nodded in agreement, while the sound of a distant marching band emanated from his mid-section.

"Pauline packed a container of egg salad in the basket for us," I told him, "along with bread slices, lettuce and pickles. Let's make sandwiches and have lunch before you go."

Since there was no argument from him, I went out to the truck to fetch the food. I tried ignoring the implacable bluff as I stepped outside, but it seemed to elbow its way into my consciousness. So I paused to give it another gander, while also checking on the weather. It was a sunny, windless day, perfect for climbing down a rock-face, one would think. A loon flew rapidly only five feet above the lake, then splash-landed and disappeared underwater. At my feet, a big bumblebee had nearly pulled the head of a wildflower to ground-level with his weight, so he now sported a sprinkling of golden pollen. But the normalcy seemed interrupted by the massive outcropping; it was a dark grey cloud in an otherwise blue sky. I'd had a close-up view of it with my binoculars; I could see the two long diagonal cracks which were going to be Trevor's route to the ledge. The image of him up on that rock wall popped into my mind as I hastened to the truck.

He only had one sandwich, saying, "I don't want to fill up, maybe I'll have the rest when I get back." Smiling calmly at me, he added, "Don't look so nervous, I'll be fine."

The Climb

I could understand why he hadn't wanted to tell the women. They simply wouldn't allow him to do such a dangerous thing; they'd physically restrain him if necessary. But all that stuff about a man 'having to do what he has to do' is mostly true, so I kept quiet. Anyway, I don't think I could hold him back by myself. We're both about six foot and our lifestyles keep us fit. While he's certainly no muscled 'Mr. Universe' type, he has the sort of strength needed to actually tear a stick from Pooch's mouth during a spirited game of tug-of-war. Though I'd been thoroughly impressed at the time, I'd also made a mental note to avoid participating in any sort of wrestling match with the guy.

Intruding upon my troubled thoughts, Trevor indicated the compass hanging from a cord around his neck and said, "I'll give you a mirror-flash once I get up there. Then you can row out to the middle of the lake and wait until I jump: duck soup." He looked at his watch and told me, "I should be going now, since I can't be late for my date with Portunus."

"Is he going to be there?" I asked.

"I don't know, but he'll be watching somehow, count on it." He smiled in what he probably thought was a casual way, and said, "I'll head north around the shore, then climb up the bluff from the side." He looked at me and asked, "Have any final and encouraging words?"

Though I'm not overly religious, I replied, "Go with God," and smiled confidently, but I'm fairly certain it was more like a grimace. Stupidly, I extended my hand, and he shook it, but I instantly felt foolish. The formal gesture had been out of place under the circumstances; maybe a hearty clap on the shoulder and shout of 'atta boy!' would have been more fitting. I'll have to brush up on the appropriate way to behave when a friend is determined to do something incautious, if not outright insane. I watched him disappear into the bush, then I went down to the wharf to stew for a while.

The lawn-chairs were still there, so I heaved one ashore and turned the other away from the bluff. Now facing the creek inflow only forty feet away, I noted again that this would be a good spot to fish on those days when you couldn't be bothered to use the boat. As the cold creek hit the more temperate lake, a ten foot semicircle of greenish white water was formed. I imagined trout within it gobbling up insects, grubs and all the other goodies the current was constantly providing, but thoughts of Trevor interrupted my fishing analysis.

By now he'd be most of the way to the base of the northern side of the bluff. I peered across the lake, but not surprisingly, I couldn't see him. It's half a mile over the water, plus he'd told me earlier that his trail was well away from the shoreline. I turned the chair to face the bluff, then kept an eye open for his signal. After about a half hour of worried waiting, I saw a number of flashes coming from the top, so I jumped into the boat and rowed to the middle of the lake. I stopped, and trained my binoculars on the highest point of the bluff. I saw Trevor conversing with Portunus, but the chat didn't last long. Our other-world friend simply walked into the bush after a few words with Trevor, then vanished from view.

Trevor stood near the edge with his hands on hips as he studied his route down. I could see him taking deep breaths as he psyched himself up, then he waved at me without smiling. He threw something down to the lake far below. It seemed airborne for a long time, then it hit the water with a loud plop a hundred feet off my starboard bow. When I rowed over to retrieve it, I discovered his small daypack in a plastic bag tightly tied shut with pink flagging tape. Inside were his moccasins, with his watch and compass nested in each. Earlier in the day he'd been indecisive about his footwear, but he clearly thought the too-tight sneakers he'd shown me would be better than his moccasins. I retrieved the bag, rowed back to my original spot and waved. So, without further ado, he started down and I held my breath. Then I leaned over the boat's side to scoop some cold water onto my face; to what end, I really don't know, since my pointless ablutions didn't help relieve the tightness in my gut. I grabbed the binoculars again and unconsciously bit the inside of my cheek as I watched him descend.

He was coming straight down the right side of the face. There were enough plants poking out that the climb had presented no problems so far (easy for me to say). I was inwardly thanking the junipers for being there, when the stem of the plant under his knee broke, followed immediately by a small avalanche of dirt and pebbles rushing down the fifty degree slope of bare rock. The evergreen part of the juniper sailed out and didn't touch the stone, but I was concentrating on him, so I didn't see, but only heard the gentle splash as it hit the water.

Meanwhile, Trevor was hanging by his hands from a plant growing just above the one that'd given way. As he fumbled sightlessly with his feet to find a place to secure his stance, I was holding the binoculars so tightly that it was fortunate they were made of hardened steel. He finally found a good foothold on another plant, then not releasing his grip above, he just stayed in that position for a moment, resting his head against the rock. Then he continued his descent, as he carefully pushed at each stem before trusting it with his weight.

He reached the diagonal fault which stretched all the way to the other side at a downward angle of about fifteen degrees. I can only imagine how he felt as he paused to survey his route. He had to leave the relative safety of the junipers, then go out onto that wall of bare rock to shuffle to the other side with no handholds at all. After taking a deep breath and getting his feet into the crack, he leaned forward on the stone with his hands splayed out on it just beside his head. He ventured a few feet down the fault, then with alacrity, he returned to the plants. I jumped to the conclusion he'd encountered a bee hive or a hornet's nest and was telling myself, 'he could probably do without stinging insects flying up his jeans or attacking his face'. My speculations about savage bugs had been wrong, but at the time, I nervously wondered what he'd do next.

He studied the way down, as I looked up at him through the glasses. I figured he'd have to put his left foot into the crack, lean forward on the wall, then carefully place his right foot beside the other. He'd repeat this process until he'd made it across, or at least, that's what I thought he'd do. But he did the sideways shuffle so quickly, that by the time he was halfway to the other side, I was angrily asking myself, "What's he doing? There's no big rush!" Just as I was thinking this, a heave in the rock-face nearly forced him backwards. As time stood still, he waved his arms out sideways to regain his balance, and flopped his chest forward onto the wall again. After slowly working his way under the rocky bulge, he resumed his quick crab-walk and I dropped the binoculars to have a drink of lake-water. I just couldn't watch.

By the time I'd refocussed the glasses on him, he'd reached the end of the upper crack and was awkwardly looking at the one under it. There was an eight foot separation between the two, so doubtlessly he'd want to make a thorough perusal, but he could hardly move. He looked down between his widely spread feet for a moment, then dropped to the edge of the lower crack. He hung there searching with his feet, until he found the line of indented rock and settled into it.

Even though he'd already climbed down most of the top half, there was still about fifty feet of raw granite to wish him goodbye if he involuntarily started the drop to the lake far below. In other words, sliding down a steep rock slope isn't very good preparation for a high-dive, or a jump or anything involving the human body, gravity and high speed.

Without hesitating, Trevor continued his rapid sideways shuffle, leading with his right foot this time. I couldn't understand why he was in such a hurry as he advanced across the high wall, but soon he was only ten feet above his destination: the narrow ledge. The rock below the upper crack ballooned out a little, so Trevor slowly slid down it as he controlled himself with his fingers hanging onto the edge of the diagonal fault-line above. He had about a foot remaining to the ledge after his clutching slide, so he dropped to it and did his teetering act again. Seeing he'd succeeded, I breathed a sigh of relief, but I knew he still had the long plunge to the lake to complete.

Not trying to turn around to face the water, he didn't stand around on the ledge for long, but pushed himself off backwards. With his black hair flapping above his head and his hand on his nose, he seemed to fall feet first forever. He hit the lake without much of a splash and I hurriedly unshipped the oars to row over to his landing spot. He resurfaced while I was still forty feet away, so I shouted to him, "Congratulations! You did it! Would you like to do an encore?"

"No thanks," he said grinning triumphantly, "I think that was enough. Now help me get into the boat." Once I'd pulled him aboard, he laughed with relief and said, "See? I told you it'd be duck soup, so here I am, safe and sound!" As I nodded happily in response, he plucked at his wet clothing and said, "Let's go straight to the cabin so I can put on some dry things, then we can talk about the climb."

I was so pleased he'd gone through the ordeal without injury, that I couldn't stop smiling at him as we headed back to the weirdly coloured wharf. After tying up the boat and entering the cabin, Trevor went to the back room to change, while I put on the kettle for tea.

When we were finally settled at the table, I noticed he had angry red blotches on each temple, along with another on his forehead. When I asked about them, he raised his sweatshirt to show me similar marks on his front, then he said, "That s.o.b. Portunus made things as tough as possible. He knows the bluff gets baking-hot on a sunny day, so that's why he wanted me there in the afternoon." Trevor showed me the same vivid colours on the underside of his arms then added with a weary chuckle, "I didn't need to hang out there much longer. It was too hot."

"Through the glasses I saw you talking with Portunus," I said. "So, how's our friend doing?"

"I don't think he expected me to make an appearance," Trevor said. "He wished me good luck, but he was smirking when he walked back into the bush. No wonder he's not liked, but I guess I proved something to him today!"

"You bet you did," I said nodding firmly, "but you should see about those burns. Pauline has just the thing for flesh fried on hot rock." Looking at him as if I was suggesting a course of action that would be difficult for him to take, I said, "It'd probably be best if we had supper tonight at Three Duck Lake. Then Pauline can take care of your scorched hide." Grinning at him, I added, "It's spaghetti night; Pauline usually serves it with a garlic loaf." Since I'd obviously grabbed his attention, I decided to lay it on thick by saying, "Her green salads are something else and you love her juice-blends, but if you want to stay in your cabin tonight, I understand." He offered me his arm to twist, but because of his tender skin, I didn't. "Should we make a couple of sandwiches here, to tide us over until supper at the lodge?" I asked, "or do you think you can hold out?"

After some serious consideration, he said, "Let's go now. We can take everything in the basket back to Pauline. I don't want food left out in the open when I'm not here."

He'd been trying to be calm, but his recent adventures at the bluff had clearly excited him. He kept pausing in the middle of saying something to stare at me sightlessly with a far-away smile on his face, so I casually suggested I should drive. Seeming indifferent to my proposal, he shrugged and handed the keys to me without any argument. Soon I was piloting the Flaming Barge slowly down the mining road, while Trevor smiled to himself and was clearly unaware of my presence.

Wedding Plans

"A penny for your thoughts," I said to Trevor as we turned onto the blacktop and I shifted up to fourth. It was easy to find yourself belting along at over 70 mph in this powerful vehicle, so I was often flicking glances at the speedometer.

Trevor took a deep breath and said, "It's a done deal now. I can tell the ladies and they'll be angry at first, but in the end they'll be glad it's all behind me." Giving me a rather sour look, he added, "I was going to call in on Sarah, but ...."

"But I'm around?" I said, finishing his sentence for him. "I take it you'd like some privacy and would prefer not to have me sitting across the room studying you two through my binoculars." I said this indignantly, as though a third party should always be expected to act this way around a couple.

"Well," Trevor answered, "I wouldn't exactly put it that way, but …. yes." Then he turned sharply towards me and said, "I'm not forgetting you were there when I needed you. Your moral support was very important to me. It was strange," he continued, "the sight of you far down on the lake looking up at me with the glasses, somehow gave me strength. Thanks," he said, punching me lightly on the shoulder, "I owe you one."

"Twarn't nothing," I replied as I stopped for a pedestrian who seemed lost and was apparently trying to regain his bearings by wandering aimlessly in the middle of the street.

We were going through town now, and Trevor was waving at all the people he knew. Some of these folks were the same ones he'd acknowledged this morning; they were clearly puzzled to see me in the driver's seat again. Maybe they thought I was kidnapping him and part of my dastardly scheme was to spend all day driving back and forth through town. Anyway, I nodded to them perfunctorily, as if I had more important things on my mind, and this caused an occasional furrowed brow.

After our parade-like progress through town, I sped up as we got to the blacktop on the other side. Trevor said, "I can phone Sarah from the lodge," then he added hurriedly, "after supper, of course." Suddenly changing topics and turning dead serious, he added, "I noticed Portunus wasn't there to congratulate me for completing the task successfully. I don't think he was very happy for me. I trust him, but I don't."

"I know what you mean," I replied, "I haven't even met him yet, but he gives me the creeps anyhow."

Just before turning onto the dirt road leading to the lodge, I stopped to let an elderly man cross the blacktop. He seemed so overwhelmed by my politeness that at one point I thought he was about to display his gratitude by making me open the door and shaking my hand. Thankfully he didn't, but he made a big production of it nonetheless. He carefully looked both ways, even though all traffic had stopped and all the universe was on pause. During his arduous trek across the road, I nodded and smiled in a familiar way at the total stranger who'd been heading in the opposite direction in his car, but had also stopped for our elderly friend. When I saw the guy behind the wheel hadn't recognised me (gee, I wonder why?), I rolled down my window, stuck my head out and shouted, "It's me!" as if this would remind him. He continued giving me the baffled eyeball, so I rolled up my window and tried to look sulky. Then he took in the full beauty of the 'yellow with violent orange flames' motif of our paint job and was doubtlessly wondering if any acquaintance of his would drive such an atrocity. When I finally got going again, I shrugged and gave him a disappointed look, while he still appeared puzzled. You might think this is a really tiresome way to get one's kicks, but you have to remember that we don't have TV or go out very much. We usually have to make our own entertainment and sometimes it's rather feeble: so sue me.

Continuing our conversation about Portunus, I said, "I think you're right, he won't go back on his word and that's a positive thing." I grinned at Trevor and told him a little judicious posterior-smooching might work wonders. "Even if you don't see him, you can bet he's keeping a close eye on you. So appease him by getting a new wharf-covering. You can afford it."

"Do you think he believes I'm being disrespectful?" Trevor asked with a worried frown. "Well, I'm not. The orange and black carpeting was on special, so I bought it. End of story."

"Yeah sure," I replied insincerely, "I believe you." After a thoughtful pause, I added, "There's always the chance you love the colours; you're not going to show up soon wearing a bright orange and black shirt, are you?"

"Only on holidays," he answered as we pulled into the lodge's parking lot.

Obviously familiar with the sound of the Flaming Barge, the dogs were there to greet us. They gathered at the driver's door of the truck, but when they beheld me behind the steering wheel, they wagged their tails and gave me a nice welcome. Then they scooted to the other side and made much more of a fuss over Trevor.

They frisked around him as we walked to the lodge; outwardly I was my usual gracious self, but inwardly I was a trifle miffed. We bumped into some clients returning to their cabin after supper, and I stopped to chat as they played with the dogs.

When we finally entered, Pauline turned from the sink where she'd been washing dishes and smiled, saying, "You're back! Just a minute while I finish up here. Hungry?"

Probably because the fragrance of her spaghetti sauce permeated the room, Trevor's gut, relatively quiet until now, squawked loudly in response. Then she saw the blotches on his face and instantly turned into Florence Nightingale, asking with concern, "Whatever have you been doing?"

Before he could explain, I gave Pauline a kiss and said, "We'll go wash up, and over supper we'll tell you what's been happening."

"I'll put on the pasta," she said, pushing me away. "I'll cut a leaf off the aloe vera plant. Those burns look nasty."

She was no longer aiming her stunning blue green peepers at me, but seemed more intent on seeing to our guest's injuries. Doing this was clearly the correct priority, but I felt left out nonetheless, just like with the dogs. Poor me:

the paragon returns home and gets ignored. Keeping well back so I wouldn't get in the way, I watched Pauline apply the fluid from a cut leaf to his face, then his arms and chest. Since I was still hanging around in the kitchen area and they were at the table, I yelled over to them once the procedure had been completed, "I'll wash up now. I'm looking forward to your spaghetti."

Without turning, she said, "Yes honey," while Trevor just smiled at her and looked grateful. When I returned from my ablutions and sat, Pauline told him not to clean off the fluid as he headed to the washroom in turn.

When we were finally at the table, Trevor was too busy eating to properly describe our day. It wasn't until his second plate that he told Pauline about Portunus's demands and the gut-churning climb down the bluff. "My God!" exclaimed Trevor, interrupting himself through a mouthful of spaghetti and garlic bread. "This sauce is terrific!" With an admiring gaze at her, he asked, "So, what's the secret?"

Responding with a humble shrug, Pauline said, "No big mystery, really. Just some onions, tomatoes, beef and spices. Did Sarah know you were about to do such a foolish thing?"

Looking guilty, but clearly not overcome with shame, he answered, "No, she didn't and she still doesn't know. I plan to phone her after supper." Seeing he'd finished off his large bowl of salad and momentarily was quelling her indignation, she asked if he'd care for another helping. Silly question.

As we watched him steadily consume his third plate of spaghetti, I was thinking of Ted, our neighbour a mile up the road. Since he too had a cargo ship hidden under his belt, I was trying to imagine the two of them eating at the same table; it'd probably be very quiet except for the constant masticating sounds.

Since Moon was absent, Pauline had apparently taken on the chore of telling Trevor the main course was over. "I have something new for dessert," she informed him the moment he finished his third plate. Hurriedly grabbing it and heading to the sink, she added, "I'd like your opinions." Returning shortly, she put two bowls on the table and said, "It's lemon custard with stewed apple slices, sprinkled with walnut pieces." Before she'd finished with her description, he'd already heartily sampled a spoonful and was rolling his eyes in awe.

By the time he'd finished his second dessert, it was dark out. The dogs had clattered in, so he'd gone over to their place by the wood-stove to say hello. Since he was particularly enamoured of the man, Banjo started to excitedly croon his 'aarrrooo' song as Trevor approached. But when he realised no one was joining in, he tamped down his urge to tunefully vocalise and just looked glad. After visiting the canine crew for a few minutes, Trevor called over to us and said, "I have to phone Sarah; I'll be right with you."

While he was chatting with his bride-to-be, Pauline and I discussed his new place as we washed the dishes. "From what you've been telling me," she said, "it sounds beautiful, but that business with Portunus and the bluff is frightening. It puts a black cloud in the sky, don't you think?"

"We believe Portunus will be true to his word," I answered, "and he'll leave Trevor and

Sarah to live their lives in relative peace. Nonetheless, since he probably isn't going elsewhere, it's likely he'll be watching them. And there's all that gold on the claim, so there's no way Trevor would simply abandon it." I kissed her on the nose as we stood at the sink and said, "Don't give him a hard time about his climb. I'm sure Sarah will find a way to make her opinions clear to him. I think he was just proving something to himself, so let's forget it." She slowly shook her head then grimaced, but she begrudgingly nodded in the end. Finished with his call, Trevor went back to his chair at the table, and we joined him.

Grinning sheepishly at us as we sat, he said, "Sarah didn't seem pleased or proud when I told her about my day's rock-climbing. In fact, I'm glad I told her on the phone, otherwise she'd have done me violence." Chuckling drily, he added, "She's familiar with the bluff."

Pauline reddened a little and said, "She has every right to be angry." Then she remembered our agreement and said nothing more, though she clearly had an indignant speech ready. After a quiet, internal fume, she asked, "What's new with Sarah?"

Smiling widely, he answered, "Oh, nothing much: she's still looking forward to her wedding day."

She tried to stop herself from scolding him about the lengthy delay, but a wee bit of peevishness leaked into her voice nonetheless, as she asked, "And when's that going to happen?"

Still smiling hugely, he winked at Pauline and replied, "That'll depend on how quick you can get the lodge ready for us. How about the Monday after next?"

"It's about time!" Pauline responded, "Sarah must be excited, and you too!"

"Yes," he answered, "I'm tingling all over. And she says hello to both of you. We figured we should have the ceremony on an off-day at the lodge, but the date's not set in stone. Whenever's convenient for you is fine."

Pauline had become flushed with enthusiasm as all thoughts of Portunus plainly evaporated. "I haven't made a wedding cake before," she said to herself, "but with Moon's help, it won't be a problem." Grinning at me, she added, "and you can wear that nice sports coat which has been hanging unused in the closet for years."

"I'm really looking forward to it," I answered with a distinct lack of eager anticipation, "I'm the one who's all a-tingle now." My response clearly hadn't diminished Pauline's excitement: she was still positively glowing at the news.

"You have ten days to sort out the details," I said, "wait until Moon gets back the day after tomorrow and she'll certainly help. You two will be bridesmaids of honour, as I recall."

Pauline looked about ready to get up from the table: to what purpose she likely didn't know, but she obviously needed to do something.

Before she could stir, Trevor said, "There's no way I feel like driving out to the cabin now." She seemed mildly irritated he'd pulled her back to the present, but she got herself together and focussed on him.

"Can you put me up for the night?" he asked her.

Before she could open her mouth, I displayed my generosity by answering, "Sure, there's lots of room in the shed out back, so the resident family of mice shouldn't be much of a bother to you."

Giving me a dirty look and thus interrupting my outpouring of hospitality, Pauline said, "Don't listen to him: we've never had a mouse problem here. And you can stay in Sarah's room, that is, if you don't mind the mess."

This had been a bone of contention between the two women on many occasions, until Pauline had finally told Sarah that maid service wouldn't be provided any more. "If you want your room looking like it has suffered severe hurricane damage, then so be it. I'm not going to clean up after you; I'll just shut the door and let the rubble heap take care of itself." It'd been a number of weeks since she'd promised this, so the present state of Sarah's abode was a mystery for everyone. In all fairness though, I think Pauline had been exaggerating about the condition of the room. On one occasion I peeked in and saw no permanent hurricane damage, although a strong wind seemed to have rearranged things a bit in there.

Trevor turned to me and asked, "Want to go out to the claim tomorrow morning? I'd like you to try a wetsuit: you can follow me out there in your own vehicle, work half the day, then return here sometime around noon. I should be able to repay the loan by then, but that depends on how much gold we find."

"Sounds good to me," I replied, "I'll take along Pooch and his saddlebags."

I asked Pauline if we could have breakfast at 5:30 or 6:00 tomorrow morning and this was no problem for her. Since Moon was temporarily absent, Pauline had to feed the chickens, so she said, "I can give them their chow, then come back here for you two."

I dispassionately noted her priorities: birds first and husbands second, but I dismissed this slight, instead saying cheerfully, "Good! The prospect of wearing the right gear in that cold pool is very appealing: all that gold!" Thankfully, I refrained from cackling and greedily rubbing my hands together. I could tell she was back to thinking of the wedding again, so anything I'd said had probably been just the buzzing of bees to her. Looking at the kitchen clock, she said, "It's already past 9:30, where does the time go?" Turning to Trevor, she asked, "Would you like a mug of cocoa?"

"No thanks," he answered, "it's been a long day and I'm tired. If you don't mind, I'll just wash up, then hit the sack."

Since I'd never before seen him refuse sustenance of any kind, I flattened my hands on the tabletop to prevent myself from falling out of my chair. After Pauline told him not to clean the aloe vera fluid from his burns, he headed to the washroom. When he returned, he wished us goodnight, then stepped without mishap into Sarah's disaster zone and softly closed the door.

The Stroll to the Creek

Pauline started to write something on a pad, before yawning loudly. As the dogs were awakened from their snooze-fest near the wood-stove and looked over at us curiously, she threw the pencil onto the table. "I can't do this now," she said as if she was being forced, "and I don't feel like making cocoa. Let's just go to bed."

"You go ahead," I said, "I'll join you soon."

I lit a candle, shut off the two gas lamps, and said goodnight to the dogs. After a few minutes, Pauline left the washroom down the hall, went into our bedroom and closed the door. This left me with the sound of someone pull-starting a chainsaw which would nearly cough into life, then die. Trevor was outdoing himself in regard to the sheer volume of the snoring coming from behind the door, so I wondered again how Sarah would handle his nocturnal vocalisations. (She's always been a big fan of the guillotine.) Before I doused the candle, I went to the table to read what Pauline had written on the pad. It was the beginning of a wedding list: 2 rolls of film for her camera, the cake and which reverend to use. The thought of Sarah and Trevor getting hitched made me smile as I entered our bedroom. Pauline was already asleep, so I crawled quietly in beside her.

The following morning, I had to practically pull Trevor from the scrambled eggs we had for breakfast: the guy always has an empty cargo hold.

Pauline said to him, "Those burns are healing nicely." She gave him two of the fat leaves from the aloe vera plant. "You'll wash everything off being in the creek with your wetsuit," she added, "so apply the fluid after you finish." She eventually fed doggy-biscuits to Banjo and Grace to distract them while Pooch, Trevor and I snuck out to the parking lot.

I always have a superior attitude when I'm up and about early in the morning. The thought that most people are still lying in bed somehow gives me the feeling that I'm a real whiz-bang, no matter how unfounded this notion might be. Pooch jumped into the back of my International Harvester pickup, I threw his saddlebags aboard, and we followed Trevor as he drove the Flaming Barge out to the road. Keeping the windows closed because of the rooster tail of dust coming from Trevor's vehicle, it wasn't until we reached the blacktop that I rolled mine down to smell the morning air. While we stopped curbside so he could buy a newspaper, the fragrance of brewing coffee emanated from a nearby restaurant as probably their first customer of the day wandered in. Seeming too young to be smoking a pipe, the guy who ran the little kiosk on the corner spent a few minutes yammering in a familiar way with Trevor: another close friend, no doubt.

We got going again and it didn't take long to get through town. There were a few people on the sidewalks, but there was hardly any traffic on the road: the place obviously wasn't fully awake yet.

After driving through town and making the left turn onto the dirt road, we travelled over the uneven surface slowly. As we reached the mining road, Pooch leapt out of the truck and ran behind. After about fifteen minutes, Trevor stopped at the start of the trail down the ravine, then got out of his vehicle. Waiting until I pulled up and joined him, he told me he'd decided to leave the initial rough patches of the dirt road leading up here to themselves. "If things are smoothed out and repaired," he said, "people will want to know where it goes and we can't have that."

"I noticed you've removed the flagging tape marking the way down to the creek," I commented as I looked around.

"Yes," said Trevor, "highlighting everything could lead to problems, so I took it down. Anyway, I know the trail's location."

The best route down the ravine was well-trodden and marked with flagging tape. While I religiously kept to the trail, Pooch often made twenty-foot leaps straight down the rock face, supposedly to cut down on those tiresome zigzags. As I watched his casual derring-do, I made a mental note to find out if he sometimes moonlights as a mountain goat. Trevor was nearly as bad a distraction: he kept leaving the trail and fussing with the flagging, but he was keeping well ahead of me all the same. In a startling moment of deja-vu, I could see the two of them gazing up at me as they stood by the raging creek. After I'd worked my way down, we all hiked upriver to the pool with its gold pellets.

A wide shaft of sunlight shone through a gap in the trees at the top of the ravine, accentuating the billion specks of mist created by the creek. The tumultuous water falling over the rocks was a vivid contrast to the tiny particles hovering silently over the noise. As usual, Pooch was investigating everything that presented itself to his nose. Inevitably, something in one of his saddlebags had come loose and was making a racket as it shifted around. I wondered idly if the resultant rattling and clanging bugged him, but he didn't even seem aware of the ruckus.

A Dip in the Pool

Trevor had hidden the wetsuits under thick bushes near the pool. After retrieving them and spreading them out on the rocks beside the creek, he said, "I bought everything but the tanks and masks. We don't need them; anyway, goggles cloud up when they go from cold water to warm air, so they're not worth the hassle." The violent aquamarine colouring, along with the crumpled humanoid outline, made the suits seem incompatible with the wild setting. I was trying to decide whether or not they looked like two very thin space aliens resting in a most uncomfortable place, when Trevor said, "There's a rubbery smell at first, but you'll soon get used to it. Are you wearing swim trunks under your jeans?" After I nodded, he handed me a suit and told me to strip down to my swimsuit, then to get into the thing. As he did likewise, I was glad no one else was around to see me. I called Pooch over to take off his saddlebags and he seemed mildly alarmed at my appearance. But he obviously wasn't overly bothered, since he shortly wandered off into the bush again.

The attached hood of the suit fit tightly over my chin, while the top half of the rubberised face-hole came snugly down to my eyebrows. It felt as if my stretched-out headpiece was squeezing my face outward and elongating my features, but I tried acting as though I was used to wearing shrink wrap. I quickly concluded that seeing my own lips was entirely incidental to the purpose of all this: gold!

Holding a pair in each hand, Trevor showed me the sock-like boots completing the ensemble. "Just put them on like ordinary shoes," he said, "then make sure you stretch the uppers to a few inches below the knee." After following his instructions, then standing there in my electric-blue togs, he told me the initial stage of immersion was the toughest. "The moment you get into the pool," he explained, "it'll seem like the suit has leaks everywhere. That's the way it was designed: cold water will dribble through the zipper at the front and the various other apertures, then form a body temperature layer that'll insulate you. It works well, but it's a little uncomfortable at first." We were watching the melt water tumble down the rock face and into the pool. I was happy to delay my cold plunge as long as possible, so it was a relief when he started speaking again.

"I've been concentrating on the area just under the falls," he said, "plus I've occasionally looked here and there." Having to raise his voice to be heard over the torrent, he told me he wasn't going to be so haphazard in the future. "I'd like to thoroughly pan all around the outer edges of the pool, then work my way in. The water's only three feet deep there, so we'll be spending most of the time kneeling." Going back to the saddlebags and reaching in, he said, "I almost forgot," then he chucked me something: knee pads. "These'll make it more comfortable for us, plus, we don't want to wear holes in the legs of our new outfits, do we?" Grabbing his spade and colander, he told me he'd brought two of each. Handing me a strong-looking canvas bag about half the size of a pillow case, then taking another for his own use, he told me that now we could work separately. "I'll do the far side," he said, "while you start here. We'll meet halfway around, then do another strip of ground a few feet closer to the falls." With that, he grabbed all his utensils and simply walked into the pool with no further comment. The water came up to his shoulders at the deepest point, but he soon reached the other side. As he was getting ready to work, I took a tentative step into the pool and was pleasantly surprised. I felt no cold wetness or any of the other joys the frigid water could bestow, but I knew this was a feeling of false security.

It didn't take long for me to see I'd been right. As I knelt in water coming up to my chest and started digging, I could feel icy dribbles entering the suit. The sensation was similar to having a melting lump of snow slide up and down your spine: not very pleasing. At one point, I stood up to do a number of shoulder twisting gyrations and side steps, which didn't help relieve my discomfort at all. As a matter of fact, my newly-invented dance (it could be called 'The Wetsuit Shrug') had made things worse. Like lowering oneself in underpants into a bathtub of icy water, a bum freezing wetness seeped forward to my privates. Again: not very pleasant. From across the pool, Trevor paused to observe my antics. He didn't say anything, but he was smiling widely and shaking his head as he resumed work. I guess he was dazzled and bewitched by my dance moves.

After a few minutes, the water in my suit got up to body temperature, so I felt less like a bipedal bag of iced tea. The dirt and gravel I was scraping off the bottom then dumping into my bag had a few visible signs of gold, while the stuff from directly under the falls had been much richer. The lovely yellow pellets from there could easily be seen, even before panning.

As I dug with the spade and scraped with my colander, I felt protected by the suit from the cold embrace of creek water, but I'd come to a number of negative conclusions about its effectiveness. My feet were freezing: surely some sort of insulated underwater boot had been developed. My hands felt like insensitive claws as I rubbed my frigid nose to see if icicles were hanging from it. The suit did an admirable job of keeping my mid-section unfrozen, but it was a different story for my extremities.

I lasted about forty minutes before shouting across the pool to Trevor: "I'm getting out of the water to build a fire. I can't feel my feet."

"Yes," he responded rather unsympathetically, "I noticed you were stumbling and falling a lot."

Not bothering to dwell on the tedious fact that he was outlasting me again, I yelled back, "My bag's nearly full of pay dirt anyway."

He nodded, turned his back to me and fell to his knees in the waist high water. As he started digging at the bottom with his spade, I clumsily went about preparing a fire on the rocks by the pool. After it was going, I sat near it to take off the wretched boots portion of my colourful attire, then I looked at my feet. They were dry, but they had the pale, unliving pallor of a corpse's appendages. As I sat there trying to warm myself, Trevor was still slogging away in the pool, drat him. I'd decided I'd had enough and was just about to get out of the clammy wet-suit, when I saw someone sitting casually on a windfall about twenty feet to my left.

He was leaning back on the steep ravine wall seemingly nonchalant, but he'd probably been watching me for some time. Just how long, I didn't know: I certainly hadn't noticed him as I'd searched for fuel for my fire.

It was Portunus, of course. There could be no mistaking the silly hat or the big teeth as he grinned at me. I didn't know what to do. Should I call over to Trevor and tell him we had a visitor, or should I do my best to handle the situation?

Barring the need for any personal action from yours truly, Portunus came over and sat across the fire from me. He was wearing a long sleeved white shirt with bone buttons down the front. His lower half was clad in tailored looking brown pants he'd tucked into tan riding boots. He looked dapper and harmless, but his dark eyes gave him away. They were piercing yet shifty, so you just knew that this guy was no gentleman.

He glanced over at Trevor, who was still working in the pool and unaware of his presence, then he closely perused my startling aquamarine ensemble with a sneer on his face. To get the conversational ball rolling, he said, "Nice outfit."

"Nice hat," I wittily riposted. My glib rejoinder had clearly caused him vexation, so I understood that referring to his lid in any light-hearted manner was a no-no. This was Trevor's claim after all, and me cracking wise wouldn't help matters for him. Therefore, I decided to be respectful to Portunus and to sheath my wit for the time being.

As we sat there waiting for the other to speak, I noticed one of his eyes was darker than the other and also that he appeared to have no hair. Unless he had a scraggle of growth forming a topknot under his hat, he was probably as bald as a bowling ball. "So, how're things going?" he asked pleasantly.

I think he'd made a conscious decision to be civil, and I followed suit. "So-so," I answered, "we're just exploring the outer edges of the pool. Kind of slim pickings."

He nodded in response, but he clearly hadn't been listening to me. He'd been watching the creek as it rushed over the rocks to disappear around a nearby bend. "It's wilder here than at Three Duck Lake," he muttered pensively, "don't you think so, Henry?"

I was aware he knew my name, but his use of it was startling nonetheless. He'd turned from contemplating the angry water to face me. He seemed comfortable in his pale brown skin as he sat there, but something unnamable and unsettling was in his eyes as he said, "The right people have to live here; it doesn't look good if folks get lost or dead."

I was tempted to ask, 'To whom might it not look good?' But instead I said, "Trevor and Sarah love this place: you don't have to worry about them being disrespectful or taking their good fortune for granted. And they aren't city slickers who think unpaved country is just an amusement park."

He was attempting to be polite, but he clearly felt so superior to me that he couldn't disguise his patronising attitude as he said, "They're

friends of yours, what else are you going to say?"
He was now acting as though I was privileged to
be in his company: me, a mere human being and
him …. not. His condescension was so apparent that I wanted to be rude in return. I could
say something like, "Portunus, I notice you're
always wearing the hat. Is that because you're
actually a pinhead with a comb over?" But then
I remembered that I might make things difficult
for the couple, so I didn't ask.

I was glad I'd kept my mouth shut, because
he was back to being pleasant again. "I like your
dog," he said, "he understands. I met him earlier
this morning in the bush: he's a good beast."

This was all very nice, but he seemed to be
implying that a nitwit like me couldn't possibly
fathom what Pooch had easily understood. Was
Portunus being nasty again, or was I being overly
sensitive? And what was the precise nature of the
'understanding' he shared with the dog? There'd
been a definite self-pitying tone to his voice when
he'd spoken, as though he'd been irked that only
a canine could truly grasp the importance of his
outlook. No wonder he wasn't popular among

his peers; he kept you so off balance with his frequent changes of approach, it was difficult to know where one stood with him.

"The fire needs more wood," he said, then got up. Telling me to stay put and saying, "There's a dead branch lying on the rocks a few feet behind you: I'll go get it," he carefully walked around me. Suspicious of his suddenly helpful attitude, I turned to look ten seconds later, but he was gone.

I took off the uncomfortable wetsuit and lay it out on the rocks to dry. Then I did likewise with my swim trunks and got into my nice dry clothes. By the time I'd refurbished the fire, Trevor had exited the pool and was heading my way.

Carrying his bag of paydirt plus his utensils, the first thing he said was, "My hands and feet are freezing, so let me at that fire."

As he took off his boots and sat as close to the flames as possible, I told him about Portunus' unexpected appearance on the scene. Trevor listened patiently, then said, "It isn't so surprising: he wants me to know he's watching and he also wanted to meet you." Grinning at me while dodging a stream of wood smoke by jerking his head to the side, he added, "It's hard to tell, but I think he likes you."

"The feeling's mutual," I gushed in response, "I'll be pressing wildflowers, so I can send him a proper Valentine's Day card."

Trevor chuckled, then reached for the bag of pay dirt he'd retrieved from the pool. "I don't think this is as rich as our previous finds," he said as he looked at the contents, "but it's good to know what's here." He looked appraisingly at the pool, then turned to me and said, "I see you've decided not to go in again. Didn't the wetsuit help at all?"

"It was fine," I replied, glancing at the aquamarine corpse lying on the nearby rocks, "but I had the same problem you're having."

Sitting with his chin on his knees, he had his feet propped up on a stone and was wiggling his toes at the fire. He was also holding his palms out to the flames as he nodded ruefully and said, "Yeah, I've got to get better boots and some good gloves: I should've known by now."

"Don't worry about it," I responded, "you've had a lot on your plate recently. A little forgetfulness is totally understandable."

He nodded and smiled at me, saying, "Once I get some feeling back in my hands and feet I'll work some more, then I'll have something to eat by the fire. Maybe I'll go back into the pool after lunch: it depends on how I feel." Suddenly, he asked, "Where's Pooch? I haven't seen him for some time."

"Perhaps he's having tea and crumpets with Portunus," I suggested.

"I wouldn't think so," replied Trevor as he lazily scanned the immediate area, "I'm sure the dog prefers water and a ham sandwich for his midmorning snack."

Speak of the devil, Pooch appeared and gave us each his usual effusive greetings. He had burrs tangled in the long hair of his chest to under his left foreleg, and as I tried removing them, he took this excellent opportunity to lick me lavishly on the face. Holding his head, I looked deep into his happy dark eyes and posed a most reasonable question: "How can I see what I'm doing with your big tongue on my eyeballs?" I asked. He answered by licking me on the nose and wagging his tail, so he'd obviously understood every word.

"I don't want to leave the fire," Trevor said, "could you unpack the saddlebags? There's a camouflage tarp in there that I can use to shelter the gear, plus there's my container of food." After I respectfully placed the precious box of sustenance at his side, he handed me his pay dirt bag and said, "Put this in, will you, along with yours. We'll let the dog carry them up to the truck." We arranged for me to take the pay dirt I'd collected back to the lodge, to be cleaned there later. "Leave mine leaning on the left front tire of the Barge," he continued, "I have two empty ones here, so I might have three bags to go through at the cabin tonight. Let's hope it's a pleasing chore!"

"Amen!" I responded happily, and finished putting the saddlebags on Pooch. "I know you do it all the time," I sermonised, "but you shouldn't be out alone in a wild place like this. I'm guilty too, but at least Pooch is usually with me. Be careful: I hope Sarah comes down here with you in the future."

Trevor grinned at me and replied, "Yes Mommy, I'll try not walking off a cliff."

"Good!" I said, ignoring the sarcasm, "now, is there anything else we should go over before I leave?"

"Make a note of today's gold prices and leave the newspaper in my truck," Trevor answered, "then we'll see where your loan to me stands." I nodded and he started pulling on his diving boots with an unthrilled expression on his face. As Pooch and I headed downstream to the stepping-stone crossing, I turned to see Trevor walking resolutely towards the pool in his aquamarine suit. Brrrr!

Wolfhounds and Shoelaces

*A*fter the dog and I had climbed up to the vehicles, I made the arrangements I'd discussed with Trevor. Since there wasn't any room to turn my truck around, I had to back up for a mile down the mining road. Sitting in the box and clearly enjoying our backwards progress, Pooch was quietly alert as he watched the scenery go by. There was a hundred percent certainty that branches would whip me in the face, so I didn't stick my head out of the window as I reversed. Using the outside rearview mirrors, I managed to slowly steer the International Harvester down the road without major mishap.

As I turned the vehicle around to carefully drive along the heaving and pot-holed dirt road,

I was thinking that Trevor had it right. Some guys go into deep hock by buying expensive equipment and hiring crews, so finding gold is an absolute necessity for them. While Trevor was more than happy with his claim, the cabin downriver and the upcoming marriage were his priorities. Discovering he had a rich source of gold under his control, he hadn't wanted it all immediately. He was just taking what he needed and not crowing about it: smart guy.

As I turned onto the blacktop and picked up speed, I glanced in the rearview mirror at Pooch. With his massive front paws draped over the side of the box, he was eagerly leaning into the rush of air. He had his mouth open, so the wind had plastered his tongue in a most unbecoming way along the outside of his jaw. His eyes were half-closed, his whiskers were bending in the breeze and he was slowly wagging his tail. Clearly, he was in doggy heaven as I drove along.

We soon got into town and almost immediately, I hit a red light. As we sat waiting, a pickup stopped not right beside me, but a little back. Supposedly this was done so the driver could have a close up look at Pooch, who didn't seem enthralled that this gawker had suddenly become part of his life.

The dog is big, plus he looks like the offspring of a grizzly bear and a wolf, so he's accustomed to the curious gapes of strangers. Keeping his window rolled up and pressing his nose against the glass, the driver inspected Pooch from about three feet away. The dog didn't react at all, and just stared through his new buddy at nothing in particular. After his rather rude perusal of the hulking beast in the back of my truck, Mr. Rubberneck drew up even with me and cranked down his window about a third of the way. Gesturing at Pooch, he poked his nose out and yelled over to me, "What kind of dog is that?"

"He's an Orkney wolfhound," I answered by shouting over the bench seat and through the open passenger side window. The driver raised his eyebrows and nodded knowingly, as if he was familiar with the breed. "Careful!" I added, looking concerned, "he gets …..skittish sometimes."

As Mr. Rubberneck hurriedly rolled up his window and thus ended our brief chat about

canines, I noticed one of the pedestrians crossing in front of my truck had slowed to look at
me. He was one of those who'd waved at Trevor
this morning, but then he'd regarded me quizzi-
cally as I'd sat behind the steering wheel. Now
I was driving a different truck and Trevor was
nowhere in sight, so this was obviously giving
the pedestrian pause. I waved cheerily at him as
he went by, but he looked suspicious and only
nodded hesitantly in response.

I stopped at the post office to pick up my
favourite form of written communication: bills.
Amongst all the bad news was a personal letter
with a Danish postage stamp, so at least Pauline would be happy. She loves news from home,
especially as related by her mother

I drove to the lodge and the dogs were there
in the parking lot to welcome us home. I grabbed
the bag of paydirt after Banjo's and Grace's
unrestrained greeting, then we all headed
towards the path. Pauline had probably gone
up to the garden after lunch, and no one was in
the lodge. I made a couple of cheese sandwiches
and a pot of tea for my midday repast, then sat

at the table and thought of Trevor currently working in the cold creek water. I concluded that finding gold was all very nice, but if it's not really needed, then drinking tea in the lodge is much more rewarding. Interrupting my quiet contentment, a large frowsy woman burst through the main door and skewered me with a judgemental gaze.

"Do you have any shoelaces?" she demanded. "Little Robert managed to break the lace on his left shoe."

Since I was sure she was about to tell me how the little tyke had accomplished this, I cut her off by saying, "No, we don't have any new ones, but wait here for a moment." I hurried to the bedroom and found an old pair of shoes in the closet. Their laces were used looking and a bit fuzzified, but there were no breaks. After taking one out of a shoe, then peering at it as it hung from my fingers, I noticed it retained its zigs and zags no matter how straight I tried pulling it. Since poor little Robert was likely anxious to get back his shoe, I hastened from the room with the lace hanging crookedly from my hand.

My large female client was wearing sky-blue shorts so tight that they'd forced lumps of pallid flesh down towards each of her knees. Topside, she sported a dark red haltertop blouse contraption, which I hoped was securely affixed to her person. "This should work," I said as I closed the bedroom door and showed it to her, saying, "it's a bit frayed, but it should do the job."

She regarded the lace with revulsion, as though I was offering her a thin and hairy snake. Raising her substantial hooter snittishly, she said, "That's the wrong colour," as if I should have known. She finally took it as though doing me a favour, then she departed without saying thanks. It was so nice being at the lodge again!

I walked up to the garden after my little interlude with the client. Not knowing I was watching, Pauline was on her knees weeding, while the two cats were nearby, pouncing on any insect foolish enough to show his antennae. Even though they'd had interactions with me for years, upon seeing me on the patio, the felines scurried to their hedge-caves. Then they regarded me suspiciously, but from safety and comfort. I was disappointed to see that the demented Siamese seemed to be a bad influence on Mr. Robertson, the large marmalade cat. Normally friendly and easygoing, he was obviously jittery as he leapt into a cave after seeing me: he should know better, the silly beast.

Pauline noticed me, then stood as I made my way towards her. After I'd put an arm around her shoulder and given her a kiss, I gestured at a small weed that'd been partially hidden under a drooping cabbage leaf. "You missed one," I pointed out helpfully.

After looking me up and down in a speculative manner, Pauline said, "Hmmm. I could use a labourer with eagle eyes: you're hired!" She handed me her trowel, smiled brightly and added, "I'll be right back," then headed towards the equipment shed near Moon's composters. I looked at the tool I was holding and also at the weed coyly peeking at the sunshine from under cover. Then I said to myself, 'You should know better'. I hadn't yet learned to make myself scarce when this disagreeable chore happened to be underway; I silently lamented my obtuseness.

Carrying shin pads with attached knee protectors in a bucket, Pauline returned shortly. I took the pads out, and buckled them on over the legs of my jeans like she'd done. The hockey equipment made excellent kneelers, but I immediately spotted a problem with mine. "They're mismatched," I whined, "and anyway, neither colour goes with my outfit."

Handing me the bucket, Pauline said, "Yes, that's terrible. Cry into this: no salt water on the plants, please." Although her sincere sympathy had somewhat mollified me, I remained irritated with myself. The little weed under the cabbage leaf had started all this, so it was first in the bucket.

Pauline went off to a nearby section of the garden to work, but she was still close enough to comfortably converse with me. Unusually, she talked nonstop, mostly about the wedding of course. "We'll need lots of flowers in the lodge," she informed me. She was looking at me through the particularly robust leaves of a potato plant as she paused in her weeding and said, "Moon'll be back tomorrow and that'll be a big help." Even though Pauline had been addressing me, I don't think I'd been part of the conversation: I'd been just a sounding-board for her. "Let's see," she said as she tapped her hand with the trowel, "there's the Reverend, the guests, the food, the presents …." She suddenly stopped talking and fixed me with a stare, asking, "What are we going to give them for a wedding gift?"

"I was thinking maybe an extra-large lunch bucket for Trevor," I replied enthusiastically, "along with a few bucks in cash for Sarah."

"Those are very thoughtful and romantic ideas," Pauline said. Then she cursed softly as she had difficulty with a weed refusing to be cleanly uprooted. Rolling her eyes at me, she said, "We'd better discuss other options."

"Okay," I replied doubtfully, "if you say so." We worked for another two hours, until Pauline went down to the lodge to prepare the evening buffet and I went out in the boat with the dogs.

Phil Frutt and Isaac

Trevor phoned a day later to test the C.B. radio phone system he'd rigged up with his friend in town. I was amazed: there were no rude 'horse with digestive problems' noises in the background, nor the sound of a number of people singing different songs in a variety of languages. There was only a soft hum and a click before he spoke: "You have to say 'over' when you finish speaking," he told me, "I'm using a radio, so we can't both talk at once, over."

"You're coming in loud and clear," I responded, "your buddy could probably give the phone company a clue or two, over."

"I know you meant that as a compliment, but assisting them in any way would be the very last thing he'd ever do," Trevor coughed dryly and added, "He's had an ongoing dispute with them, you see: something about being billed for services not provided. His name's Eric, by the way, and I'm sure he'd be happy to give me some details if you'd like to know, over."

"I can well imagine all the pleasant chats and written communications he's had with service representatives, so you don't have to tell me," I hurriedly replied. Quickly changing the subject, I asked, "How's Sarah? Over."

"She's thrilled," he reported, not sounding delighted himself.

He told me he'd gone to her place to pick her up, but she and her mother had still been fussing with the wedding dress, so he'd parked the Barge in the driveway. Unexpectedly coming home from a meeting with a colleague, Sarah's father Rick apparently hadn't been super-pleased to see the bright yellow and orange chariot sitting in his driveway. Having to park on the street, he'd angrily rushed through the front door to confront the Native guy who was marrying his daughter, but they'd seen him arrive and were just leaving. The three of them had an awkward moment on the front steps, as Rick tried half-heartedly to hide his dislike for Trevor by hugging Sarah. She clearly wouldn't be embraced by someone with such negative feelings for the man she'd chosen to marry. She'd broken away from her father, as she said, "We're leaving now, see you later." There was a long pause, then Trevor chuckled as he quoted Sarah's opinion of her dad: " 'He's an idiot who can't see past his own prejudices.' Over."

"You shouldn't go around tearing families asunder," I said scoldingly, "try being a bit more circumspect. When are you coming over? Over."

"Not until the wedding day, I guess," he answered, "Sarah has me running in circles so much that I can't think straight, but I don't believe there'll be any spare time in the near future. Over."

"Well, your phone set-up is working," I said, "so if you have any doubts or questions, you'll always have me with whom to talk it over. Over."

"That's very reassuring," he said, but he didn't seem grateful that he'd be privy to all my advice about marriage and life in general. After a pause, he told me they were visiting a kennel just outside town on the following day. "We both want a dog. I like Labs and she does also, so maybe we'll get two. What do you think? Over."

I answered, "It sounds like a good idea, but it'd probably be best to never name a dog 'Rover'. Over."

"I'm glad I called: you've been such a big help!" Trevor said.

"Don't mention it," I replied grandly, "you can call any time you want." We signed off shortly after our chat, and I didn't see him until the big day.

Life at the lodge changed a bit after Moon's return. The women spent a lot of time making lists or having intensely whispered conversations. The Scrabble board stayed in its box, while the normal party atmosphere was missing during our paydirt cleaning. The bag I'd brought from Trevor's claim yielded less than an ounce, so no one was impressed. I pointed out that most of the gold was in powder form, similar to the stuff I'd found at Three Duck Lake. They certainly hadn't been galvinised by this observation. In fact, it was clear they couldn't give a fig if the precious metal appeared out of the black

sand in 5 pound bricks, since the wedding obviously occupied all their thoughts. Nonetheless,
I tallied up the totals and found that Trevor still
owed me a few bucks, so I decided to give him
a hard time about it later.

The first thing Pauline said after she'd gotten
out of bed at 5 a.m. on Monday was lost in the
rustling of sheets and blankets as I shifted around
in bed. "Rise and shine!" she said cheerily, supposedly repeating her previous utterance, only
louder this time. "It'll be a long day," she continued, "so get up! I'll start the coffee brewing."
She bustled out of the room while I watched
her from under cover, then I tarried for a few
minutes more in my warm horizontal position.
It suddenly clanked into my brainpan that this
was the wedding day: yippie! Heaving a self-pitying sigh at having to remove myself from my
comfy nest, in a half-conscious state I sat on the
edge of the bed thinking of nothing in particular. The fragrance of perking coffee livened
up a few neurons; therefore, I was able to get
dressed without injury. Pauline had opened the
bedroom shutters, allowing me to look out at the

new day. Even though the sun hadn't risen yet, a few birds were chirping and sounding lonely in the dark. About ten minutes later, the stars had disappeared, the eastern sky had a golden tinge and more of the feathered beasts were singing. Fully awake now, I turned from the bedroom window to join Pauline in the kitchen area.

As soon as I made my appearance in the lodge proper, she pointed at a felt marker sitting on a piece of paper beside my bowl of fruit salad and said, "You'd better write a notice to our clients about the wedding; they've been told, but they'll probably forget. You know the details."

While I started eating, I carefully printed out the message: 'The buffet will be early today (3:30 p.m.), because a wedding will be taking place in the lodge this evening. Sorry for the inconvenience.'

Reading it as I started on my pancakes, Pauline said, "That'll do," then she asked rhetorically, "guess what Sarah wants to serve her guests after the wedding?"

'Oh oh', I thought. Pauline obviously disapproved, so was there an undercurrent of friction among the womenfolk?

"Moon agrees with me," Pauline continued, "she thinks fish and chips have no place at a wedding. What do you think?"

I love Pauline's fish and chips, but treading carefully, I responded, "You're both right: the meal seems totally inappropriate, but if that's what Sarah wants, then so be it."

Since she had a faraway look in her eyes as she filled my coffee mug, I knew she hadn't been listening to my rock solid reasoning. Confirming the fact that she'd been elsewhere, she made no disparaging comments about the bucket-size of my morning drinking vessel. Instead, she said, "I'm going up to Moon's to get our dresses ready. Lay out your evening clothes on the bed," she told me, "then take the dogs for their walk. I'll see you later."

"Yes dear," I responded meekly, not accustomed to seeing her in a 'Sergeant Major' mode.

Worriedly glancing around at the lodge's interior, she muttered something about flowers being delivered later in the morning, then regarded me as I sat at the table. I'd returned to my own little world and was lovingly slathering a thick layer of crabapple jelly onto a piece of toast. Interrupting my little pre-coffee ceremony, she said, "Get your clothes ready," and left.

As I ate my toast, I noticed six eyes and three black noses were pointed in my direction. "I'm not sharing a crumb with a greedy bunch like you," I told the dogs, "but don't worry, we'll go for our perambulation soon." (It's best to avoid using the 'walk' word around here.)

After I'd finished breakfast, I washed the dishes, and headed to the bedroom. Opening the closet door and riffling through apparel that seldom saw the light of day, I found the sports jacket at the end of the rack. I lay it on the bed for a good look at it, and it appeared as attractive as it'd been all those many years ago when I'd bought it. It was a pleasing shade of brown wool, but I remembered the shocking yellow silk lining had, for some reason, convinced me to make the purchase. I picked it up from the bed, gave it a shake, then tried donning the garment. It fit quite well I assured myself, except for a minor snugness around the shoulders and upper back. In truth, the woolen material in these areas was stretched tight, but I blamed this on the sweatshirt I was wearing. 'This is too bulky,' I said to myself, 'things'll fit fine with an ordinary shirt.' I had some difficulty taking off the jacket: I ended up with my hands trapped behind me in the sleeves. After finally releasing myself, I dug my only necktie out of the sock drawer, and found my pale yellow dress shirt on a hanger. While I was in the closet, I grabbed my tan cotton pants too, admiring the sartorial splendour of my outfit as I spread everything out on the bed. Pleased I'd sorted out my wardrobe for the big day, I left the bedroom and asked the dogs if they cared to go for a walk: a very silly question.

It was still before 7 a.m., and we had the trail around the lake all to ourselves. I love these early morning hikes: going past the sleeping cabins, then around the open patch of the eastern shore, is very satisfying. Entering the large pines across the lake from the lodge, I usually quicken my pace. The sun's rays can't get through the canopy; therefore, the light's always dull in there. This, combined with a cathedral-like hush, makes the place a bit unsettling, but we were soon out in the sunshine again. I paused at the Narrows to watch the dogs take an unneeded drink, then engage in a game of 'let's hassle Banjo, no matter what he might be doing'. Pooch and Grace were always disrespecting him by shouldering him aside when he found something interesting on the ground. His sister was by far the worst: sibling rivalry, I guess. If he displeased her in any way, she'd flatten her ears and snarl, all the while giving him a threatening sidelong look. Sometimes she nipped him hard enough to make him howl briefly in pain, but Banjo clearly didn't hold grudges and went about his day with not a care in his 'mind'. This might be rather uncharitable, but frankly, I think he's probably too dim to take offence.

When I got back to the lodge, the dogs disappeared into the bush. A few minutes later, Betty, our neighbour from up the road, pulled into the parking lot and exited her vehicle with a large sealed bowl in her hands. After shouting 'good morning' to each other, she approached me on the path and nodded at the bowl she was carrying. "These are the pike fillets for the fish and chips," she said, shaking her head. "Imagine wanting this for your wedding!"

Actually, the end results of Pauline's magic touch with the spuds weren't 'chips'. They were thinly-sliced potatoes fried golden brown in olive oil, while the fillets were coated with a whole wheat batter that was delicious after deep frying. And you could write home about the red-cabbage coleslaw; the meal was rather elegant, really. I mentioned none of this to Betty of course, but rolled my eyes and shrugged.

"Young people!" I asserted, as if I was an old codger sitting in his rocking chair, "sometimes there's no accounting for their wishes." Then I heaved an indignant sigh and shook my head, but I think she saw through my pretended outrage.

Looking at me doubtfully, she said, "Well.... yes," and told me she'd put the bowl into the cool room, then go up to Moon's. "We'll be getting our dresses ready, so what're you going to be doing?" she asked. When I told her I didn't know, she said in a distracted way, "That's nice," then hurried into the lodge. I was still standing there when she reappeared minus the bowl and gave me a somewhat worried smile. "See you soon," she said, and went up to Moon's, leaving me alone outside the lodge.

I figure weddings are mostly for women. I'm not complaining, but I'd been left out of the fussing and planning for the ceremony. Most guys would probably prefer a handshake and a shared glass of beer with their loved one, but how then could mothers get involved?

Pauline and Moon came down to prepare the breakfast buffet for our clients. Ten minutes after the last of them had left, the flower delivery van pulled into the lot. Pauline and Moon soon had the lodge looking festive with daffodils and tulips, plus the wild flowers they'd picked themselves. After they'd festooned the place with blossoms, I volunteered to help in any way possible. Since they appeared shocked to see me hanging around and didn't reply to my generous offer, I made a pot of tea and didn't offer any to them.

As I sat at the table, they were in the kitchen area discussing the Reverend. Pauline was

stirring in the spices Moon had slowly been dropping into the batter in a big bowl. "His name's
Harris: he's a new guy and apparently this is his
first wedding," said Moon, "but he'll be fine."
She snickered and added, "They were annoyed
when I phoned the church, since they usually get
a month's notice."

Pauline shrugged and said, "He'll like it here.
When's he due?"

"About 4:30," answered Moon.

Pauline was just about to say something
else, when she seemed to become fully aware
of my presence. Glaring at me as I sat munching
a peanut butter cookie with my tea, she asked
sharply, "Got your clothes ready?"

"Yes ma'am," I replied, "they're laid out on
the bed."

Wordlessly, she went into our sleeping cham-
ber, then reappeared shortly after and said,
"Everything looks nice, but do things fit?"

"The jacket's a little snug, but nobody's going
to notice," I assured her. I didn't waste time by
telling her I hadn't tried on the pants, since
they'd been fine the last time I'd worn them.

She nodded in a preoccupied way, then paused as if she was crossing out an item on a mental check-list. She smiled at me and came over to the table to give me a peck on the cheek. "We're going up to Moon's to see how Betty's doing," she explained, "we'll be back soon." They left and since the dogs hadn't reappeared, I was alone in the lodge as I finished my tea.

Since it was plain my assistance wouldn't be needed, I'd decided to split some logs out back, but the phone rang. When I picked up and said hello, a cheerful voice responded by saying, "Hi! I'm Phil Frutt (I instantly forgot his name, so I've rechristened him) and I'd like to outline some of the financial services my company can provide for you." Without allowing me to get a word in edgewise, he described how he could make my business much more efficient. "Our advice on the proper investments and bonds will make you a wealthy man," Mr. Frutt promised me. I hadn't said anything other than 'hello', so he supposedly took this as a positive, since he then enquired, "Will you sign up for our two-month trial offer?"

Letting a few seconds go by, I answered by asking in a slow and moronic voice, "Do you like soup?"

"Er, pardon me?" responded an obviously mystified Phil.

"I like soup," I stated happily. "My friend Marcie grows her own tomatoes, carrots, peas, onions, all kinds of vegetables, really. Then she makes soup that's nothing like that canned stuff." After this joyful account, I asked, "Do you like soup?"

"Yes, yes I do, it's very nice," he responded in a placating voice, "is there someone else I can talk to?"

"I have a Winnie-the-Pooh soup bowl," I said in answer to his query, "it has pictures of dancing Piglets all over it."

"That's fascinating stuff," he replied, "I have to ring off now."

"The bowl's yellow with green drawings," I informed him as he hung up gently. Hopefully, he wouldn't call again.

I went out behind the lodge to slip out of my 'moron-mode' while I cut some firewood.

The dogs magically materialised and balefully watched me swing the axe for a while, then disappeared into the bush once more.

I thought of Trevor and Sarah as I worked. Pauline says they bring out the best in each other and I agree: they belong together. But I didn't care for the blasé attitude Sarah had for Portunus. While she'd been angry at Trevor for jeopardising everything with his scary bluff-climbing episode, she seemed to have disregarded the fact that he'd been forced into doing it by a spirit with questionable motives. I hoped their home in the wilds would be good for them, but the image of Portunus's unsettling dark eyes under the brim of his silly hat, made the picture seem less rosy. The bounty of gold pellets in the creek was a bonus: a rewarding way to start a marriage, but still I had my worries.

As usual I lost myself in the wood cutting, until Pauline poked her head out of the rear door and called over to me, "Early lunch today. Come in before the hungry horde arrives!" Then she limited me to only one ham and cheese sandwich, plus two rather small pickled onions.

When I asked for more, an image of Trevor eating at the table suddenly burst upon my consciousness. He was casually inhaling vast quantities of sustenance while wearing a large blue tarp for a bib. I wondered if this unflattering depiction of my friend had something to tell me: like maybe he'd been a bad influence on me in regards to my food ingestion. So I didn't complain when Pauline said, "You don't want to be stuffed at the wedding; anyway, there'll be lots to eat after the ceremony."

As I was eating my meager lunch, a client came in with her little boy. "Mrs. Mendelssohn!" Pauline exclaimed as if she was overjoyed. She briefly hugged our guest, then hunkered down to be at the kid's level and said to him, "You must be Isaac; how old are you?"

"I'm three and a half," he answered as if someone was going to dispute it. He'd momentarily been pleased to have pretty Pauline so close, but his glow definitely diminished as he focussed on me. I'd just taken a bite of sandwich and he was regarding me disparagingly, like I had a glob of mustard on my face. Since he was still rudely staring at me as I finished chewing, I took a sip of tea, and stuck my tongue out at him when his mother wasn't looking. The little snitch immediately raised his head to his mom to tell on me, but she was talking with Pauline. "It looks so nice in here with all the flowers," Mrs. Mendelssohn was saying. She leaned over to put her sniffer into a cluster of purple and white buds displayed in a cut-crystal vase. "I love lilacs," she said, "and they look so nice with the yellow daisies."

While the ladies were engaged in their blossom-fest of a conversation, Isaac took the opportunity to look huffy and to return the favour by sticking his tongue out at me. Of all the nerve! But his mother caught him in this obvious disrespect and chastened him by batting him once on the head-bone. "He started it!" the loveable little tyke whined as he pointed at me.

I shrugged and looked puzzled, as though I was a serious adult with weighty matters on my mind. Supposedly, I couldn't care less about the accusatory ravings of a three-year- old, as I sat calmly drinking my tea. Pauline said to Mrs.

Mendelssohn, "You're a little early for lunch; can you come back in twenty minutes?" As the boy and his mother left, Isaac scowled at me for getting him into trouble, so I smirked at him in return. He was insistently bleating something to his mother as she closed the front door behind them. Though I didn't catch his exact words, he certainly didn't sound like a happy camper.

Betty came down from Moon's and declared, "The dresses are hemmed and I'm already late." Looking worriedly at her watch, she said, "Ted's useless when it comes to preparing his own meals: he'll probably end up having moss and pine needles for lunch. I'll be back at 4:30." Smiling ruefully at these personal responsibilities and then at us, she hurried out.

I distinctly felt that Pauline and Moon would like to see me haul my carcass elsewhere, as they gawked at me in the ensuing silence. To be honest, I thought the feminine touch had been a bit heavy-handed with all the flowers around the place. Their overall effect had me feeling out of place, like a wrench lying on a lady's bedside table. So I had no problem in leaving: "I'll be right out back if you need me," I said, glad they didn't roll their eyes and sigh with relief at my departure.

Chopping wood always sets me adrift: maybe it's the power of a good stroke with a razor-sharp axe or the smells and sounds of the endeavour, but it doesn't take long to lose myself. Pooch appeared without the other two and intently watched as I added to the neat wood stack just outside the lodge's rear door. After a while, I chunked the axe into the chopping block and called the dog over for a chat. "Pauline is starving me to death until after the wedding," I complained to him, "so I'm distracting myself." His eyes were sympathetic, and I knew he understood. If you're ever in need of a dose of empathy, just lament to a dog about the lack of food. As far as he's concerned, life should be a never-ending feast of rare fillet mignons with a tub or two of cool water on the side. A canine will always commiserate about food or the lack of it.

Pooch's presence made me feel less hard-done-by, so I picked up the axe and he backed up a few paces. I was about to resume work, when Pauline popped her head out of the back door and called over to me, saying, "You don't have to skulk out there with the dog any longer. The lunch buffet is over and all our clients have left." Pausing to unemotionally behold my usual summer attire of jeans and teeshirt, she said, "It's time to change into your 'best man' clothes: it'll be nice seeing you in a tie and jacket, for once." She'd muttered the last bit in a weary voice, as though we'd had frequent heated discussions about me dressing up for supper and she'd been stymied by my pigheaded stubbornness every time. Anyway, after telling Pooch I'd see him later, I went inside. Pauline was loading a roll of film into her camera as I headed for the bedroom. "I'll be ready for you in all your glory," she said, as she snapped a 'before' picture of yours truly.

My Snazzy Outfit and the Guests

My clothes were laid out on the bed, just as I'd left them. Even though I'm certainly no clothes horse, I found myself looking forward to getting stylishly well-dressed. I stripped to my underwear, and put on the shirt. I noticed the buttons seemed reluctant to go into their holes, while the threads attaching them were stretched tighter than violin strings. And there was NO WAY the collar could be fastened closed: 'Oh well,' I said to myself, 'the tie will secure everything, plus it'll hide all the distressed cordage running down my front.' Mildly surprised I had no difficulty with the knot, I donned the useless garment, then peered into the mirror. Everything looked peachy, but I was concerned that the tie could flap aside and thus reveal all the shabbiness. So I found my never-used clip and made sure the neckpiece wouldn't go astray.

I sat on the edge of the bed and pulled on the tan trousers. I was instantly reminded of an uncomfortable incident I'd shared with a girl-friend, many years before I'd met Pauline. My female companion had been so enthused by the yoga instruction at a course she'd been taking, that she'd finally convinced me to attend a class held in the local high school gym. Showing the pants to me, she said, "These are leotards for men. You can do exercises much better when you're wearing them, plus you'll fit in with everyone else."

After putting them on and experiencing their skin-tightness, I'd said, "I can't go out in public like this. I may as well hang a sign around my neck with an arrow pointing down to my crotch and the script reading, 'Care to indulge in the bulge?' I'd found this notion amusing, but she hadn't. Not coincidentally, we'd parted ways soon after.

I don't have much belly fat, but once I'd used brute force to get the waist button fastened and

I'd zipped up, the pants were pushing everything upwards quite unattractively. The restrictive shirt was no help in hiding my deformed midriff; in fact, it was highlighting the swells and valleys of flesh with pale yellow cotton. Thinking the jacket would hide all this, I put it on, then felt its tightness again on my shoulders and back. At this moment, Pauline came into the room with the wedding ring in her hand, saying, "You can't forget this! Put it into your pocket until ....." Then she stopped dead as she got an eyeful of my attire: especially the pants. After looking me up and down in a rather stunned silence, she said, "Oh my God, nothing fits. Didn't you check things out before today?"

"I thought everything would be fine," I replied weakly.

Looking down at my tight trousers again, she informed me that codpieces had gone out of fashion long ago. "You must have other pants," she said, obviously frustrated.

"Yes I do," I responded, "but they're from the same era, so they might be a tad snug too." Shrugging as though there was nothing to be done about some realities, I said, "I usually wear jeans or work pants. You know that."

She'd come around the bed to put the ring into my jacket pocket and to fuss with my tie. Discovering the trip-wire zone of straining button-threads hidden beneath it, she rolled her eyes without comment, then she cinched everything firmly down with the clip. She stood back to further peruse my garments, while I said conversationally, "Nobody's going to even notice me: all eyes will be on the bride."

Clearly unconvinced, Pauline nodded anyway and said, "Come out to the table with me," then left with purpose, like a school principal having invited a particularly recalcitrant student to the office.

The squeezing embrace of my outfit slowed me down as I strode into the lodge proper. My usual graceful stride had been reduced to tentative, short paces as I shuffled up to her. She took a picture of me and I noticed it wasn't full length. Handing me a bouquet of daisies and baby's breath, she said, "Hold this to cover your front trouser area." I felt like a too tightly stuffed wiener holding a spray of blooms, as Pauline again studied the way I was presenting myself to the world. "Hold the flowers lower," she ordered, then snapped a picture of me when I complied. We giggle now at the photo of me with a garland hiding my crotch, but it wasn't much of a yuckfest at the time. "Betty's due soon," Pauline said as she glanced up at the kitchen clock, "tell her I'm at Moon's." Giving a headshake to my wardrobe and probably to yours truly also, she left me standing there with my daisies.

Ted and Betty were the first to arrive, each carrying a large cardboard box. He was his usual grumpy self, but he looked nice in his shirt and tie. As he put his carton on the kitchen counter, he asked me, "Do you think seven or eight bottles of my wine is an appropriate gift to give them? Neither drinks very much." He didn't look overly concerned about committing a social blunder; actually, I think he was just making conversation. Thankfully, they hadn't said much about my wardrobe. Ted probably hadn't noticed my tight wrapping, while Betty had said, "Don't you look nice!" then appeared to regret saying anything as she got a close up view of me.

"Look at this!" Ted said to me, clearly unaware of any discomfort in the air. He handed me a small square of paper picturing stalks of rhubarb lying in a wicker basket. Written in flowery script above the image was 'Rhubarb Rosé, while beneath it in a slender and flowing font were the words 'From the Merriwether Winery'. "I designed the label myself and Betty did the drawing. It turned out nice, don't you think?"

"Perfect!" I responded, even though I knew that the 'Merriwether Winery' was just a dozen plastic garbage cans in a barn. "And the wine's a fine gift for them," I added, "it's always good to have a few bottles in the house."

"Yes, yes," said Betty dismissively, as if our chat about wine was of no import. "Where's Pauline?" she asked as she rather suspiciously looked around. I was about to tell her that Pauline had decided to take a short tour around the lake in her hot-air balloon, when Betty said, "She's up at Moon's, isn't she?" Without waiting for a reply, she left the box she'd been carrying on the counter, then hurried out of the lodge.

The dogs had picked up on the excitement in the air, but obviously they didn't know what might happen next, so they were watching us closely. Maybe they were expecting Ted and I to break into a tap-dancing routine, but no such luck.

After knocking politely, the Reverend Harris came in and said, "It's nice around here," then smiled as he introduced himself to everyone. I'd been expecting someone in dark clothes and clerical collar, but this guy was dressed as a normal human being. He was wearing a short-sleeved blue shirt and pleated grey trousers: he looked appropriately respectful, but not too formal. He went over to the unlit stove to say hello to the dogs, who clearly liked him, then I invited him to sit at the table. Clutching my bouquet of daisies and holding it below waist-level as I poured glasses of wine for the two men, was not only odd looking, but just seemed to draw attention to the area I was trying to hide. So I ceased and desisted with the flowers as I carefully lowered myself onto the chair beside Ted. Feeling that the pants couldn't take the strain of me sitting, I quickly got vertical again and wished my daisies were within reach. Thankfully, Sarah and Trevor came in just then, so I rushed to the door to greet them.

After hugging me and taking a casual glance at my attire, Sarah asked me, "Wearing your kid brother's clothes?"

"You know I don't have a kid brother," I replied, trying to act unhurt by this aspersion cast at my apparel.

"That's too bad," she responded, "otherwise he might have told you that in order to be debonair, your garments should be approximately the correct size."

Ignoring her rude comments, I shook Trevor's hand, then clapped him on the shoulder and said, "Congratulations! Today's the big day! But are you sure you want to be handcuffed to this female forever?"

"I'm mostly comfortable with it," Trevor responded as he put an arm around her shoulder and kissed her on the forehead, "I think things will work out," I shrugged in response and said in a doubtful voice, "If you say so," then I grinned at her.

We male-gendered folk seemed to suddenly fade away as she said, "My gown's up at Moon's, so I should be getting changed." I motioned the Reverend Harris over for a quick introduction to the couple, and she left.

I was wondering whether I should risk sitting at the table with the others, when Dot and Rick arrived. Sarah's parents were gracious enough, but it was easy to tell that he didn't want to be present. He smelled strongly of booze as I shook his hand, and I hoped his wife had been driving. I hadn't liked him from the first time we'd met and there was no question that the feeling was mutual.

As I was hanging Dot's coat on the peg near the door, he blearily gazed at my 'best man' outfit and said, "Nice duds," then he laughed. I smiled in return, but I'd been gritting my teeth under all my outward niceties.

As usual Dot needed a chin, so again I wondered where Sarah had obtained her good looks. Maybe from her dad, I surmised. He was tall and well put together, plus he even had a chin! But in the end he was always mean-spirited and judgemental towards others. While Sarah could be somewhat harsh with her opinions, there was usually a spark of humour in her outlook, something Rick clearly lacked.

Looking over to the table where Ted was saying something to a seemingly spellbound Reverend Harris, Rick spied the wine bottle and said, "At least there's something to drink." He left my company without a further word, walked unsteadily to the table, loudly introducing himself to Harris as 'father of the bride'. Since Ted hadn't stopped speechifying to him and was now speaking louder to drown out Rick's irritating interruption, the unfortunate reverend didn't know which way to look. He solved the problem by smiling and nodding at each man in turn, then taking a glass-tilting swallow of wine.

Rick had plopped himself down and was reaching for a glass before he realised he was sitting right next to Trevor. His first reaction was to change seats, but he stopped after rising halfway from his chair. Being patronisingly magnanimous, he draped an arm over Trevor's shoulder and started acting all buddy-buddy. I stopped watching when the semi-inebriated lout started referring to his daughter as a 'ball and chain' as he told unfunny dirty jokes. The reverend drank more wine and seemed fascinated with the ceiling: he was intently studying its construction as I turned back to Dot.

She sighed as she watched her husband, then jingled car keys at me and said, "I won't let him drive when he's been drinking." Shaking her head and looking embarrassed, she continued, "Sorry for the way he's bulldozed through your little gathering; I shouldn't have insisted he attend his daughter's wedding." Rick still had his arm around Trevor's shoulders and was apparently telling him another joke. There was a feeling of forced merriment about the table that was plainly at odds with the normal relaxed atmosphere of the lodge.

After grimly regarding his intrusive presence at the table for a while longer, Dot apologised again, then said, "The girls must be up at Moon's, so I should join them."

When the majority of people relate even the most mundane of information, they somehow manage to convey the fact that there's a solid reason for their verbiage. Not so with Dot. She could yell 'fire!' into a crowded room and folk wouldn't take her seriously or even notice her. No matter what she had to say, she seemed able to dust all her words generously with boredom and apathy: a gift! The fact that she had some control over her loose cannon of a husband was highly impressive, but I was glad when she left.

As I was closing the door, Trevor got up from the table and approached me. He was wearing dark grey dress pants, a beige leather jacket and a pale blue shirt. He'd loosened the knot in his tie, but he still appeared spiffy and comfortable in clothes that actually fit. Looking flustered and annoyed as he gained my side, he said, "Let's go outside for a while and bring the dogs along."

When we were all out on the path under the brightness of the moon, he said angrily, "Rick's drunk and he's spoiling things. Right now he's telling the reverend how the fuse-box had been set up on a drag-line he'd worked on last year, so I had to leave before I said something I'd regret." He gazed up at the stars as he took a deep breath, then exhaled slowly. After doing this three times, he turned to look me up and down. "Nice threads," he murmured, "know many midgets?"

Since I knew he was stressed and probably didn't realise what he'd been saying, I chose not to answer the rude question. As I reached down to give Banjo a friendly thump on his side, I noticed an inch or four of shirt-cuff that shouldn't be poking out of my jacket sleeves. Plus, the moonlight made the yellow cotton thus revealed almost phosphorescent white, so I quit patting the dog and got upright again.

Trevor said, "Let's go down to the wharf before we go back inside," proceeding silently to the pebbly beach. Not overly fond of being out after sunset, the dogs stayed close-by as we approached the inky water. Finding Pooch's leather hoop, his favourite toy, nearby, I frisbeed it into the lake and he splashed in to retrieve it. Trevor threw in sticks for the other two, so we soon had a canine water fest underway. After a few minutes of this, I could almost see the tension falling away from him. I'd been momentarily worried that he was simply getting cold feet, and his animosity towards his prospective father-in-law was just a convenient excuse. But I should have known his dislike for Rick was genuine and that Trevor really wanted to marry Sarah.

While an enthusiastic and wet Banjo watched eagerly, he flipped a stick in his hand and smiled over at me. "That's a really sharp outfit," he observed, as he nodded at my sausage-casing with socks, "It makes you glow in the moonlight. Wherever did you get it?"

"Nowhere special," I replied humbly, "I threw it together myself."

"Did you think of throwing it far away?" he asked as though he was about to write a report.

Since there could be no mistaking the flagrant disrespect of his query about my wardrobe, I responded by gazing out over the lake and looking hurt. He finally chucked the stick into the lake for Banjo and I heard someone at the fire pit ten feet behind. As I turned to look, a blue flame sparked to life at the bottom of the hole, but there wasn't any fuel there. Then I saw a figure sitting on the big log near the pit: it was Portunus.

My shocked first reaction was to ask him indignantly what he was doing at my lake. But I stopped myself from making any kind of emotional outburst that might cause trouble for Sarah and Trevor in the future. Portunus was sitting on the log oddly: his hands were together prayerfully as he held them between his knees. He was leaning forward to stare fixedly into the weird fire, as if Trevor and I were secondary to the blue flame. Strangely, the dogs hadn't seemed to notice his sudden appearance and they'd run back to the lodge when we quit playing fetch with them. This was very unusual behaviour for the canines: normally, they'd hang around, then return with us as soon as we went inside.

I could see the edginess on Trevor's face as he acknowledged the sitting figure with a single, curt nod. Portunus grinned at us, and invited us to sit on the log across the fire from him. As we complied, I felt something pop or tear in the posterior portion of my pants and hoped no one had noticed the subtle ripping sound. Portunus was wearing the same shirt and pants as on our previous encounter, so I wondered if he ever had a laundry day. No words had yet been spoken as we sat down with our uninvited guest, but there was no doubt that Trevor's unfriendly manner was a reflection of my own feelings.

"Don't look so glum!" Portunus said to Trevor, "today's your wedding day!"

"Why are you here?" asked Trevor, trying to be unemotional.

Disregarding the obvious lack of joy his presence had brought, Portunus answered, "I couldn't let my newest tenant get married without showing up to pay my respects." He'd sounded reasonable and hadn't taken offence at our cold welcome, so I was highly suspicious of him. When he'd finished speaking, he gazed down at the woodless blue flame in the pit. His eyes were hidden by the brim of his ditzy and unbalanced-looking hat, plus I saw a horseshoe design on its crown that indicated exactly nothing to me.

"What do you mean by calling me a 'tenant'?" Trevor asked him in an annoyed voice. "You're not my landlord."

"You're right," said Portunus, "it was a poor choice of words." He'd been looking into the pit, but he raised his eyes to Trevor and said straight-faced, "After all, you have a piece of paper granting you ownership of the land." There'd clearly been a mocking and derisive tone to his voice that set Trevor mouth in a grim, tight-lipped line. But before he could respond, Portunus dismissed the topic by saying, "Anyway, I'm not here to upset you. If that'd been my intention, I could've joined the little gathering indoors: I'm sure that would've caused some consternation." He chuckled at the thought and grinned at us, apparently unaffected by our unhappy faces. "I just wanted to give you my best wishes," he said to Trevor in humble good fellowship.

"Well…..thanks," he responded without any warmth. After an uncomfortable moment of watching the pebbles supposedly burn in the pit, Trevor asked, "So, when are you leaving?"

Portunus quickly quit the 'hale and hearty' bit. With his face appearing mask-like in the spooky blue light, he stopped smiling and narrowed his eyes. For a moment I thought he was about to have some kind of a conniption, and I braced myself. But he only looked misunderstood as he got up from the log. The fire instantly went out, leaving us eyeballing a silhouette until our eyes adjusted. He stood there for a long moment staring at Trevor sitting beside me. Once I could distinguish things more clearly, I could see Portunus had a rather scary smile on his face. "Too bad I didn't get to give Sarah congratulations," he said, as he bowed his head slightly. "Oh well," he continued in a more upbeat way, "I'll see you both soon enough!" With that, he unhurriedly headed towards the parking lot and disappeared in the moonlight.

After watching his departure, Trevor said with a snort, "He says he doesn't want to upset me with his visit: yeah, sure. And I own a horse who likes to pole-vault in his spare time." Looking into the murky distance and frowning, he added, "I should've been more obliging to him, but he bugs me so much that I couldn't. Do you think he'll be a danger for me and Sarah in the future?"

"He's a drama queen," I responded, "he craves an emotional scene. I think you handled him just right; you kept your cool and didn't give him the opportunity to fly off the handle." We stared up the incline where he'd wandered off, then I said, "Never mind him; there's something else that might require some attention, let's see, what was it?" As though finally seeing the light, I snapped my fingers and answered myself, "Oh yeah! You're about to get married and I'm the best man. Let's get indoors before the ladies make their grand entrance."

Although he'd obviously been rattled by Portunus's unexpected little visit and wanted to pursue the matter further, he said nothing. Turning his back to me, he looked into the night sky and breathed deeply for a moment. When he faced me again, he was smiling as he said, "You're right: let's go inside."

The Blessed Event

When we returned to the lodge, the first thing I noticed was the Reverend Harris sitting at the head of the main table with a flushed and slightly frightened look on his face. To his left, Ted was saying something about wine-making, while to his right, Rick was clearly getting ready to interrupt. Two empties and a newly-opened bottle were on the table, so it appeared that the trio of gents hadn't been shy about sampling the wine. As we approached, the good reverend hurriedly drained his half-full glass, then grabbed the bottle as though 'last call' was about to be announced.

The florid man-of-the-cloth clearly wasn't accustomed to hitting the sauce so hard. He smiled at us gratefully, then stood with the bottle still in his hand. But the sudden upward movement had apparently scrambled the grey cells that'd usually keep a guy vertical, so the reverend abruptly sat down again. "Do you have the ring?" he asked me, trying to be all business and probably assuring himself that no one had noticed his momentary conflict with gravity. After I nodded and patted my jacket pocket, he invited us to sit with them, but then the women came in.

We all stood to watch the procession: the bride was first through the door. Her brown eyes were shining but looking down modestly, as Sarah entered with her mom a step behind. Since Rick had refused to be part of the ceremony (silly man), Dot was 'giving the bride away' and was completely ignoring her husband. Sarah was wearing a white gown with a tinge of blue to it: Pauline told me later that the dress was Dot's and Sarah had made some drastic alterations to it: especially to its length. Apparently it'd been almost down to the floor, but now it was just below knee-level. Pauline gave me more details about all the stitching that had to be done, but frankly, I was only being polite in listening.

Descriptions of construction projects involving any kind of clothing leave me cold: I'd rather watch grass grow.

Anyway, Sarah had a garland of daisies in her hair and looked very pretty. As bride's maids of honour, Pauline and Moon followed wearing outfits identical to each other: long-sleeved white blouses and maroon floor-level dresses. They were solemn, but their eyes sparkled and I noticed the bouquet Moon had in her hand was the same bunch of daisies and baby's breath that'd recently been used for a different purpose. Nonetheless, the beribboned blooms had managed to keep themselves presentable.

Dressed in her Sunday best, Betty was last through the door, then stopped smiling when she saw the reverend still holding the bottle and standing at the head of the table. "Oh Christ!" exclaimed Harris as realised it was his turn at centre stage. He immediately looked up at the ceiling and said, "Sorry about that," then guided Trevor and I to the 'common room', where the ladies had stopped. After stationing the groom alongside the lovely Sarah, with me close to his right but a bit behind, the reverend started without preamble.

"Dearly beloved ....", he was saying, when the door opened and in came Mrs. Mendelessohn with Isaac. Everyone swivelled their heads around, while time seemed to stop for a moment as she stood there with her son, looking surprised. "Oh!" she exclaimed, "the wedding! I'd completely forgotten."

'Fat chance', I thought as I regarded her and the adorable little Isaac standing halfway through the front doorway. The boy looked as formal as a three-year-old could: his blonde locks were neatly brushed and he was wearing a natty blue jumpsuit with a big zipper down the front.

His mother happened to be dressed to the nines and had obviously just applied a layer of makeup to her visage. I'd recognised her as a wedding crasher right from the start, so I wasn't shocked. She stood there uncertainly with her son, until Betty invited them in and the ceremony commenced.

I must say that Reverend Harris comported himself well: he was pious but joyful at the same time and no longer seemed to have trouble staying upright. This in itself was admirable, since Ted's 'Rhubarb Rosé is about 16% alcohol, so if it's drunk too enthusiastically, it'll cause the floor to tilt alarmingly. Although the wine apparently goes well with food, Pauline had insisted on serving a much weaker white with the fish and chips.

When Harris asked the bride and groom if they'd prepared statements of love for one another, I nearly chortled out loud. Since I didn't want to put further stress on my tight garments, plus I certainly didn't need everyone gawking at me, I stopped myself. The reason for the suppressed laughter was simple: Sarah's reaction to wedding vows uttered damp-eyed on the altar. Pauline told me what Sarah had said and I quote, 'If I hear the words 'love, cherish or forever' spoken again by some twerp in a wedding gown, I think I'll puke'.

'That's not a very romantic attitude', Pauline had responded unemotionally. Sarah had opened her mouth to say something, but in the end she'd only snorted haughtily and shrugged.

Since Trevor hardly ever speechified enough for his words to fill a thimble, there was an awkward silence after the reverend's query. Sarah shook her head minutely, so Harris asked, "Is there anyone here who objects to this sacred union?"

Rick was somewhere behind me and I was half-expecting him to say something stupid. Instead a child's voice loudly proclaimed, "I think I peed my pants."

Not missing a beat at this startling revelation, Harris sounded annoyed as he said, "No, no, no, I wasn't asking about that." Looking over at a red-faced Mrs. Mendelssohn and raising his eyebrows, he asked, "You're the mother? Perhaps you can take care of his problem."

She nodded and seemed in a hurry to leave. She grabbed the incontinent little rascal, smiled ruefully at the gathering, then rushed outside with her damp and increasingly obstreperous child held not-so-tenderly in her arms. Poor thing: she didn't get to see much of the wedding.

Giving me a significant look, the reverend asked me to hand the wedding ring to Trevor: a straight-forward and uncomplicated task. But I blew it by fumbling in my pocket and dropping the ring to the floor, where it rolled somewhere behind me.

Reflexively, I shot my left foot out to stop the thing from going walkabout, when a loud ripping sound occurred and my trousers suddenly felt more comfortable. Thankful that my jacket was hiding all the split seams and shredded material at the posterior of my pants, I squatted to retrieve the ring. Unfortunately, Rick was doing the same thing, so we knocked our heads together hard. Surely, the hollow thud caused by our colliding coconuts hadn't been audible to the rest of the folks, but nonetheless, I found myself lying on the floor beside Rick. We were both moaning and rubbing our noggins: it's amazing how quickly things can fall apart. I fleetingly wondered how Trevor felt upon seeing his best man, plus his father-in-law, injure themselves during his wedding, but we both got up after a moment, and proceeded with the ceremony as if nothing had happened. Trevor put the ring on Sarah's finger and kissed her, so the reverend pronounced them man and wife. After this tender and special moment, Trevor turned to me and said, "I'm starving! When do we eat?"

As Sarah rolled her eyes and shook her head at him, I replied, "In about a half hour, after you open your gifts," then I rubbed the sore spot on my skull.

As it happened, we'd all decided to give practical presents. Ted and Betty gave them a bread box, cutlery and a battery-operated wall clock, while the proud parents had a beautiful down duvet for them, along with an envelope that Rick wordlessly put into an inside pocket of Trevor's jacket. Pauline gave the newlyweds matching toques and a wool blanket that fit nicely in the ice-cooler I'd gotten for them. I'd also bought a selection of hooks, lines and lures for him, which he clearly enjoyed more than the homey stuff.

A while later, Sarah had a large helping of fish and chips with her husband, but since he was far from finishing, she left the table, saying, "I'm going up to Moon's to change into normal clothes."

"We should be going too," said Dot. Since she'd noticed Rick had been more interested in the wine than in the food, she was regarding him without affection.

"Busy day tomorrow," said the reverend, "I should be heading out too. I'm happy for you and Sarah," he added as he lay a hand on Trevor's shoulder, "it sounds like you'll be living in a nice place."

"Thank you sir, we'll do our best," he responded, but since he'd just shovelled a large forkful of chips into his mouth, the words had been slightly garbled. So, the fabled evening ended with Pauline and Betty struggling to keep up the supply of fish and chips. While Ted and Trevor dedicated themselves to making the food disappear, I watched as I drank my tea. It was just as I'd envisioned: fork from plate to mouth with the regularity of a metronome and no conversation. After a few minutes of this busy quiet, I asked Trevor, "So, do you think you'll enjoy married life at the cabin?"

I'd asked only for something to say, but he paused with a large fork-load halfway to his mouth and seriously considered the question. "I guess that unfortunately depends on Portunus," he finally replied.

"Who's he?" Ted asked through a mouthful of coleslaw. He'd been entirely concentrating on feeding himself and hadn't even raised his head to speak, so Trevor doubtlessly figured that Ted didn't much care.

"You don't know him," answered Trevor, while at the same time giving me a concerned look, "he's just an acquaintance of mine."

Betty came over with two heaped plates, put them on the table and addressed Ted crossly: "Since this is a special occasion I haven't said much, but really! This is your fourth helping and you're not getting any more." I noticed she hadn't berated Trevor, who'd been matching her hubby plate for plate. I guess she figured it was the groom's right to pig out, but that didn't mean Ted had to join in.

I observed the men's marathon-like feeding for a few minutes more: it didn't take them long to consume the last morsels and to cast somewhat guilty glances towards the kitchen area.

"What's for dessert?" asked Ted, as Betty collected their empty plates.

"A piece of the wedding cake of course," she answered, giving Pauline a smile, "a single piece," she emphasised and seemed to be including Trevor this time.

Sarah had chosen the recipe: chocolate with raspberry swirls and white, almond frosting. Very nice. Although I'd already had my dessert, I asked for a small chunk just to keep the guys company. They seemed to enjoy the cake too: after the second forkful, Ted paused his steady masticating long enough to say, "Good stuff!" then he resumed eating. I couldn't help notice that they'd each received gargantuan wedges, while a pathetic little cube graced my plate, but I didn't complain. That'd be unhostly and anyhow, one shouldn't whine at a wedding.

Ted was carefully using the tines of his fork to press and lift any crumbs remaining on his plate, as if he'd waste away without their nourishment. The poor creature obviously needed more food, but he'd been cut off by a well-intentioned person who still didn't understand after all the years they'd spent together. Never renowned for his scintillating wit or his conversational skills at the dinner table anyway, now Ted gazed into the middle-distance as he rested his choppers.

I was about to say something cheerful and manly to a thoughtful Trevor, when Sarah and Moon came in. They'd changed into jeans and blouses: obviously they'd abandoned their wedding garb for something more comfortable. After a quiet chat in the kitchen area with the other women, Sarah came over to sit on Trevor's knee. Handing me Pauline's camera, she said, "Take a few shots of me with my beau just after the wedding." As I did so, I wondered how the other snaps looked, since the camera had been available for anyone to use. Hopefully, the evening's events had been recorded without the fuzzy image of fingers on lenses, or too many photos of the startled looks from folks just realising the moment would forever be memorialised in colour.

After I'd taken some posed pictures of the newlyweds, Sarah yawned and said, "It looks like the host and hostess are still dressed for the wedding, while we aren't." Trevor and Ted had removed their ties and jackets to better facilitate the heavy lift of food from plate to mouth, so they were hardly paragons of spiffiness. "Pauline tells me she's perfectly comfortable in her 'maid of honour' outfit and Betty looks nice as usual, so you're the only one who's…" Sarah paused, then finished by saying doubtfully, "er…. still dressed up." She scanned my fashionable 'squeezed look' with something approaching wonder on her face. Showing insight beyond her years, she said to me, "I bet you'd rather be in t-shirt and jeans: we don't mind, since we'll be leaving soon anyway."

I grinned at her and hurried to the bedroom, where first off were my skin-tight trousers. Happily, they were beyond repair in the seat and crotch, so I spent a vengeful moment visualising them wrapped around a burning log in the stove. The jacket and shirt could be given to charity or buried in a deep hole, as long as I'd never see them again. After I'd donned my normal clothes, I joined the others, feeling relaxed and loose, as if a full-body cast had been cut away from my person.

Betty came over to the table and shot a scolding look at her husband. He'd been patting his pockets, apparently searching for his box of toothpicks, when she said to him, "Never mind the dental kit. Anyway, I thought we'd already discussed this: no one's interested in watching you dig in your pearly whites." She regarded him with an obvious lack of adoration, as he sat there trying to look hurt and misunderstood. "Come on," she said more fondly, but in a tone of voice usually directed at a dog who'd spent too much time sniffing at a scent. "I just wanted to see the newlyweds together before we left," she smiled at Sarah, who was still sitting in Trevor's lap, "I'm sure they don't need us hanging around, so let's go!" As Ted got his things together, Betty went around the table to hug and say a few words to the couple. "I can't wait to see the wedding photos," she told Sarah, "give me a shout when they're ready."

Worriedly searching through his pockets again, Ted was muttering, "I must have left them somewhere around the lodge."

"Is this all about your stupid box of

toothpicks?" asked Betty as they headed for the door. Not waiting for a reply from a rather sulky Ted, she added irritably, "Maybe Henry will find them and build a new wharf." Hustling him out of the front door, she turned to give us a smile, then they were gone.

Moon hadn't said a word since she'd joined us at the table. She took a sip of tea, then chuckled as she took in the closed front door and the receding voices of our guests as they bickered their way to the parking lot. "I hope you two were paying attention," she said to Sarah and Trevor, "that's what married life can be like: there might be disagreements, but nonetheless, it's filled with joy." Apparently unable to say this with a straight face, Moon chortled under her breath and took another sip of tea.

"Henry and Pauline have their act together here at the lake," Sarah replied brightly, "they've given us a good example to follow."

"What a nice thing to say!" exclaimed Pauline, then she regarded me appraisingly and added, "although there's still lots of room for improvement."

Since I know I'm only a smidgen away from perfection, I didn't bother responding to her slight. Anyway, I was comfy in my normal clothes and wasn't in the mood to act indignant or miffed. So I smiled at her in a loving and probably slightly unctuous way, then I nodded as if in complete agreement with her untrue statement.

Moon seemed to doubt the veracity of this display of marital diplomacy, but she turned from Pauline and me to refocus on the newly-weds. "Are you worried about Portunus?" she asked them. She'd tried making the query sound casual, but the trepidation in her voice had been unmistakeable, so an alarm started sounding behind my complacency. Then Trevor told the ladies about Portunus's visit to Three Duck Lake: by the time he'd finished his description, Moon was gazing unemotionally into the distance and this somehow made me more uneasy than any hysterical reaction ever could.

"No one knows much about him or why he's here," said Moon, still not looking at any of us, "he just showed up some time ago." She sighed, then added after a while, "But he's known to be obsessive and something of a control freak, so be careful if you have to deal with him."

Probably because he'd personally experienced Portunus's polite but scary presence, Trevor nodded slowly, but Sarah responded, "He can go stuff himself into his hat. Who cares how some homeless Spirit feels?" She dreamily studied her wedding ring, then said to her husband, "We should be heading out soon." Looking gratefully at Pauline and Moon, she added, "Thanks for everything: it was perfect, but we have to be going." After she'd gone over to praise the dogs for being so well-behaved during the ceremony, she gave them some doggy- biscuits as a reward. Since they're very fond of her, much tail-wagging and excited canine vocalisations ensued. They also very much liked the cookies, so the lodge was momentarily filled with the sound of fervid chomping.

Eventually, we all walked out into the bright summer night. Taking a deep breath and looking skyward, Sarah said, "It's so nice here, but our cabin's closer to the stars."

I was just thinking that she'd expressed her mood well, when the pragmatic and clearly unromantic Trevor looked up too. "It's a clear night," he said, gazing into the heavens, "so it'll get cooler as we head up to the cabin." Putting an arm around her shoulders, he half-asked her, "You forgot to leave a sweater in the truck, didn't you?"

When Sarah gave him a guilty nod in answer, Pauline said 'no problem', then rushed back to the lodge. She returned shortly with a cardigan for the bride and handed it to her, saying, "There's no big hurry: bring it back when you can."

While Pauline had been fetching the sweater, I'd noticed Trevor had casually walked to the rear of the Flaming Barge as it sat parked facing out. Seeing no empty cans or other noisemakers tied to the bumper there, he'd rejoined us without comment. Then he saw that I'd been watching, so he shrugged and said, "Just checking."

As she closed the lodge door and headed back to us, I lowered my voice to tell him conspiratorially, "Pauline wanted to attach three 45 gallon drums, but I dissuaded her. I told her that all the racket would probably disturb our guests, so we decided to give that particular tradition a miss. It's a good thing I'm on your side," I murmured to him as she approached us, "she can be quite rambunctious at times: the innocence and caring bit is just an act."

"Yeah sure," he replied, "I believe you," then he grinned as if he knew I'd been telling whoppers about my partner in life. He winked at Moon, who'd been standing there with a big smile on her face and saying nothing: she obviously hadn't heard the fibs I'd been flinging around about Pauline.

With the dogs staying close-by, the three of us waved to the couple as they drove out of the parking lot and towards their new life together. But there'd be no honeymoon. When Pauline had asked, Sarah had replied without any hint that she expected marriage to bring her rainbows and strawberries: "There's no time for that romantic crap," she'd said with feeling, "we have work to do." With promises they'd see us again soon, the Barge rumbled out, and Pauline and I returned to the lodge.

The Cabin and Garden Plus Two More Dogs

I spent lots of time at their cabin: I was there regularly until the fall. I suggested to Pauline that she use a baseball bat to pacify some of our more unruly clients while I was away, but she and Moon didn't seem to need my sage advice. Business at the lodge ran smoothly without me, so it's a good thing I have strong underpinnings; otherwise, I'd feel slightly unnecessary around here.

On her first visit to the newlyweds' cabin, Moon regarded the hulking bluff across the lake, rolled her eyes and turned to Trevor. "You climbed down that.....cliff?" she asked him angrily, "you're an idiot!" Although I had similar feelings about Trevor's day of adventure,

I'd not use the same words to criticise him: I prefer 'numbskull' rather than 'idiot' for example. When Sarah showed her the patch of ground adjacent to the cabin where a garden was planned, Moon got to her knees to study the earth. "You'll need some good topsoil," she declared, as she stood up and spanked her hands, "this stuff will only grow evergreens." After scanning the area again, she added, "The ground needs levelling and all those rocks will have to go, but no problem. We'll be ready to plant by spring."

On the following days, Moon had us all digging the earth behind the cabin, until a shallow depression of about thirty feet square had been formed. She suggested we use all the core samples as the bottom layer of the garden, so soon it looked like a large grill of rock bars covered the ground. After we shovelled on two-inch thicknesses of crushed gravel then sand, the patch was ready for the topsoil. Moon had no problem in getting friends to provide the necessary materials at cost, so the cleared mining route had lots of traffic for a while. I also helped Trevor with the myriad of chores involved in getting the cabin ready for winter.

This included the addition of new insulation to its tiny attic, plus the installation of a few cedar shakes to its roof. Moon had been indispensable as usual: without her, Trevor probably would've been running around like a chicken relieved of its head. He's a strong guy, but the constant stream of important decisions he had to make would get to anyone, so his normal calm outlook had been disrupted to a degree. This reminded me of my own periods of cluelessness when I first moved to Three Duck Lake, but at least he knew long ago that Moon could be trusted.

Although no thoughts of Portunus sullied our busy days, we were always aware of the huge bluff across the lake. Sitting on the cabin roof as I replaced some of the shingles, the rocky monolith seemed to lean towards me aggressively, so I chastised myself for seeing things. But being up there made me feel exposed and vulnerable, silly me, so I finished the job double-quick, then climbed down the ladder quickly to go inside.

Pauline stayed at the cabin for a night, as did Moon. Getting up with the sunrise and going down to the lake one morning to behold the blinding reflection off the bluff, Moon tried acting ho-hum about it, but she'd clearly been impressed. Trevor told me she didn't seem willing to discuss it, instead she told Sarah that tomatoes or melons probably couldn't be grown. "It gets too cold up here at night," she'd said, "stick to spuds, carrots and leeks for the first year, then we'll see how that works out." Smiling at the couple, she added, "We can always barter: your potatoes for my tomatoes, no problem."

By the time a few tentative snowflakes were being hurried along on a cold wind, the garden was ready for a spring planting and the cabin had hopefully been properly prepared for winter. Too busy to work his claim, Trevor went down to the creek to gather the wetsuits and the other gear; he obviously didn't want to leave things out for the long freeze. He bought a small tracked vehicle with an enclosed cab and room for one passenger; it'd be needed to travel over the deep snow the mining road would likely be wearing. Then he could drive down to the parked Barge and transfer to the truck; it was a hassle, but it was better than getting stuck.

Sarah and Trevor got two Lab puppies from a friend in town. When they'd been immediately christened 'Jerome' and 'Ralph', I asked if there was any particular reason those names had been chosen. "Long before I met Trevor," Sarah answered brightly, "they were boyfriends of mine. The dogs reminded me of them, that's all." Apparently, her new husband hadn't had a say in the matter, but he seemed okay with her choices. Nonetheless, I wondered how those two former paramours would take it if they knew a couple of Lab puppies had been named after them.

The Lights at Sarah's Lake

When the newlyweds came down to the lodge for a visit, they brought along the Labs to introduce to my dogs. As soon as Sarah put the puppies among my 'mature' beasts, the newcomers spied the massive Pooch, rolled over on their backs and whined plaintively. Showing her motherly side, Grace licked them all over, then lay down beside them. Banjo was ecstatic, since he seemed quick to understand that he was no longer last in the pecking order. But his happiness faded later on, when he discovered the puppies had taken a shine to him and were always underfoot. Since this supposedly messed up his contentment as he bumbled through the day, Banjo spent a lot of time alone in the bush when Jerome and Ralph were visiting.

Sarah said, "It's so nice spending the night relaxing, without having to worry about all the things that need doing." We were sitting at the table an hour after our clients had eaten and Moon didn't seem overly impressed by Sarah's proclamations of all the work she had to do.

"All the backbreaking labour must be tough," Moon said. She'd likely tried sounding sympathetic, but she hadn't seemed particularly heart-broken. "Any sign of Portunus?" she asked much too casually.

"We haven't seen him, but we know he's around," answered Sarah. Turning to Trevor, she was clearly annoyed as she said, "Tell her what you've seen."

Although he'd recently had two large wedges of blueberry pie for dessert, Trevor had been chomping through the plateful of chocolate-chip cookies Pauline had put on the table. When he realised he'd been addressed, he stopped in mid-munch and said, "Hah?"

After a weary sigh, Sarah told him to describe

the lights he'd seen late at night. "And don't forget to mention those two flying cubes you saw one morning just before sunrise. I don't think you were supposed to witness them, since it was much too early to be out of bed."

Trevor was attempting to be offhand about the matter, but he wasn't convincing. "Don't you think you're being a little dramatic?" he asked her. "The cubes were only fist-sized and did no harm."

"You told me they were so bright that they lit up the cabin along with its surroundings," Sarah said in response, "tell them about it."

Trevor shrugged and said, "It was weird: something woke me up and I was rolling over in bed, when I thought I heard a faint scraping sound. I got up to see if some critter was living in the cabin with us. But the vague noise seemed to be coming from outside, so I put on my bathrobe and quietly went out." He'd stopped his idle ingestion of cookies and was now paying himself full attention: "It was cold and a little breezy, but I could still hear the indistinct sound. It'd changed into a sort of soft fluttering and seemed to be coming from above." Appearing newly-astonished by his own words, Trevor said, "Suddenly, two bright white lights lit up the outside of the cabin one was slowly circling the building, while the other was going up to about fifty feet, then coming down and hovering at roof-level. They were so intense that I couldn't keep my eyes on them, but I think they were cubes." He wasn't trying to hide his concern any longer as he asked Moon, "Do you know what the lights mean?"

"Not really," she answered, "I've never before heard of such a thing happening. You can bet that Portunus is responsible though; it's probably just his caring way of keeping an eye on you."

Since this reply hadn't helped at all, he gave her a long, somber look, but she didn't say anything else. He turned to Sarah, who was wearing her 'inscrutable look' and said, "Then there's the 'campfire' we occasionally see on top of the bluff, just after sundown." He chuckled nervously, as if he thought we'd have difficulty believing him, adding, "The flames are blue."

I think Moon was irritated that she knew so little; this sort of thing was supposed to be in her bailiwick, after all. She stared worriedly at the couple for a moment, then loosened up and grinned at them. "Portunus hasn't made a personal appearance recently," she told them, "so that's a good sign. Maybe he's more respectful or afraid of the absent Overseer than he'd have us believe. I don't know. Obviously, he wants you to be aware of his presence, but perhaps that's all he can do." She sighed, then added, "I've felt 'out of the loop' for a while, especially with the Overseer gone indefinitely. But I think you'll be okay: as long as you don't throw wild parties or pitch your garbage into the lake, that is." We all laughed and pretended to make light of the matter, but not one of us truly convinced the others.

A Scintillating Chat

A week before we shut down for winter, I was resolutely performing my lodge duties by fishing with a client. The angling's good this time of year: the trout are fattening up for the fast-approaching cold slowdown, I suppose. I think my client, Gordie Galway, was somewhat relieved to be out in the rowboat with me and away from the loving presence of his wife and two teenaged sons. Glancing furtively behind as I rowed to my favourite spot, he asked, "You don't mind, do you?" as he took the cellophane wrapper off a cigar. Without waiting for a response, he scratched a wooden match on the sideboard and made a big production of lighting up his stogie. With a contented expression on his face, he exhaled a cloud of blue smoke, then jabbed his arms out sideways in an exaggerated yawn. "This is so nice," he said, "let's just sit here for a while." So, making sure the breeze would blow the smoke away from me, I stopped rowing and shipped the oars.

Gordie took another drag as he relaxed on the stern seat and I noticed how boney and grizzled he looked. Although skinnier than a starved worm, Mr. Galway had an impressive bearing about him. Something in the way he held himself shouted authority, so I surmised he was a military officer, or someone accustomed to issuing orders in his line of work. I found out later that he's an accountant working for a big law firm, so I wasn't even close with my guess. These faulty assessments of mine might help explain my losing nights at the poker table, but that's a topic I'd rather not pursue.

After a few minutes of silence and slow drift, he fixed on me with his intense grey eyes, then informed me he'd bought a brand new car a month ago. He'd spoken as if I should be astonished and maybe leap overboard to splash around in delight, but I hadn't brought along my water-wings, so I just nodded. "I was very careful," he told me, "I researched a number of different vehicles before I bought. My final choice runs fine." Shaking his head in a world-weary way, he added, "It doesn't seem to matter how good it might be; a car's a cash pit. All the expenses!"

He was now looking at me as if it was all my fault and he wanted an explanation. So I sighed sadly and shrugged, then gave him a head-shake in return. "Ain't that the truth," I said, "you'd probably be better off just taking the bus."

"No, no, no," he responded forcefully, "that's not what I meant. I need a vehicle to get to and from work." He gazed at the slowly-passing shoreline fifty feet away as we drifted along, then he seemed to relax. He took another long draw from his cigar, then with a satisfied expression on his face, he looked up at the blue sky and exhaled expansively. Somehow a basketball-sized cloud of his tobacco smoke remained intact, so we watched it as it sifted calmly five feet above the water and disappeared into the trees onshore. Finally turning to me, he smiled in a slightly querulous way, then told me he'd run an idea past his wife and kids which they'd thought was 'half-baked'.

"I'd like to hear your opinion," he added, "after all, you're a businessman, so you know how things work in the real world."

'That's me,' I thought to myself, 'I'm an astute galoot!' But at the same time, I wondered which 'real world' he had in mind.

Out loud, I asked him to describe his idea, then I furrowed my brow as I paid rapt attention. "Everything's expensive," he began, "whether it's insurance or gasoline prices or repair costs. Lots of businesses seem to exist only to relieve drivers of their hard-earned cash." Seeming buoyed by my studious manner, he continued: "Since so many people make their livings by screwing car owners, why not just give away the vehicles? New businesses would pop up like mushrooms and everyone would be gainfully employed. Easy! Who says politics can be complicated?"

"What about the folks working in the car factories?" I asked, "how'd they get paid?"

Clearly having anticipated the question, he replied breezily, "No problem: the government already heavily subsidises the auto industry, so paying wages wouldn't be so different."

"Who'd get the high-end cars?" I asked.

"It'd solely depend on income," he answered, "those who could afford it would get a Rolls. Others down the line would receive less pricey vehicles, while those on extended and self-imposed welfare would get roller skates." He chuckled, but I could see he was dead serious. He was regarding me in a semi-belligerent way as he waited for my response. Even though I could see a number of Grand Canyon-sized flaws in his scheme, I'd, decided long ago that it's not good policy to bicker with the guests. So I nodded and smiled, then picked up my rod to commence fishing.

I think smoking cigars is forbidden behaviour in the Galway clan, because he nervously glanced back towards the lodge and asked, "We can't be seen out here, can we?"

"Does your Missus carry around a pair of binoculars so she can keep an eye on you?" I asked.

Startled by the question and flicking an irritated glance in my direction, he muttered, "Of course not!"

"Well then," I said, "we should be okay."

He reached into his shirt pocket for another cigar and lit it. Apparently, he'd finished outlining his grand economic plan and was nodding to himself as he puffed on his cheroot. Pooch usually comes out in the boat with me, but Gordie isn't a 'dog person' (we all have our faults), so the canine had been left behind. We fished without enthusiasm or luck, until the drift took us to the Narrows and I unshipped the oars. As I rowed back to the wharf, he relaxed on the stern seat as he finished his smoke, then he flipped the butt into the lake. I don't like my lake being despoiled, but I figured giving him a tongue-lashing along with a hefty on-the-spot fine might cause a bit consternation, so I didn't say anything.

As I rowed in, I could see Pauline sitting on the wharf in a lawn chair. Wearing cutoffs, a blue blouse and shades, she only nodded curtly at my shouted greeting, then studied us intently as I drew the boat up onto the beach. Seated crossed-legged and sipping a glass of juice, she looked too elegant for the likes of me. She took off the sunglasses and smiled at Gordie as he said goodbye. As usual in her presence, I'd ceased to exist for anyone of the male gender, so there wasn't even the hint of a 'fare-thee-well' for me.

After we'd watched him disappear down the path, Pauline said, "This'll probably be the last time this year that I can sit out here in the sun. What a nice day! But sometimes there's cold in the wind: winter's coming for sure. Sarah told me on the phone this morning that a half-inch of snow fell last night at her lake." Pauline got up from her chair and said, "I'll go inside with you before I get chilled. It's a good thing Trevor cut all that firewood: they'll need it."

Dogs

*T*he arrival of fall and the cessation of clients arriving at the lodge always puts me in mind of the happy feelings connected with the start of the summer holidays. It'd been a joy to slack off then, and even though it was now the seemingly endless winter ahead, the sense of relief was the same.

I enjoyed cleaning and shuttering the cabins, while the dogs poked around outside. The path goes through a spinney of poplars between the two furthest buildings and the trees had left a carpet of leaves. They were dusted with frost and brittle in the cold, so as we walked through, they rustled loudly. Something had left an interesting scent there; as the dogs sniffed vigorously, I watched. Their breath was visible in the frosty morning air, while their tails were standing at attention. They were accustomed to the smell of rabbits, so maybe a bear or a moose had wandered through.

Just as I was heading on my way again, my old buddy Gus the Canada jay landed on my shoulder and peered at me with his intense black eyes. I'd like to think he was fond of me and was just wishing me a good morning, but I knew he'd land on anyone, the feathered little hustler. Since there wasn't any food available, he gave me what I thought was a scolding look and flew into the trees. Previously, I'd told him his iffy birdly morals would get him into big trouble one of these days. Landing on everyone and anyone, he was bound to run into somebody who'd instantly convert him into a badminton shuttlecock with a beak. But no! he obviously hadn't heeded my advice and was still perching on any Tom, Dick or Henry who happened along. He's been warned, but it won't do any good, he's a loose bird.

Ten days later we awoke to find a foot of snow on the ground, and according to Trevor on the phone, they'd got twice that at Sarah's Lake.

Since the road to my place was still usable for four-wheel drives, he picked up Pooch and me in the Barge. There wasn't room for three guests at the cabin, so he'd also invited either Pauline or Moon. But they were busy with a mysterious project that I suspect had something to do with Christmas. They'd both refused and promised to visit soon.

❧

The gravel road leading to the blacktop was unploughed as usual, but it had a few fresh vehicle tracks. As I was idly wondering who'd been using my road, Trevor turned onto the 'highway' and immediately pulled up behind a hapless driver who'd obviously just guided his chariot into the ditch. Pooch jumped from the bed of our truck to greet him in his normal effusive way. Heaven knows what the driver must have thought. We got out, and Trevor asked him, "Need a hand?"

Looking embarrassed, he answered, "I should've put on snow tires. Thanks for stopping," then he turned to ruefully regard his vehicle. It was tilted so the two passenger-side wheels were free of the snow, indicating he'd probably gone into the ditch at some speed. I was just thinking of what must've been a thrilling but brief plunge from the road, when he asked about Pooch.

The dog was now sniffing the two exposed tires of the car and looked huge with the snow background. "Oh," I explained to him casually, "he's an Asian elephant dog." Making it up as I went along, I added, "Alexander the Great used them as camp guards for a while, but they ate too much, so he switched to terriers." Because of the knowing smile on his face, I instantly knew he hadn't believed this nonsense, I found out later that he was a Kennel Club member who'd also been a judge at some meetings. So he'd probably be quite certain there weren't any 'Asian elephant dogs' running around. Maybe it was time to quit with the wit; some people, Sarah for instance, have characterised my imaginings as being 'half-wit'. Anyway, Trevor used the winch on the Barge's front end to pull the car out of the ditch and there wasn't any more talk of unusual canine breeds.

After completing our good deed, we drove through town, then up to the tracked vehicle he'd parked in the bush near the start of the mining road. The snow had been getting progressively deeper as we'd driven up, so I was relieved to transfer to something without wheels.

It was cramped with two men in the cab, but the snow presented it with no problems as we eventually travelled up the road at walking pace. The little Sno-Cat, Sarah had dubbed it 'The Doodlebug', was ideal for going over all the white stuff. It was a smooth ride. Thankfully, the steep ravine on our right was hidden by snow-laden evergreens, so it could be dismissed. Pooch had been loping easily behind as we'd moved along, then he'd leapt onto the truck's bed just as Trevor slowed to study the spot where the ravine trail started.

He stopped, then turned to me with a serious look on his face and said, "I've put most of the gear into the core-shack for the winter, but I left a couple of spades and pans near the creek. I could probably find them, so we could clear a patch beside the running water, then dig around and see if we can find anything." He resolutely turned off the ignition while still wearing a dead-pan expression and added, "There's lots of time,"

"What a good idea!" I responded ardently, "those icy ravine walls will make the descent to the creek even more exciting! We could laugh it up with a snowball fight on the way down."

After witnessing my display of ironic eager-ness, he chuckled and switched on the ignition again. "Maybe not," he muttered, then sighed and slowly shook his head as if he'd seriously con-sidered going down there himself. We motored on in an easy silence until we got to the cabin, where Sarah plus Jerome and Ralph greeted us.

⚘

The two Labs were half-grown now, but still obsequiously respectful to Pooch. The younger dogs briefly touched noses with him, looked ecstatic to be in his presence, then backed off. This was doubtlessly the canine way of saying 'your wish is my command', so no warning growls from Pooch were necessary.

It was good seeing Sarah again; I missed her frequent visits to the lodge. As I gave her a hug and a peck on the cheek, the big rock across the lake hulked behind her shoulder and marred my glad feelings a little. The bluff somehow seemed less vibrant; perhaps this was because its shoulders and head were covered in white. But despite its washed-out appearance, it still had the same brooding, angry quality. Snow had been blown into the two diagonal faults Trevor had used in his descent and for some reason, I found this unsettling. While Jerome and Ralph watched enviously, Sarah patted Pooch and spoke fondly to him, then she said to us, "Come on in and I'll put on the kettle." I tried to ignore the huge slab of rock, and we all went inside.

While we sat at the table and Sarah got the tea things ready, I noticed the CB radio had its own shelf, with pens and notebooks scattered around. Apparently, she'd been spending time talking with friends, but she clearly wasn't lonely. A framed sketch of the bluff adorned a wall, and this simple drawing seemed to make the place homey. Jerome and Ralph had stayed outside with Pooch; I could hear the three of them frisking in the snow.

"They're good dogs," said Sarah as she put the tea pot on the table. "They don't go wandering off into the bush, plus they also have a very possessive attitude towards the cabin and its surroundings. Moon doesn't think we'll have any problems with animals raiding the garden." She put a plate of peanut-butter cookies beside the teapot and gave Trevor a frosty look. "Try leaving one or two for our guest," she said to him as she pushed it a few inches closer to me. After he'd raised his eyebrows in hurt innocence, she snapped her fingers and muttered something about 'almost forgetting'. She hurried into the bedroom, then returned shortly with something in each hand. "Trevor carved a mate for the figure of a loon he gave me after we'd first met." She put them on the table and gazed at them fondly, saying, "Aren't they beautiful!"

Since one had its head turned, it looked as if it was viewing the other. Trevor had imbued his carving with life, as usual. The two figures were each only about one third actual size, but they appeared ready to go fishing. I nodded with approval as I looked at the meticulously-painted feathers while Sarah smiled lovingly at him. But in truth, I felt a little jealous of his talent.

I'd once found a vaguely fish-shaped piece of driftwood on the beach that I figured was halfway to being a work of art. All it'd need would be a few careful cuts with my hunting knife and maybe some sandpaper work. After I'd applied my magic touch to the piece of wood, my 'fish' looked like a garter snake that'd been squashed on the highway. Probably because of all the salt it'd absorbed during its sea-journey, the driftwood burned with a pretty blue green flame when I chucked onto our fire. Anyway, after Sarah had returned the two figures to her bedside table, she joined us as we drank our tea.

"So, what do you think?" she asked me as she looked around the room in a house-proud way.

"Very nice," I answered as I regarded their snug home in the woods, "but will there be space for the piano?"

Sarah snickered and said, "No, we'll have to give that a miss for the time being: the chandeliers too."

I chuckled, but I felt a bit sad at the same time. It seemed like only yesterday she was just a friend's daughter who Pauline had promised to care for during one summer. Now that she was married and was clearly committed to be living at the cabin, through no fault of her own she made me feel ancient. She looked at the cookie plate, where a single large one was skulking on the porcelain. In fact, all three of us were viewing it with varying degrees of intensity. Finally, she offered it to me, but when I declined, she said to Trevor, "You'd better take it. We can't have you starving to death before lunch: it might take the shine off the day."

As he snagged the last cookie, I said, "That reminds me," then I went out to the Doodlebug to fetch my duffle bag from its small deck. When I returned, I said to her, "Pauline sends you a goody bag with her compliments," then I handed her the small pack I'd taken out of the bigger one. Among many other things, was a big jar of beef stew and some spuds.

"Perfect!" said Sarah, "I was wondering what to have for supper. Turning to me, she asked, "You're not staying here overnight, are you?"

"If you ever have other guests," I replied huffily, "I advise you not to pose that particular question: it's sort of unwelcoming."

Accustomed to my japes and pretended hurt feelings, Sarah replied, "Yeah sure, thanks for the etiquette tip. So, will you be staying?" After telling her that I was just visiting for the day, she said, "Good!" then apparently realised her response had been slightly inhospitable. "I don't mean to say it's not nice seeing you," she hurriedly explained to me, "it's just that I'm not prepared." I nodded as if I understood, but I sulked and sighed anyway. Since I obviously wasn't going to help her out, she changed the subject. "What do you boys have planned for the day?" she asked, but I could tell she wasn't much interested.

She was now looking at the radio, then she cast a glance at the wall-clock as Trevor answered, "I just wanted to show Henry our new vehicle and maybe we'll build a doghouse for Jerome and Ralph. It depends on how we feel."

Though she clearly hadn't been listening to him, she muttered, "That's nice," and without pausing or even looking at him, she added, "I'd better call Eric: it's past nine."

She radioed in every morning to let Trevor's friend in town know that things were okay. Apparently, this daily call had turned into increasingly long chats, with Sarah doing most of the talking. After Trevor'd told me this on our trip up here, I'd asked, "Can you trust that Eric has no ulterior motives concerning Sarah? To me, he sounds like a smooth operator." Having introduced this seed of suspicion like a good friend should, it was now my turn to change the topic. "Let's go down to the wharf while Sarah makes her call," I suggested to Trevor, "It's probably better that we don't hear what's said."

When we went outside, I was surprised that the edge had been taken off the cold. Low clouds hovered over the bluff, there was hardly any wind and the snow underfoot had lost its powdery dryness. The dogs accompanied us down to the lake, but when they saw that nothing interesting was happening, they soon disappeared.

Sarah's Lake had a dark, unfrozen path about fifty feet in diameter right in the middle, so the sissy in me went 'brrrr'; I try to hide this side of my personality, but it often minces into the limelight anyway. We carefully negotiated the narrow walkway and stepped onto the frozen-in wharf. Our weight made it loudly break from the encompassing ice, so it was floating freely again. It was no longer sporting its Halloween colours either, but was now clad in more appropriate dark green outdoor carpeting. After gazing out at the rather forlorn white surface for a while, Trevor said, "I was afraid the dogs would get themselves into trouble, but they clearly avoid going out onto the thin ice. Natural instinct, I suppose."

I was just about to tell him that Pooch had been the same, when I heard a movement behind us. Thinking that Sarah had finished her radio call and was joining us, I turned to greet her happily, but I was shocked to see Portunus.

Portunus Visits

A s Trevor spun around to regard our uninvited guest without any hint of a glad
welcome, Portunus smiled at him. But I think
he was just showing off his big teeth, since the
friendly expression didn't reach his black eyes.
He was standing onshore with his hands on his
hips and was observing us clinically, like we
were unpredictable but harmless specimens and
he was curious about what we might do next.
He was wearing the same shirt and pants, so I
was beginning my internal rant about cleanliness, when I stopped myself short as I realised
something. Portunus is hardly the type to stand
in front of his closet, furrow his brow and ask
himself, "Now, what should I wear today?" The
poor guy probably doesn't even have a closet or
a selection of snappy styled changes, so I ceased

my judgemental thoughts. As if it was a sentient creature quite apart from himself, his ridiculous hat somehow seemed more out of place in the winter day. He was also wearing a jacket. The unbuttoned short coat was his concession to the cold I guess, but the garment was insubstantial and showed he didn't feel the day as would an actual human being. As I was thinking that he appeared almost like a person, I noticed he was standing on the carpet of snow and hadn't sunk in, so I quickly revised my opinion of his normalcy. I glanced at Trevor and could tell he was highly irritated by Portunus's sudden appearance. The two stared at each other and didn't say anything, so I whispered to Trevor to be careful not to get our guest excited.

Having heard this warning, Portunus said to us, "Don't worry, I didn't come here to explode." Seeming to be in a contemplative mood, he regarded the mostly-frozen lake, plus the sullen bluff. Nodding at the wharf, then gesturing at the cabin (even though it couldn't be seen from this level), Portunus said, "I like what you've done so far; you've built a good place to live."

Not only was he being positive, but his usual patronising air wasn't apparent, so I got really suspicious of him. While I was busily thinking ill of him, he said to me in a friendly way, "Hi Henry. How's Pauline?"

It gave me the heeby-jeebies as I realised how much he knew about me. Nonetheless, I answered casually, "Oh, she's fine. I'll tell her you asked about her."

He chuckled and told me, "I bet that'll make her day!"

This self-deprecation wasn't his style, and I could see that Trevor had also picked up on the change. We were still standing on the wharf, so clearly neither of us wanted to get closer to him, while Portunus hadn't even stepped onto the walkway. So, we gawked at each other across twenty feet of snow and ice for an uncomfortable moment.

He didn't in any way seem affected by the weather or the time of year. It was hovering around freezing, which we view as being balmy during the winter months, but even then, we don't run around in summer jackets and shirts. I looked at his shiny riding boots and it fleetingly occurred to me that footwear probably wasn't a problem for him, since he'd never have to worry about the damp of the snow.

After our pregnant silence, I thought he sounded a bit apologetic as he said, "I just dropped by to wish you well for the winter and to tell you that things have changed." Now he was speaking as if he couldn't believe what'd been happening, but I suspected his bewilderment was false. Maybe my skepticism was misplaced, but the more I saw him, the less I trusted him. "Don't ask me to explain," he said, wagging a finger at us as though we were frantic to know. He looked up at dreary low clouds with obvious displeasure, then at the snow-clad surroundings in general. "I don't like the winters here," he muttered and shot us a look as if it was all our doing. He heaved a hard-done-by sigh, then regarded us sharply and said, "I'll be leaving for a few months; I have to find out what's been going on behind the scenes."

"Gee, we'll miss you," Trevor replied, "things around here just won't be the same without you."

I thought Portunus would take exception to this sarcastic utterance, but he didn't. He only gave Trevor a hurt look and said, "There are a few things I have to consider, so I'll see you in the spring." He walked soundlessly a few paces down the shoreline and paused to rummage for something in his jacket pocket. His Spookiness then turned ninety degrees into the bush and disappeared among the trees without a fond farewell or a friendly wave. We stood on the wharf and stared stupidly at the spot where he'd gone from view. There weren't any footprints leading there and only the quiet remained.

Since Portunus is always such an exciting guy, I had to wait a minute to calm myself after he'd departed. Finally, I asked Trevor, "Don't you think it was rude of him to leave so quickly?"

"Maybe he was getting chilly," he answered straight-faced; it was plain he had other things on his mind. As he opened his mouth to say something else, there was a scream from the cabin, a short pause, then an angry bellow. Since it was obviously Sarah's voice, my first thought was that Portunus had dropped in to say hello and had startled her. Although I quickly realised she wouldn't react in such a way, I knew our friend in the peculiar hat was up to something.

Without a word, Trevor scrambled along the walkway with me a pace behind. Making haste while heading up the path to the cabin, he got his feet tangled and fell backwards onto me. Just as we both got vertical again, Pooch came belting out of nowhere and knocked us down again. Not stopping to apologise for his boorish behaviour, the dog rushed away and we didn't see him till later. As we got upright again, another loud vocalisation erupted from the cabin. Since there hadn't been fear in her voice but only rage, my concern had turned into curiosity by the time he flung open the door and we charged in.

We saw Sarah angrily standing over Ralph, as she brandished a headless loon at him. Most dogs can't hide their shame and he wasn't an exception. Ralph had everything on the droop: his stationary tail was inches from the floor and he'd bowed his head. With his ears flopped forlornly down, he was regarding the agitated human female with trepidation. In other words, he looked guilty as hell. The flecks of paint I could see on his chops also hinted that he was probably the one who'd done it.

Sarah was holding the decapitated loon carving in front of his nose and yelling, "Look what you've done, you stupid dog!" Thinking she was offering the defunct figurine to him, he tried taking it from her hand. She snatched it away and regarded Ralph disbelievingly, as if she couldn't fathom how a supposedly intelligent beast could be so obtuse. Actually, the dog reminded me of Banjo, but I thought it best not to mention this, since it's not my place to be casting aspersions on members of their household.

The half-chewed and half-painted chunk of ragged wood she was waving in front of Ralph's face, no longer bore any resemblance to a pretty bird. Its head and neck were now likely only small splinters scattered somewhere, while the body had a carelessly-sampled and a half-cooked chicken look to it. Jerome had been watching his brother's extreme discomfort from a few paces away, as if he was saying, 'I don't know this guy: what a boob!' He kept glancing at us, then at Ralph. Finally he lay down and sighed, which is probably the doggy equivalent of rolling one's eyes. The lack of brotherly sport was even apparent to a beast like Ralph with hardly any grey matter between his ears, so he knew he had to take Sarah's outrage all by himself. After loudly recounting a not-so-glowing history of his lineage, Sarah went to the door and opened it, saying to the cringing dog, "I can't bear looking at you any more. Get out."

Ralph scurried through with obvious relief, while at the same time staying as far from her as possible. He was quickly followed by Jerome, but there was no sign of Pooch outside. My dog plainly hadn't wanted to get involved in the sordid 'chewed loon' affair, so he'd made himself scarce. This rapid exit had shown cogent thought, so it was just bad luck that Trevor and I had gotten in his way. Perhaps the dog might consider that not everyone enjoys being bowled over by an accelerating and four-legged defensive end-type dressed in a fur coat.

As Sarah slammed the door shut and gazed at the critically wounded loon in her hand, I thought she was about to start crying. But she just angrily shook her head and handed the raggedy lump of wood to her husband. As he distastefully surveyed the damage to his artwork, he was clearly upset too. After his scrutiny, he marched over to the woodstove and said, "All the time and effort it took, oh well." He opened the firebox door and casually flipped it into the flames. Then he went into the bedroom and returned shortly, saying to her, "Its mate somehow escaped the dog," he said as he put an arm around her shoulder, "so it's fine, I'll carve you another."

A coating of anger covered her heart-break, so I'm sure she was torn between either throwing a fit or crying. I think she was about to do both simultaneously, but Trevor interrupted her dramatic moment. Addressing her with a fondly scolding tone to his voice, he said quietly, "You have to remember to keep the bedroom door closed. Dogs will be dogs."

Stifling her emotions, Sarah laughed unconvincingly, then shrugged and said, "You're right, it's spilled milk. It won't happen again." Even though she was now acting as if she'd accepted the fact that Ralph had destroyed her wedding gift, she was obviously still upset. Since momentarily there was no love lost between herself and the absent Ralph, plus there was no one present to berate, she looked at us helplessly and shook her head again.

"What's been done is done and there's nothing we can do to change it," said Trevor. He was trying to be calmly philosophical, but it was plain that he was still highly displeased. Breaking himself out of his angry funk, he turned to me and asked, "Feel like building a doghouse? It's not so cold out there."

Doing something nice for the two canine brothers seemed inappropriate, given the circumstances. But I was glad to leave her lingering and room-filling wrath, so I nodded, then went out the door. Trevor didn't follow immediately, but closed it softly behind me and I could hear his consoling voice as he spoke with Sarah for a while. I scanned the surroundings as I stood there waiting, but there was no sign of the dogs. Idly speculating, I was coming to the conclusion that Ralph had at least a half-clue more than Banjo. The adolescent Lab knew his presence wasn't appreciated at the moment, so he'd left. But Banjo would be totally unaware of the bad feelings he himself had invoked; he wasn't clever enough to hide. As usual, he'd probably leave dog spit and nose prints on everything, as he ineptly travelled through his day. He could be counted on not to dwell on past happenings. Put another way, it was unlikely to have been a learning experience for him. So Ralph is probably more intelligent, but that's hardly a ringing endorsement of his mental keenness. It's like saying a tree stump is smarter than a traffic sign; nothing can be proven and anyway, who cares?

After this interlude of slightly fractured internal dialogue, I tried shaking my head to clear my mind. Instead of clarity, I got an image of Ralph taking the loon figure off Sarah's bedside table, then lying down so he could have a good chew.

Thankfully, this unhelpful picture of canine bliss vanished as Trevor came through the door and closed it softly behind him. "She's gonna call a friend on the radio," he explained to me, "so she can tell her what's happened." Rolling his eyes, he added, "Lucky friend!" He smiled at Sarah's supposed overreaction, but he was obviously still angry that the dog had eaten his wedding gift to her.

Trevor had taken apart the boxes of stone rods, so sheets of plywood leaned against the core shack's walls. He'd glued some of the wood into double thicknesses, so we used these to construct a rather snazzy two-dog house. Its roof could be lifted off to facilitate cleaning and it was carpeted with the wharf's former colourful covering. "The dog's won't mind the orange and black," he said, as he cut it to size with his hunting knife. He'd clearly dismissed the loon incident and was once again his steadfast old self as he asked, "Do you think we should add a couple of windows with flower boxes?"

"That'd be too much," I responded, "how about simply hanging a framed picture on a wall?"

"A picture of what?" he asked.

"A cat?" I answered, "or maybe a nice landscape."

Seeming to consider the perplexing problems inherent to the interior design, Trevor wrinkled his brow and finally said, "I'm not familiar with their taste in art, so I'll have to ask. Meanwhile, let's just leave the walls blank."

After we finished construction, Trevor took me for a hike down one of the trails he'd been cutting. It started snowing hard; large and complicated-looking flakes reduced visibility to a few yards and the wind got stronger. Since neither of us was wearing skis or snow shoes, we turned and headed back to the cabin. The dogs magically appeared, greeted us as if they didn't have a care in the world, then joined us for the return journey. I noticed our inward-bound tracks had been covered by the heavily falling snow and Trevor must have seen the same thing.

"This is the first real dump we've had at the lake," he said, "the weather around here is highly localised." Grinning ruefully, he added, "So far, most of the snow seems to want to fall on the mining road, so I'm glad I bought the Doodlebug." By the time we were kicking snow off our boots at the cabin's door, I was concerned that I'd be prolonging my visit indefinitely. Seeming to read my mind, he said confidently, "Don't worry, I'll get you home."

Sarah fed us each a bowl of vegetable soup, then two egg salad sandwiches with gherkins on the side. "Sorry about the bread," she told me earnestly, "it's two days old." Giving her beloved a meaningful look, she said, "Since I don't have an oven yet, I can't do any baking. So I disguised what was available by toasting it. Is everything okay?"

"The sandwiches are very good," I opined, "but a cook should never tell on herself. You should act like everything's hunky-dory as you watch your latest victim choke and die." Feigning outrage, I added, "Have you learned nothing through all your years of work at the lodge, about serving the public?" She giggled and punched me playfully on the shoulder, but I think the lack of a stove was still really bugging her.

Trevor used his sleeve to clean a peephole in the window. After gazing out for a minute, he said, "It's coming down harder now, if that's even possible. Maybe I'll have to re-think my plan of working at the garage during winter. I wonder what's happening to the mining road now?"

"It's probably buried under forty feet of snow," I answered cheerfully, "so we're likely all doomed." Turning to Sarah, I asked, "How much food do we have?"

She looked a bit startled as she opened her mouth to reply, but Trevor interjected. Clapping me on the shoulder and regarding me fondly, he said, "We can always count on you to say something comforting, so it'll be a drag to have you leave."

"You want me to go?" I asked, acting surprised and not helping the social discomfort at all.

Sarah sparked up a gas lamp as Trevor glanced out the window again and said, "It's dark out there and it's only just noon. I think we're in the middle of a big storm. I'd better get you out and now."

"Will you bother coming back?" I asked as if Sarah didn't exist, "or are you planning to stay at the lodge a few days?"

"No, I'd better return," he answered, then he gestured nonchalantly at her with his thumb and added, "Can't leave the wife out here by herself; doing that sort of thing might ruin a guy's reputation."

Sarah clearly hadn't listened to our conversation with anything approaching a humorous outlook. She knew we were only joking, but I could see she was getting ready to blow. Before she could endow us with a dramatic scene, I hastily grabbed my duffle bag off the floor and zippered it closed. Then I hugged her around the shoulders and kissed the side of her head as I told them I was ready to go.

After Trevor and I got settled in the Doodlebug, he said to me, "I didn't think informing Sarah of Portunus's little visit would be a good idea, especially considering the circumstances. I'll tell her later."

Back to the Lodge

As we got underway, it was so dark that he switched on the headlights. But the heavily falling snow just reflected the brightness back into our eyes, so he finally doused the lights. The windshield was constantly being coated with snow and the wipers couldn't handle it. Trevor frequently had to crank down his window and reach around to clear the windscreen on our slow way down the road.

I could just see the pink of Pooch's tongue as he loped easily behind. He likes the snow, which is diametrically contrary to his feelings about rain. The only sign of the buried road was the ribbon of gaps among the tree trunks, so Trevor guided the vehicle carefully. At one point on our slow journey around the side of the hill, we lost track of the road's perimeters, so Trevor stopped and with difficulty walked ahead for a look. When he returned and slammed the door closed, he said, "No problem, we aren't about to plunge down the ravine."

I hadn't been thinking about the steep walls with the raging creek below, but it was nice being reminded, and his confidence really put me at ease. My side of the windshield was a blank white: the wiper had given up trying to shift the heavy snow and was now ensconced in a thick layer of the white stuff. Since my window wasn't much better, I was frequently glancing over my shoulder to see where we'd been. Pooch had decided to jump onto the bed of the vehicle and was intently watching the tracks the Doodle-bug was making in the snow. The rear window was accidentally being swept clean by Pooch's slowly waving tail, but I found this close-up view of his hind end particularly uninspiring. As we motored to a lower elevation, the snow gradually stopped coming down with the same intensity, but it was still falling steadily.

At the bottom of the hill where the ground is rocky and firm, Trevor'd spent a day cutting a parking spot for his two vehicles. Though its location is only a few yards away from the mining road, it's hidden in the trees. As we pulled up alongside the Barge, he said, "All our tracks will be covered up by the falling snow and anyhow, no one else comes up here, especially in the winter." He shut off the engine, and we quickly transferred to the truck, where Pooch happily stretched out on the rear seat of the crew-cab.

Driving through the ten inches of accumulated snow at this elevation was a drastic change from the Doodlebug. The truck was roomier and much quieter, maybe because the engine wasn't housed in a thin metal console like in the Sno-Cat, and wasn't in the cab with us. Trevor turned on the radio and we listened to a sad song about lost love. The heart-broken female singer had a high-pitched nasal voice and sounded like she'd been huffing helium between her teardrops. Soon Trevor turned off the musical accompaniment, and we continued on our way in blessed silence; the four-wheel-drive had no problem getting to the 'highway'. As we turned onto the blacktop and headed into town, he asked me, "Notice anything different about Portunus?"

I nodded as I offered him one of two wrapped mints I'd found in my pocket. Since refusing sustenance of any kind just isn't his thing, he took it, then tooted his horn and waved to the driver of a pickup going the other way. "Sorry," he muttered, "you were saying?"

"I noticed our friend in the silly hat was less hostile than usual," I replied, "he seemed aggrieved, if anything."

"Yes," said Trevor, "I felt that too. And he's leaving for the winter, so what's going on?"

"I have no idea," I answered, "maybe Moon has more details."

The snow was still falling as we drove into the lodge's parking lot. Pooch jumped out of the backseat as soon as I opened the door, then he joined Banjo and Grace as they welcomed us home. As the dogs disappeared into the bush after their glad greetings, Trevor said, "Say hello to Pauline for me. I should get right back to the cabin: Sarah might get out of sorts if I stay here for a visit." Chuckling at this understatement, he added, "I'll phone tonight."

I grabbed my duffle bag and waved as he drove away, then I headed to the lodge.

I could see Pauline's footprints in the snow going up to Moon's, so I knew the place would be empty when I opened the door. I made a pot of tea, then I sat at the table and thought about Trevor's return journey along the snow-packed mining road in the noisy but efficient Doodle-bug. At least they wouldn't have the pleasure of Portunus's company for the winter, and this was doubtless good news. But his promised reappearance in the spring wasn't something to anticipate with glee. In fact, it seemed an ominous pledge. But Portunus wouldn't be showing his face for months. In the meantime, the couple was very busy getting settled and his vow seemed lost in all the activity.

Trevor built a proper ice-fishing shack which was much roomier than the cramped, two-man coffin he'd constructed at Three Duck Lake. He also bought a wood-burning oven and set it up in a corner of the core shack. Now Sarah could bake the cookies, pies and bread necessary for his survival.

Thanks to Pauline's and Moon's strict kitchen instructions, Sarah quickly learned to play the stove like a piano. After sampling a walnut and raison oatmeal cookie she'd brought from the cabin, Pauline said, "Humm, not bad," which was actually high praise, coming from her about someone else's baking. Slightly burned on the lower edges with scorched-looking and golden brown undersides, they were presenting themselves exactly how good cookies should, so I tried one too. I liked it very much, but I didn't gush about it; this might be pure fabrication on my part, but I think my wife is a bit touchy about me going gaga over a friend's cooking. Pauline's always encouraging and she'll praise when it's deserved, but I get the feeling that sometimes she's not as pleased as she seems. Anyway, I nodded and said, "Very nice," without much enthusiasm, then I added unctuously, "but not as good as yours, my sweet." Not easing my discomfort in any way, Pauline informed me that she'd given the recipe to Sarah. "The cookies are the same as you get here," she said, not letting me off the hook.

"But they don't have your magic touch," I replied, then I hastily exited to chop some wood that suddenly needed my attention.

All three dogs knew that when snow lay on the ground at Three Duck Lake, human visitors would no longer be arriving to crowd up the place. The canine crew seemed to relax and no doubt knew that anyone they might encounter on the trail would probably have four legs. Although they plainly enjoyed being out in the white stuff, they spent a lot more time than usual sleeping on their rug near the stove. I suppose they were in partial hibernation, like us.

Moon came down to the lodge in the evenings to play in our ongoing Scrabble tournament. Pauline had put an end to Moon's winning streak, but she'd unintentionally made me feel like an also-ran in the process. It just wasn't right that the women won most of the time, since I'm supposed to be the wordsmith around here. And it doesn't help that Moon regards me with pity as I pack up the board after another of my losing games. "Never mind," she tells me soothingly, "you did your best." On one occasion, after a kindly and compassionate perusal of my supposedly befuddled face, she wrinkled her brow and helpfully suggested, "Maybe you should eat more fish, you know, for brain-food."

Thanking her avidly for her unsolicited advice, I added brightly, "See you tomorrow!" even though she hadn't yet searched out her boots from under her chair.

"You want me to leave before I can give you some more useful hints on how to sharpen up your mind?" she asked huffily.

Having used the 'hurt and insulted' routine many times myself, I knew enough not to be shamed. So I grinned bravely, as if I'd just overcome the defeat and wanted nothing more than to go to bed. Thinking I hadn't noticed, Moon rolled her eyes at Pauline and left. After she'd gone, we had a mug of cocoa and chatted about all the newlyweds' efforts at Sarah's Lake. Portunus's name wasn't mentioned, but his presence seemed to lurk behind our words, nonetheless.

They joined us for Christmas that winter, but other than that, we didn't see the couple until spring. But we didn't lose touch; Sarah phoned often and Trevor called me every ten days or so. "I've decided not to work at the garage for the time being," he told me. "My replacement is working out fine and anyhow, it's a hassle for me to get down there every day," I noticed he hadn't mentioned his gold claim as being an alternative source of income. He clearly didn't want to announce this happy state of affairs over the radio-horn and I understood.

"Have you been doing much carving?" I asked. I felt silly saying 'over' after each question and since the reception was still clear as a bell, I'd abandoned radio protocol.

Giving a miss to proper procedure himself, he answered, "Yes, and that reminds me. Is the offer to buy my carvings still a go?"

"Of course!" I responded, "they'll sell well at the lodge; that is, if they're not masticated and shredded before the public can see them."

Trevor chuckled and said, "It's hard to be sure, but I think Ralph now knows that objects sitting on tables shouldn't be chewed. Sarah's been quite forceful with him about this," he observed soberly, but then he chortled again.

After a moment, he added, "I'm now working on a hunched-down fox looking at a grouse. It's tricky, using just one piece of wood, but I enjoy the challenge. The carving will be about a foot long, with heights and widths half that."

"I like it and I haven't even seen it yet!" I enthused, "I'll buy it! As a matter of fact, consider it, along with your next five pieces, as being commissioned by the lodge. Is that okay by you?"

"Sure," he responded happily, "since I've already made another mate for Sarah's Loon and I probably won't be working at the garage any more, that's a good motivation for me to keep busy." He finished off talking by saying, "Don't worry about Ralph and his chewing necessities, the dogs are under control."

"Famous last words," I intoned in a doomsday voice. We agreed to discuss prices face-to-face, then we signed off as Pauline shouted a hello to Sarah.

Skiing with Pauline is one of my favourite ways to take the dogs for their morning walk. One day, we'd stopped to take off our jackets and to look at the lodge across the melting ice of the lake. She whipped out her camera and smiled, saying, "Remember the photo I sent to my mom, which she then turned into Christmas cards? Let's see what she does with this shot: same subject, but the end of winter, plus you'll be smiling into the camera, off to the side of course."

So she set up the picture with me looking relaxed and with the lodge in the background. As I posed, I felt my skis lose traction on the easy slope down to the lake, so I slowly succumbed to gravity and started sliding backwards. I'd only moved a foot or two before my back edges dug in; I had time to squawk in surprise as I fell awkwardly into the slushy snow. During this rather peaceful interlude, I heard the clicking of her camera, so I suspected that my loved-one had abandoned any thoughts of posed shots. A big lump of wet snow let go of its branch and fell onto my chin. Then it slid under my sweater as, I suppose, it searched for a nice warm place to melt. I said, "Oh darn!" (or something like that) and got out from under the tree. But since my skis were crossed, I instantly returned to the spot where I'd been lying before, and I studied the sky some more. I also made some feeble movements to rid myself of the cold pool of snow water forming around my belly-button region.

Pauline took the skis off me, then helped me regain my feet and checked me out. After her casual perusal of my form, she said, "You could've been hurt, but luckily you fell on your head. So you're probably okay." I found her caring nature really put a glow on the day, so I didn't grab her camera and throw it out onto the melting lake-ice. A week later, she showed me three photos she was sending to her mother in Denmark. The first showed me smiling in a self-satisfied way, with the lodge across the lake in the background. In the second one, I was wearing a startled look as I started on my brief journey down the hill. The third photo didn't show my visage at all. It was only a shot of a figure lying in the snow with his face hidden under the branches of a small tree. In her responding letter, her mother hardly mentioned me, but she did say I looked healthy and fit. 'Has he ever thought about taking skiing lessons?' she asked, as if she was only being politely curious, then she went on to other things.

Overpriced Lemons

We'd already had two weeks of clients at Three Duck Lake by the time the snow surrounding the couple's cabin had melted. One evening Trevor phoned to tell me he'd driven to the start of the scary trail down to the creek. "Not much sunshine can get into the ravine," he said, "so there's still a lot of ice and snow. It's too dangerous to climb down there now; I'll probably have to wait for another ten days or so."

Although I knew he was anxious to start panning gold again, I told him to be patient. "I'm glad you're being cautious," I told him, "wait until it's safe." Since I was beginning to remind myself of a granny giving overly-protective advice to someone who didn't need it, I changed the subject. "Your carvings are selling well," I informed him, "and I'm keeping the fox and grouse tableau for myself. I'll buy any figurines you make in the future."

"Glad to know that!" he responded, "it's been good of you to help us out, we sure appreciate it."

"No problem," I replied, "we're happy to be supportive; you and Sarah have worked hard, so you both deserve a helping hand. Have Jerome and Ralph been behaving themselves?"

Chuckling as he answered, he said, "They love their house, but I guess it's still too nippy around here for them to overnight in the place."

Up until now, the radio-phone connection had been impeccable. Eric had been doing a bang-up job. But now the sound of a small herd of shoed horses running on pavement suddenly came down the line. The noise grew in volume for about five seconds, then the clippity-clop ceased as abruptly as it'd started. After a brief silence, Trevor asked, "Did you hear that too, or was it just on my side?"

"I heard a voice saying something in French to a whinnying horse," I answered, "is that what you mean?"

There was another much longer silence, doubtlessly as he mulled over my observations. Finally, he said, "Never mind all that; we were talking about Jerome and Ralph. I built a dog-gy-door for them and so far they've abandoned their house for the cabin with its stove. What a couple of powder-puffs!" Then he added fondly, "But they're good dogs. Just to be careful, I try to keep chewable valuables out of Ralphs reach, but thanks to Sarah, I think he knows by now."

"That's good," I replied, "we can do without crippled moose figurines attempting to stand on a shelf in our gift shop. Did you get a painting to hang on the doghouse wall?" I asked as if I was serious.

"Of course," he answered, "the place needed some classy art. So I got a picture of a fire hydrant standing beside a lawn on a tree-lined street. In a strange way, it kinda goes with the carpet."

Unless the houses were bright orange with black lawns, I imagined the colours of the paint-ing would clash horribly with the Halloween tones of the floor-covering. But I let it pass. Instead of further discussing the doghouse living room and its colour scheme, I asked, "Any sign of Portunus?"

He was trying to be blasé, but I could hear his voice tighten as he said, "No, I haven't seen him this spring. Moon recently found out more about the …. er, situation and I guess she hasn't told you yet." He paused, but he was still depressing the 'transmit' button on the microphone, so I heard Sarah in the background call Portunus a rude name.

When I finally got the chance to speak again, I raised my voice and said, "Hey Sarah! I know you're listening, so you can stop pretending to be busy! If you persist with the barnyard language, you'll go cross-eyed and all your teeth will fall out." I finished by adding scornfully, "Not even your own husband will want to be seen with you, so going to nice restaurants or night spots will be out of the question."

After a rather startled silence, she came on the line and said with a distinct lack of sincerity, "I'm glad you're around to give me these life lessons. I don't know what I'd do without you!"

"You'd be lost," I said as if this was a self-evident fact. "Just heed your elders, young lady," I carried on snippishly, "and you can lose the sarcasm too. Now, put Trevor back on before I get angry enough to tear a kleenex asunder with my bare hands."

She giggled, then tried to reply, but she gave up and just laughed again. After a bit of dead air, she returned and said, "Thanks for the etiquette tip; I'll try to clean up my act. Here's Trevor."

"I couldn't agree with you more," he said to me as soon as he came on the line, "sometimes her bad language even embarrasses the dogs." Since there was a hoot of indignation from Sarah at this pronouncement, I thought it best not to indulge in a discussion about her occasional tendency to express herself like a hung over longshoreman.

Instead I asked him, "What did Moon tell you about Portunus?"

"Not much," he replied. After only uttering those two syllables, I could hear the tension return to his voice. "I don't want to talk about it over the radio," he said, suddenly sounding tired, "can we get together soon?"

"Whenever you're ready, give me a shout," I responded, "and don't forget to bring along any of your finished carvings." We chatted briefly about the mining road and how the now unnecessary Doodlebug was parked near the cabin, then we rang off.

Just as I was hanging up the phone, Moon came in. Pauline fetched the Scrabble box from a cupboard and said, "I'll put on the kettle." Moon had the board and pieces all set up by the time Pauline came to the table carrying a tray. They arranged mugs, tea pot and plate of cookies around the board without a word; they were obviously well-practiced at the routine. After settling at the table, I told Moon about Trevor's phone call, then asked her what she'd discovered about Portunus. "As I said before," she replied, stirring honey into her tea, "everyone finds him … disagreeable. And the Overseer wasn't pleased to have to return from his sabbatical, or whatever." She chuckled drily, then said, "Apparently, he heard about Trevor climbing halfway down the wall, then jumping into the lake. The Overseer viewed this ultimatum from Portunus to

Trevor as being directly contrary to orders." She stopped talking, looked at the plate of cookies, raised an eyebrow at Pauline and asked, "From Sarah's oven?" then took one without waiting for a response. After taking a bite of it and nodding to herself, Moon continued by asking me in a forthright manner, "If someone on the staff of a big company is causing problems, but there's no concrete reason for firing him, what usually happens?"

"The trouble-maker is transferred far away," I answered promptly, "so he'll be someone else's concern."

She smiled grimly at me and said, "You got it right the first time; I think the Overseer is doing exactly that." After shrugging slightly and taking a sip of tea, she added, "This would be good news for the couple, but I don't believe Portunus will be ecstatic to cross the Atlantic and return to Gibraltar. He knows he doesn't fit in around here and I'm hoping he won't make his departure a dramatic one. But who knows? He's a peculiar being with an attitude problem, so I'm worried about Sarah and Trevor. They've seemed to dismiss him as a tiresome presence, but he might show them what happens when he's upset."

"You haven't met him, right?" asked Pauline.

"That's the problem," Moon answered, "I'm relying on second-hand information here. I've never had the pleasure of being in his company."

Since there was nothing we could presently do about this situation, we talked idly of other things as we played Scrabble. Without seeming to expend much mental effort, Moon won all three games, with me coming in a distant last each and every time. At one point in the proceedings, I whined about the lousy letter-tiles I was getting from the bag. She regarded me with her maddening, saintly look and said, "It was only bad luck, one of these days you'll get better letters, then maybe you'll win a game or two. I know it's frustrating, but keep trying!" After this patronising pep talk, she winked at me encouragingly, and told us she was heading back to her cabin. Giving me what I interpreted as a smirk, she said as she left, "Keep me updated on any news coming from Sarah's Lake." The dogs joined her for the short walk to her place, and Pauline and I were left alone in the lodge.

"When are you and Trevor getting together next?" she asked, obviously not wanting to pursue the topic of my dismal performance on the Scrabble board. The game's simply a challenging pastime that we all enjoy, so I didn't want to sulk or to indicate my peevishness in any way. With the force of will, I tamped down the memory of Moon's blithe manner and forced myself to be civil. "It's up to him," I answered, "we'll probably meet soon after the upcoming weekend."

Pauline nodded in a pre-occupied way as she prepared our cocoa, then sat with me and looked worried. "I wish we knew more about Portunus," she said, still clearly concerned about him, "what's his game anyway?"

She was studying my face as if I might have the answer, but she quickly accepted the fact that I didn't have a clue; doubtlessly she knew that already. "Maybe Moon can give you a better idea of his character, but I think she's told us all she knows about him." After a pause, I added suspiciously, "Speaking of Moon, I think she's recently learned Braille. Notice how her hand is in the bag when she takes out her letter-tiles? She's obviously just been selecting the ones she needs and that's why she's been winning most of the time."

Patting my hand comfortingly, Pauline said, "Yes dear, she's cheating and that's why she's been so victorious lately. You'd better have a word with her about her devious ways." Although she's the light of my life and I can't imagine existence without her, I had robust doubts about her sincerity. "Finish your cocoa and let's go to bed," she said, "it'll be a long day tomorrow."

I won big at poker night on Friday, so the guys were raining aspersions upon my person and I found this to be quite uplifting. Ted, my neighbour from up the road, was particularly upset that I'd relieved him of a large bundle of cash. As I was standing near the door bidding him goodnight as he left after the game, he opened his mouth to say something supposedly devastating, but he only shook his head sadly and sighed in exasperation at me. I gave him a display of my pearly-whites and told him we'd also have fun at the next game. He responded to my jolliness by giving me a hostile look, then tramping wordlessly into the night. As I watched him fade into the murk, I happily thought of how rewarding it is to bring joy to a guest's heart. His wife wouldn't allow him to waste gasoline by driving his pickup the single mile to the lodge. Therefore, he usually pedalled over, but there wasn't sign of the bike tonight and he hadn't mentioned anything about thefts or accidents. I nearly called out after him, 'Hey man, what's happened to your wheels?' but then I thought asking that might be imprudent. He heartily disliked travelling anywhere by bicycle and he was even less fond of walking. So I kept my mouth shut and repeated the old adage to myself: 'don't poke the bear with a pointy stick.' Instead, I shut the door to help Pauline tidy up the place and also to gleefully count my winnings.

Pauline didn't seem as happy with my bounty as I was; in fact, she was quite blasé about it. "I'll be doing some shopping for the lodge tomorrow," she said, helping herself to half the high-denomination notes I'd neatly stacked on the table for the purpose of gloating. "The price of lemons is outrageous!" she added, as if this explained the instant disappearance of the cash.

Trevor phoned on Monday morning and invited me up to his cabin. "You can spend Tuesday with us," he said, "then stay overnight." As though he was really tempting me, he told me they had lots of ongoing projects, so I could join in any time I wished.

"Who could resist?" I asked, "you'll pick me up here on Tuesday morning?"

"That's right," he answered, and paused for a moment. Making it easy for him, I suggested we could have breakfast at the lodge and he agreed as if the notion hadn't even crossed his mind.

"Has Portunus showed up yet?" I asked breezily, as though I was only making conversation.

"No," Trevor replied, "we're beginning to hope he never returns." Sounding slightly agitated, he added, "That's just wishful thinking I suppose, but no, we haven't seen any trace of him."

Since it was clear that neither of us wanted to dwell on the subject of Portunus's absence, I said cheerily, "See you Tuesday morning!" then we signed off.

Revisiting the Cabin

O ur clients at the lodge were relatively civilised, so I didn't have to use the whip and bullhorn much. In fact, things were running so smoothly that I expected imminent disaster, but it didn't happen. When Trevor arrived on Tuesday morning, Pauline immediately asked him, "Will scrambled eggs and a ham steak be okay?"

He grinned and nodded, but I couldn't help thinking his response would always be in the affirmative, like that of a drowning man being asked he'd care for a breath of air. I appreciate good food, so I'm always a happy participant in Pauline's wonderful experimentations, but I don't live for it. Trevor has a more dedicated and studied attitude towards his sustenance: almost like he'd die if he didn't frequently reload the cargo hold.

After breakfast, he said, "I nearly forgot," and rushed out to the parking lot. He returned with a pillow-case-sized bag containing five of his carvings wrapped individually in newspaper. I always want to keep his creations for myself, but since we're charging top dollar for them, I can't afford it. Taking them out of the bag and standing them on the table, he looked at the figures proudly and said, "I do the carving, then Sarah does the glazing and painting; we make a good team, don't you think?"

"They're beautiful," Pauline said as she examined one of a cougar with a faraway look in his eyes, "they'll probably sell within a week." As she arranged the new items on shelves in the 'gift shop' (just a book cabinet in a corner of the lodge), I kissed her goodbye, then Trevor and I left.

The flaming barge looked particularly flamboyant as she sat in the parking lot beside less gaudy vehicles. "She needed a good wash," explained Trevor, then he chuckled and added, "her true colours were getting buried under the grime, so I thought I'd brighten her up a little."

The dogs, all excited and ready for a trip, had jumped onto the bed of the truck. I had to engage in the guilty little task of removing them and trying to explain why. Since they seemed to know there was no solid reason for our canine-free preferences, they looked sad and hurt as I gave them the old heave-ho. They followed as we drove through the trees on the single-lane dirt road, but vanished into the bush when we made the right-hand turn onto the wider gravel throughway.

Trevor is pleasantly non-talkative in the morning. I can do without someone telling me excitedly about their plans for the day, and I think he feels the same. Even after the time it takes to eat breakfast, the little grey cells are still only half-awake and tend to get bruised easily by incessant prattle. So we had a peaceful and non-verbal trip, as we turned left onto the black-top, and headed towards town. It wasn't until we reached the outskirts that he spoke. "I need more coffee," he said, "and I know where they make good stuff." After pulling over to the curb in front of a restaurant, he told me to stay put and that he'd be right back. "Want a cup?" he asked as he got out, "it's on me."

"Sure," I responded, "the price is right. Do they have honey?"

"Only in those small plastic containers," he answered.

"Pauline's warned me about those," I replied, "she says they're often just jellied corn syrup with artificial honey flavouring."

"Yes, it's criminal," he said, then he slowly shook his head and rolled his eyes, but he didn't seem overly outraged. "So," he continued patiently, "should I get you some coffee?"

"Yes please," I answered, "the smallest cup they have, black with one sugar."

He returned shortly with a cardboard tray holding two paper cups, one of which was bucket-sized. Leaning on the big one was a stack of four chocolate-frosted donuts that nearly toppled as he got back into the truck. "These are for you," he said, handing me the small coffee and a single donut. Then he settled behind the steering wheel and adopted the studied, careful way he viewed his food. He regarded the stack of three pastries thoughtfully for a moment, like a high-diver gauging the distance to the water, then pulled the lid off his cup and took a sip. "Don't get me wrong," he said after getting on the outside of two donuts as we sat there at the curb, "I love eating at the lodge, but there's no dessert in the mornings."

"I watched you ingest three thick slices of toast liberally coated with strawberry jam or crabapple jelly," I replied unkindly, "not two hours ago. What exactly would you call that part of the meal?

"It's only a part of Pauline's breakfast," he explained rather defensively, "a pie or a pudding at the end would be nice, and that's all I'm going to say. Don't tell her I've been complaining," he said, "we all know her food's excellent."

"Don't worry," I replied comfortingly, "I'll just tell her you needed topping up after her breakfast. She won't be offended at all."

After looking at me without emotion for a moment, he grinned and said, "Thanks Henry, it's good to know that you're always there to smooth things out if there's been a misunderstanding."

Acting humble, I said 'no problem' and shrugged as if it was understood that I was just being a caring friend.

He sighed as he watched customers enter the restaurant, then he turned to me and said, "I can't keep Brian my boss at the garage hanging on. He knows I'm in the middle of moving and marrying, so he's done his best to accommodate me. But he has a business to run, so I quit. There were no hard feelings about this, since he's happy with my replacement." He'd clearly liked the job and hadn't enjoyed walking away from it. "Now I'm counting on the gold and my carvings for income."

"I know you have doubts about all this," I responded, "but you'll do well." After giving him this positive reinforcement, I added, "You can really worry when the children start arriving: you know, school, vaccinations and all that other stuff. But that won't be for another year or two."

"Thanks again for putting my mind at ease," he said. I gave him my empty cup, and he put into a garbage bag that'd been lying on the floor.

On a scale of ten, with instant powdered coffee being a one or a zero and Pauline's brew as tops, the restaurant's offerings rated an eight. Not bad, but I'm spoiled at the lodge. It's all Pauline's fault I've become so picky and have elevated my gastronomic standards, but I didn't mention to Trevor that the coffee had its shortcomings.

After we got underway again, he tooted his horn and waved to various people, so I smiled with recognition at them, even though they were complete strangers to me. Trevor turned on the radio and a flourish of lively violin music filled the cab. A syrupy male voice extolled the many virtues of a fantastic new drug and the background slowly swelled with the addition of piano and a bunch of trumpets. After this inspiring musical interlude, a female voice came on and spoke very rapidly. It was almost as though she was reading out an uninteresting grocery list and wanted to get the boring task finished. "Pildynex might cause loud flatulence and warts, but this has only happened 10% of the time." Without pausing and seeming cheerier, she added, "Pildynex has also been associated with giving users homicidal rage or suicidal depression, plus nasal drip and poodle face," (at least that's what I thought she'd said). Just as the music got more upbeat, the male voice returned, but Trevor switched off the radio. So I didn't get to hear more glad tidings about this miracle of pharmacology as we left the town behind and turned off the hardtop onto the dirt road.

Most of the snow had melted at this lower elevation, but some patches of it still lingered on the sunless side of boulders and in the shadowy world of clusters of small pines. The mining road was mostly clear, so we had no problem driving up it in the powerful Flaming Barge. Stopping at the beginning of the flagged trail down the ravine, Trevor said, "Let's see what it looks like down there now." We got out and walked a few paces through the trees to the right. Looking at a particularly tricky part right at the start of the trail, he said, "There's still a layer of ice on the rock and I bet it gets thicker the further you go. No way I'd risk it; I'll probably have to wait for at least another week."

After regarding the unwelcoming way down for a moment, we returned to the truck. Trevor sat behind the steering wheel without starting the vehicle and just stared through the windshield, saying to himself, "There's no big hurry, but ….."

"It won't be long before you're panning those lovely gold pellets again," I said. "Don't be impatient, you'll have to wait for the 'all clear' from Mother Nature." Nodding as he started the engine, we slowly continued up the road, then went downhill to lake and cabin-level. There was still snow on the ground and in the branches, but it was slushy-looking and dripping. If you like frolicking carefree among the trees, you'd better choose a more appropriate time to be in the forest.

Jerome and Ralph had heard our approach and greeted us before we reached the lake. With wagging tails and a woof or two, they preceded us on the road until we got to the cabin. After we got out of the truck and were patting the dogs, Sarah poked her head out of the building's door to say hello. Trevor went over to her and had a quiet word, while I played with the two frisky Labs. They were shiny-coated and nearly fully grown now, so they were quite a handful. They paused their joyful bounding to carefully sniff at my pant-legs, where the scent of my own canines doubtlessly lay hidden. As I went to the newlyweds, the dogs remained outside. I gave Sarah a hug, then closed the door behind us.

They'd set up the main room well. By the sink stood a small table upon which was a neat row of various knives, picks and other instruments needed for Trevor's carving. Beside it was another table under three shelves filled with small bottles of artist's paint, glazes and turps. The CB radio's microphone cable had been lengthened, so now Sarah could look out of the window as she chatted with friends. While she filled a kettle using a hand-pump similar to ours at the lodge, she said, "For some reason that icy creek-water is excellent for tea; it's the same blend as Pauline's, but it's better."

Frankly, the tea was superior to Pauline's, but I'd never say such a thing out loud. After she'd poured me a mug and I'd tasted her brew, my only comment was, "Very nice, the water sure makes a big difference." Even though I'd recently indulged in a large chocolate donut, I helped myself to the topmost ginger-snap of a pile of half a dozen or so cookies on a plate near the teapot.

"They're from my oven," Sarah said proudly as she watched me munch contentedly, "I baked them the other day."

My cookie was very good, but since it was much bigger than average, I only had one. Trevor ate three and Sarah gave him a dirty look, so it was 'situation normal' for the couple.

Just as we were finishing our tea, the CB crackled into life as a friend called Sarah. While they were on the radio, Trevor said to me, "Let's go down to the wharf," so we went outside.

The dogs came down with us, but since nothing exciting was happening, they soon left. We stood on the wharf and looked at the lake; the shoreline was almost clear of ice, but a nearly circular chunk of it, about a hundred yards in diameter, floated in the middle. "I was out in the rowboat yesterday," said Trevor, "the ice floe's not very thick, so it won't be long before it melts."

The big bluff no longer seemed a rocky watchtower dominating the lake. With its scattered patches of white, plus its overall dark and wet appearance, it appeared too withdrawn to be a robust part of the landscape. After gazing at the large raft of ice for a moment longer, Trevor suggested we go out in the boat for a closer look.

As we rowed away from the wharf, the dogs appeared and clearly wanted to join us. Trevor paused and while we drifted a few feet, he shouted to them, "Too bad guys, you were late for departure and I'm not turning back. Maybe next time." He started rowing again and grinned at me as I sat in the stern seat, but this innocent little interlude somehow made me feel edgy. Adding to my irrational discomfort, a cold wind started blowing as we turned to the right and travelled about fifty feet from shore. A large trout jumped in the inlet as we slowly rowed past, so I idly wondered why there weren't any bugs around yet. Trevor saw the big trout jump too and said, "Lots of frogs in there, so that's why the fish like it." He looked up at the black clouds that'd ridden in on the strengthening breeze and said, "Storms coming, I hope we don't get more snow."

Picking up the pace a little, he rowed to where the bluff met the lake, then stopped as we reached the shelter of the rock's base. The water under the granite overhang wasn't as choppy, but rather than being grateful for the temporary reprieve from the wind, I couldn't shake the feeling of impending doom. Trevor certainly didn't improve things by looking worriedly at the large platform of ice out on the lake and saying, "The wind's blowing it towards us, we'll be trapped against the bluff."

Just then we heard the piercing warning call of a marmot from high up on the rocky outcropping. Though there wasn't any panic or fear in the sound, it seemed ominous nonetheless. The ice floe appeared to move quicker than the wind as it approached and hemmed us in. Trevor tried rowing from the bluff's base, but there was nowhere to go. The ice rapidly cut off all avenues of escape, so there we were: stuck in a narrow stretch of water with a sheet of four-inch ice forcing us ever-closer to the granite wall.

Thankfully, we weren't pushed against the rock, but there was no escaping our little canal. Trevor was trying to be casual as he surveyed our predicament, but I could see he looked concerned.

The marmot made another loud exclamation and seemed closer now, so I looked up reflexively. After seeing nothing but a cold stone wall going up to the clouds, I looked back down to watch Trevor ship the oars. "Sorry Henry," he said, "it looks like we're stuck for now." Looking at the sheet of softly bobbing ice, he added encouragingly, "While I wouldn't attempt walking on it, feel free to try and don't worry, I'll be here for you. You should be able to reach shore just this side of the inlet, that is, if you don't break through first."

"I don't really feel like going for a walk," I replied briskly, as I imagined myself taking cautious slide-steps on the thin ice. And I didn't need to dip a finger in to know the water was cold! "It's heartwarming to know you'll always back me up, but I'm going to stay in the boat anyway."

He grinned and looked out at the floe, saying, "It'll probably break up soon and we can find a channel out. But I have to say that I'm disappointed by your lack of an adventurous spirit. Don't you enjoy facing a challenge?"

"No," I responded, "not if there's a good chance I'll end up swimming in ice-water."

"Picky, picky, picky," Trevor said with a chuckle, "some guys are obviously just scaredy-cats."

I turned from regarding the ice to address this disrespect, but sitting in the bow seat still unseen by Trevor, was an unhappy-looking Portunus. Seeing my shocked expression as I gazed behind him, Trevor quickly swivelled in his seat and saw him too. Surprised and obviously nonplussed, he weakly asked our visitor, "What are you doing here?"

Acting as though it'd been a stupid question, Portunus said with a dismissive sigh, "I told you I'd return, so here I am." With a smile that didn't reach his eyes, he tipped his silly hat and said, "Howdy guys." Then he broodily scanned the lake as if it was a chore to behold us much longer. Trevor was about to say something, but Portunus held up his hand and shook his head, saying to him, "Don't speak, I have a question for you. Join your friend on the stern seat, so you won't have to look at me over your shoulder."

After the seating arrangements had been completed, Portunus gave us a condescending perusal, like we weren't worthy of his company. In other words, he appeared to have gone back to treating his acquaintances as if they were a bad smell. But there was a distinct difference in his bearing this time: his mind seemed to be on something else. Overcoming the shock of his sudden appearance, I wanted to be rude right back at him by maybe asking, 'Are you concerned about the hat being blown away? The wind's getting stronger, you know.' Instead, I stifled the wisecracks; it's one thing to face consequences by yourself, but it's quite another to cause trouble for a friend.

Anyhow, Trevor had opened his mouth to speak, so I hushed myself. Before he could utter a word, Portunus jabbed a finger towards him and said tiredly, "Shut up! I won't tell you again," he'd spoken with the authority of someone accustomed to having his orders obeyed. I don't like admitting it, but I felt cowed as Trevor didn't say anything, but stared at Portunus in a very unfriendly way. In the following quiet moment, the two locked eyes while I studied the rock wall again.

A small avalanche of slushy snow fell from the bluff to splat on the encroaching ice-floe not ten feet off our port side. Just as I was concluding that this wasn't the place to be on a spring morning, another marmot cry sounded from above. There was probably a hawk circling around up there, but all I could see was an overhanging wall of wet, dripping stone. The low clouds finally gave us a heavy downpour of hail and the wind freshened, but we were sheltered from the weather since we were under the bluff. That is, until water inevitably started to fall steadily from the rock onto our heads. Despite the strong breeze, the sheet of ice was stationary and no longer seemed intent on pushing us into the granite. But no escape routes had opened up, either.

Looking out at the dark clouds and the lashing hail, Portunus said, "It might be unpleasant here, but it's worse out there." Not seeming overly pleased by his positive forecast, he added, "It's only a small squall passing through, I'm sure there'll be sunshine soon."

"You didn't appear here now just to talk about the weather," Trevor said tensely as he broke out of his angry silence, "what do you want?"

Looking at him with disapproval, Portunus replied like a boss to a servant, "This time I'll overlook the fact that you've spoken out of turn, but don't make it a habit." He gave Trevor a warning looking and held up a finger, but thankfully he didn't wag it in his face. After another unsettled moment, Portunus asked him casually, "Know anything about death?"

The question was very surprising and seemed totally inappropriate coming from this being from another reality, so Trevor turned to me for an answer, I suppose. Silly boy! I shrugged helpfully and looked uncertain, while Portunus regarded us like we were an unfunny comedy team. "I guess it was a rhetorical question," our spirit friend muttered as he observed our puzzled expressions, "it's a concept that's obviously too complicated for you two."

Sitting on the stern seat shoulder to shoulder, our combined weight had raised the bow, so Portunus looked down at us, both figuratively and literally now. Addressing us both, he asked, "You're not very spiritual individuals, are you?" making it a statement of fact, more than a question.

This was clearly too much for Trevor, who responded with more emotion than was normal for him. "We all might get our personal comfort in different ways," he said, "but that doesn't give anyone the right to force his views on others. As long as no one with contrary opinions gets hurt, you can believe what you want."

I thought Portunus would get bent out of shape at Trevor's impertinent speechifying, but surprisingly he replied, "You're exactly right; it's a very personal thing."

It'd stopped hailing, but the wind was still brisk and cold. Even though I was wearing a thick wool sweater under a good jacket I felt chilled, so I imagined sitting by the woodstove in the cabin. As we lingered near the base of the bluff, the incessant dripping of cold water on my head didn't make my outlook any rosier. After Portunus watched the disgusted expression on my face as a drop somehow found its way down the back of my neck, Portunus chuckled at my discomfort and said, "You should've worn a hat," then he tapped on the brim of his own lopsided headpiece and appeared pleased with himself. I could think of many ways to reply, but since he might be offended by my witty rejoinders, I just looked cheesed off and held my tongue.

More dark clouds were settling over the lake and suddenly the wind stopped as Trevor asked him, "What's all this about death, anyway?"

Portunus looked at him, then smiled knowingly and said, "You don't have a clue, do you?" Shaking his head and rolling his eyes, he added, "You feel the carvings and occasional smudge ceremonies bring you closer to the truth, but you're just fooling yourself." He seemed to be more caring and sympathetic as he slowly gazed at us in turn. Apparently, he found the sight of us uninspiring, but he started speaking nonetheless. "I've been doing a lot of thinking recently," he said almost to himself, "and I've concluded

I don't belong here." He paused for any cheering or foot-stomping that might erupt from the stern, but Trevor and I just nodded politely as we waited for him to continue. "This is difficult to describe," he went on, "especially to a couple of ....., especially to you." He obviously wasn't even remotely embarrassed by his slip of the tongue and carried on by studying our faces in a somewhat clinical and insulting way. Then he asked, "Have either of you had a job that required the frequent use of a sledgehammer?"

We nodded, but at the same time we were mystified by the question. "I don't see how it matters," Trevor muttered, then he raised his voice as he addressed Portunus directly and asked, "What's that got to do with death?"

"I'm trying to put a difficult concept into terms you might understand, you dimwit!" barked Portunus, returning to his charming ways of old. "I've been more than patient with you so far," he said angrily to Trevor, "but don't push me. Just shut up and listen." After this rude admonishment a pregnant silence fell over the boat, but since he was sitting close to my side,

I could feel Trevor tensing at the blatant disrespect. From the corner of my eye I could also see that he didn't look very happy, but he managed to keep himself under control. Once Portunus saw he was uninterrupted by the two clowns on the stern seat, he seemed to relax as he said, "A long time ago, I was on a crew of four men hired to build about ten miles of fencing around a cow pasture. Sometimes the posts needed reinforcing, so we'd tie them securely to three-foot lengths of angle-iron we'd hammered into the ground." Turning to me, he said, "We haven't heard anything from Henry yet. Don't you agree that hammering in an angle-iron with force and accuracy is very satisfying?"

"I know what you mean," I answered, "it's like hitting a baseball or a golf ball well. It's sweet and seems to release the tension in your soul."

"Bravo!" exclaimed Portunus, "now there's a man who has a few clues." He was looking at me approvingly, like a professor at a student who'd just given the correct answer to a tricky question. "There's sort of a spark in that moment of contact," he continued, "it only exists for an instant, but it can be stretched out to last a century. Plus, there's the sound: call it a ringing resonance or whatever. It's obviously a part of the physical process, but somehow it's separate from it. Therein lies death and counter-intuitively, life too. Understand?" He regarded us for a moment, then he shook his head as it became clear that neither of us had comprehended what he'd been trying to describe.

"Isn't it awfully loud and ..... pressurised in the vicinity of this 'spark'? I asked, not getting his drift at all.

"You're confusing your reality with the truth," he said to me, then sighed as if he couldn't have been clearer, but we'd been too dense to grasp his meaning. Acting annoyed at our obtuseness, he tried a different tack by saying, "I've spent a lot of time in the past as a tiny droplet of mist, just drifting along creeks and rivers, then over oceans. There've been long periods of blankness in my existence, during which I might have been dead." He looked at our befuddled expressions and added, "But here I am, alive and kicking!" He was now grinning in a self-satisfied way as he regarded each of us in turn, almost as if he expected congratulations for his endurance. Since we hardly reacted, he continued: "These gaps in my past have really started to bother me, so I've decided to find out more about myself."

Unable to disguise the irony in my voice, I replied, "Your personal history is doubtless fascinating, but why are you imparting all this to us? We're just two guys trying to get on with life."

For the first time, I felt he wasn't playing games with us as he answered, "There's no one else to tell. Nobody wants to talk to me." There hadn't been any self-pity in his statement, but it began to dawn on me that he might be displaying his own version of loneliness. Even in the spirit-world, you apparently needed to spill your guts to someone sometimes, and we were his only options at the moment.

A light breeze, much warmer than before, started shifting the clouds away and a shaft of sunlight broke through the overcast. The 'canal' at the base of the bluff widened, so we were able to get out from under the cold dripping and the slushy avalanches. But the ice-floe still barred access to the cabin across the lake, so Trevor re-shipped the oars and joined me on the stern seat again.

Seemingly deep in thought, Portunus regarded the cabin and the surrounding wild countryside, and nodded to himself. "This is nice land, plus it has gold too!" he said as he gave Trevor a knowing look, "but there aren't any answers for me here. I have to go elsewhere." I couldn't help wondering if he'd make lots of new friends during his quest for self-knowledge, but since this was probably a touchy subject for him, I didn't mention it. "Anyhow, there's no reason for me to hang around for much longer." Giving us a weary grin, he added, "I'm sure you'll be like all the others: so glad to see me go that they're polite and accommodating. They even hold the door open and wish me well, but I know they're actually saying 'goodbye and good riddance'." He momentarily studied us in his lordly and maddening way, then he addressed Trevor solely, saying, "You're doing no harm here, so I'm not going to intrude any more. And I apologise for the bluff-climbing thing; I had no right to make such a demand."

Clearly taken aback by Portunus's contrition, Trevor seemed to choose his words carefully as he responded, "I enjoyed it! There's no point in rehashing something that happened months ago, so let's not worry about it." He leaned forward as if he wanted to shake hands, but then changed his mind and settled back on his seat.

Acting highly insulted, Portunus asked him, "Don't want to touch the apparition that's shown up in your boat?" Grinning sardonically, he added, "Can't say I blame you, but you should know by now that I'm harmless."

I looked up at the 'Big Rock' and imagined forcing someone to climb down it. I wouldn't characterise this as being anything close to 'harmless', while I doubted Portunus's ability to make any physical contact with us at all. He'd probably have to practise for another eon or so before adding that particular skill to his repertoire. He seemed to have blown any opportunity to get along with his acquaintances; Trevor and I were obviously the only ones to whom he could say goodbye. It was a sad state of affairs for him, but I didn't have my boo-hoo towel with me and I was glad to hear he was leaving soon, nonetheless.

Looking at me with a grim smile, Portunus said, "Henry doesn't seem very sad that I'm going away. In fact, he looks down right pleased and this hurts me deeply." He was clearly trying to be lighthearted and self-deprecating, but his mind seemed to be on something else.

I wanted to jokingly respond by asking him if he was actually in the boat, or were we just seeing some kind of spectral projection? And if the latter was the case, how come he chose that particular look, the hat especially? But I thought my eager curiosity wouldn't be appreciated, so I exclaimed with exaggerated sincerity, "That's not true! I'll forever miss seeing you around here, so keep in touch." Actually, I thought he was leaving these parts to avoid being given the boot by the Overseer, but maybe that's being a bit uncharitable. In the end, he was departing and that was what mattered; I certainly didn't want to say anything that might change his mind. "You have your challenges," I said forthrightly, "and we have ours. We have lots in common, so it's good that we're saying goodbye on good terms."

"That's a very noble and touching speech," he responded flatly, "but I don't believe a word; you're happy to see me go."

I was getting fed up with his 'poor me' attitude and I could see Trevor was getting agitated too. But before I could say something I'd probably soon regret, a marmot cried again, this time sounding terrified. We all looked up to see a hawk with a struggling bundle in his talons. The bird had just left the heights of the bluff and was supposedly heading home for lunch, when the marmot called again. The forlorn sound was cut off in mid-utterance and the hawk flew from sight: maybe Portunus would be better off describing his impressions of death to a marmot.

When I lowered my gaze, I wasn't surprised that Portunus had pulled off his disappearing act once again. As Trevor shifted himself to between the oars again, he queried casually, "Understand any of that sledgehammer and spark stuff?"

"Not really," I answered firmly, "but yes."

He considered my rather confusing response by peering at me with his head tilted slightly and a quizzical look on his face. After a moment, he asked with obviously false adoration, "O wise one, what did you glean from his words?"

Ignoring his insincerity, I shrugged and said, "Not much: Portunus is obviously uneasy in his world and I think he envies you. You've built a good life for yourself, while he's still trying to figure out the metaphysics of his existence. Jealousy along with his self-importance can't be very validating for him, so he's at odds with himself." Smiling at him after my wordy response, I added, "Never mind, let's have lunch, that is, if we can get outta here."

A few more shafts of sunlight had poked through the clouds, but we were still trapped by the ice-floe. It was ten minutes or so before it drifted towards the lake's centre and allowed us to escape. We rowed past the inlet where we'd seen the trout jump and Trevor pointed to a small cloud of tiny insects hovering over the water near shore. "First bugs this year," he reported, so I responded by pretending to happily wave a flag, then I said, "Yippie!"

Ralph and Jerome were avidly watching from the wharf as we approached. They greeted us with wagging tails, then jumped into the boat as Trevor glided the vessel alongside. The dogs clearly wanted to go for an exciting tour of the lake, but he dashed their hopes by saying to them, "You guys are welcome to sit here for as long as you want, but Henry and I are going to have our lunch."

With perfect timing, Sarah stuck her head over the embankment and looked down to us. "Pea soup's on!" she shouted cheerily, "come up when you're ready!"

As we headed to the building, the dogs realised there'd be no tour in the immediate future. They abandoned ship to join us for the short trek, then retired to their own vividly-carpeted doghouse.

Other than greeting his wife, Trevor hadn't said much, but Portunus's exit had clearly lifted a weight from his shoulders. He seemed more relaxed as we sat at the table and he talked to Sarah about the half-finished bear figurine currently on his carving-bench. He didn't mention

Portunus's little 'hello/goodbye' visit; I suppose he wanted to share the good news of the unsettled spirit's departure with her later. So, after the soup, Trevor packed in four grilled-cheese sandwiches, while I only had two.

About the Author

J im Carver is the author of 8 books, in a series called Life at the Lodge.

These books are An Almost Perfect Life, Gold Dust, Deep and Crisp and Even, Watersky, The Gold Necklace, The Mysterious Bob Larch, The Reindeer Drum, and The Cabin at Big Rock.

He is currently working on 3 new books.

Jim Carver spent many years working in geological exploration in wilderness areas all over Canada, and his books draw on his experiences.

He was sidelined from his career by the onset of hereditary cerebellar ataxia, a condition which affects motor skills in an ever-worsening way. He has been in a wheelchair for almost 3 decades, and has taught himself to type very slowly with only 1 finger. He dictates his books, even though it is difficult to speak.

He has a well-developed sense of humour, a keen interest in his characters, and to read him is to laugh out loud on every page.

He continues to inspire himself and others through his books. He loved his work in the Canadian wilderness. Now his writing is his way of interacting with others, and exploring the world.

Jim Carver lives and writes in Victoria, on Vancouver Island, B.C.

www.ingramcontent.com/pod-product-compliance
Lightning Source LLC
Chambersburg PA
CBHW050022030726
47506CB00001B/79